Dear Infidel

Tamim Sadikali

HANSIB

Published by Hansib Publications, 2014

Hansib Publications Limited
P.O. Box 226, Hertford, Hertfordshire, SG14 3WY
United Kingdom

www.hansibpublications.com

ISBN 978-1-906190-70-5

A CIP catalogue record for this book
is available from the British Library

Printed in Great Britain

Δ

Dear Infidel

For Farah –

For your derring-do; for rolling the dice; for the leap of faith; for making me stand an inch taller.

For Shehrebanu and Haider –

In the hope that you will grow into your names, and thus wear them well.

Acknowledgements

The passage on the Summer Grinch was written and performed by Zina Saro-Wiwa, on the late John Peel's BBC Radio 4 programme, 'Home Truths' (20.09.04).

Salman's final chapter, wherein he recalls an adventure as a young boy, was inspired by Micky's reminiscences of the Blue Falls in Christopher Nicholson's excellent novel, *The Fattest Man in America*.

Finally, whilst I've largely bootstrapped my own writing skills, in the early days I was helped beyond measure by Johanna Bertie, who not only gave me her time, but also the best piece of writing advice I've ever received: "Make every word count." Johanna, thank you.

Prologue

Imtiaz

It's the lows that you've got to watch out for. And the highs. The tedium of everyday is a danger, too. Sometimes I need to shut it all out and cut loose. *Escape* ... But whilst you reach for a bottle, I reach for something else.

Others take things in their stride, the background noise having dulled their senses. But my senses remain heightened and I have no answer. Touch, taste, sight, smell and sound; I receive the same data as you, but I process things differently. They say a blind man's hearing is more acute – I guess the same principle applies.

When I was a boy I loved The Incredible Hulk. I used to wait for the terror of the metamorphosis, sneaking peeks at the TV from the safety of my dad's lap. Sure, the growling green monster throwing men and cars around was damn cool, but looking back, the real power lay in the rising tension – of the quiet man seeking a simple life, but then getting disturbed.

I am The Incredible Hulk. I am the Wilderness, locked in a cage. I Am Become Death.

Nazneen

'The snow's coming, the snow's coming!' Nazneen hears someone shrill, some way down the corridor. Whoops of delight reverberate along its length, with every maid and maintenance man joining in.

'All right!' ... 'Yeah!' ... 'Let's catch some Big Air!' Footfalls rush inwards and as some girl dashes past the room Nazneen's cleaning, she sticks her head in.

'Hey, didn't you hear? The snow's coming!' She beams momentarily before darting along, thus denying Nazneen the chance to look too busy to care, throw her a patronising smile or – her latest favourite – condescend charitably.

'Honestly, it's like rattling a monkey cage,' she mutters, pissed at losing her stage to bitch. Laughter from the now-gathered cluster further sours her mood, but despite her determination to poop the party, she can't resist turning to verify the claim. And instantly her eyes sweep over Keystone Lake, basking under glorious Colorado sunshine. It lies perfectly still, but for the most gentle of rippling across its surface, confirmation of its beating heart.

A solitary bird flutters down, landing softly. Nazneen watches it drift, falling under shadows as it nuzzles its fine down. A lakefront conifer welcomes the guest with an evergreen drape. The bird accepts without fuss, head turned to the phalanx awaiting their turn. And thus drape follows drape, a seamless patchwork of green, broken only when the bird falls under the deciduous Autumn Purple Ash. Nazneen could have sworn this tree's leaves were also green, and thus despite the brilliance of the sunshine, she gets the message: nature's cycle is turning.

She traces upwards, past the lakeside trees and the hotels behind them, across and beyond the fir-lined hills close-in, and finally out towards the Rocky Mountains, tearing into the distant heavens. They sit back but dominate, with peaks like jagged teeth snarling, just waiting for God's final command to snap the world shut. And yes, just like that tree ... Those peaks, there's definitely more snow on them now. Her summer – her and Martin's summer – it's almost over. But still, behold: this *irresistible* lake, shimmering under late summer sun. Nazneen bows her head, cognising majesty. She just knows, something inside tells her – this must all be preserved: this time, this lake, this summer's end. Whatever happens from this point forth, these memories must remain vivid. Some day they'll sustain her.

Salman

Most people's growing pains are confined to their teenage years, stretching at most till their early twenties. First comes the physical stuff but alongside arrives competition, and with it the duty to compete. Subtle and not-so-subtle forces compel you to get in the ring, but unless you're a prize-fighter, you don't enter with relish. But there's no going back. You know next to nothing but this one thing you are sure of: the protection of childhood has gone for good. You must raise your fists and fight, as much for your own safety as well as to beat on others. And thus one begins clambering for a seat at life's top tables. And just like in any other race, it's the initial exchanges that count. If you mess up your schooldays you'll not get into the right university, or onto the right course, and it'll be uphill from there.

Salman recalled some graffiti, scribbled underneath a toilet-roll dispenser in his university's library: '*sociology degrees – please take one*'. All these years later and it still brought a smile to his face, but it held more than a grain of truth: he had a 2:2 in Accounting & Finance from a new uni/old-poly, and it was worth shit.

Ultimately, though, nearly everyone adjusts. With age comes the acceptance of mediocrity, and you learn to get by. Your partner might not resemble your adolescent fantasies, but it was just that – fantasy – and this is exactly this – reality – and we all know the difference, right? And anyway, you love them (or loved them once), and that will sustain you (or at least for as far as you have vision). And beyond that? Well it's nothing to worry about. You live in the Free World.

Only a few get to leave the ring outright (either through off-the-scale success or dedicated substance abuse), but it no longer matters – you all find some ground to call your own. You see yourself reflected in everyone around, and it's comforting.

Salman never got there so smoothly, though, for Salman was a Paki.

Aadam

It was 10.01 pm and most commuters were long since home, but for Aadam and a few other weary souls, the working day was only just done. His train had been due at 9.52 but it hadn't even been announced. All eyes were on the boards. Waiting, waiting ...

Aadam was near the top end of the concourse, just in from the Boadicea pub when he noticed a man stagger out, covered in blue. He was sporting a blue shirt, a blue hat and a spherical beetroot face, and he held a blue flag with intent: he was a Chelsea fan. Out of the pub he came and into the Burger King next door he went. Home from home.

Aadam looked around. No-one else seemed to have noticed the scarlet and blue clown, save for a young girl holding her mother's hand. Aadam waited expectantly and the encore duly came: out of the BK hobbled Bozo, before plonking himself into one of the plastic seats outside.

Again, Aadam checked his surroundings: still only he and the little girl were appreciating the artist at work. No matter – the show went on. Bozo sat and ate: burger, chips and shake. It was clearly a struggle, though, as successive chews were being teased out, as if he were masticating glue. And his eyes would regularly shut before he'd spring back scowling, occasionally grabbing his unfurled flag for those who ventured too close. But all on his own, Bozo could only dig deep and stay low. But then, suddenly, salvation: the cavalry arrived. Seven, eight, nine of his comrades poured out of the Boadicea, all sporting the same beetroot and blue – the colours of the King's Road. Bozo locked with each of his Brothers in Arms, relieved for friendly company. Emboldened, he walked in front of his men and, unfurling his flag, sounded the battle cry like the buglers of old: '*Who the fucking, who the fucking, who the fucking hell are you? Who the fuck-in'-hell-are-you?*' William Williams's eighteenth century devotional, capturing the march of the Israelites to the Promised Land, had found a new twenty-first century home. For the Chelsea fans were in the Promised Land, too – they'd just won a football match. The whole ensemble, a modern-day choir, joined in and sang. And in unison they pointed their arms at the commuters, who in that peculiarly British way, simply pretended it wasn't happening.

'Oh dear, the natives are restless,' quipped Aadam, deliberately loud enough for the chap nearest to hear. Aadam threw him a beaming smile and the guy stared back. *Result!* He'd long since given up caring about PR. No-one else commented and neither was there any movement – save for the woman now marching her daughter away, to the girl's obvious displeasure.

Aadam turned back to Bozo, whose expression morphed from glory to hate. And with good reason – only him and his chums were allowed to enjoy this victory, and he'd make sure those fucking suits knew it. But once on a train, Aadam knew those very same suits would prefer Bozo's company, to his own brown-skinned self. Whether Bozo be quietly dribbling spittle onto his jeans or treating everyone to a verse from '*No Surrender to the IRA*', there was no way he'd win that beauty contest. But it wasn't always thus. Things had changed. That one day, 9/11 – it had been seriously inconvenient. But he understood. He couldn't hate them back, the British – God knows he'd tried. Perhaps it was now time; time to jump ship, bail out, start again. A new life – him and Nazneen. He wondered what she'd think of it.

The British fleeing the likes of him tended to go to Australia, and so it made sense for him to head in the opposite direction. Dubai – The East served up on a Western plate. Perfect. He'd talk to her – she'd see the sense in it. It was time they refreshed their vision.

Pasha

Camphor. Tight curls of vapour spin out of control, penetrating and musty. We burn it constantly, especially at night, to keep demons at bay and our garden safe. For there will be no more trials, once you land safely on our shores. We will wipe the tears from your eyes.

Your World and our Garden. So exposed is your heart and so perilous your journey. But you have a choice. Crave knowledge and we will hold your hand. Revel in your world and we will watch you drift.

I am the Witness. I was there as your lungs took their first breath and I'll be there when ... I am closer to you than your jugular vein.

I drift in on an eternal lake. A heavy mist hangs low but my all-seeing eye is not impeded. I see Pasha, lost in the embrace of music. You may hope for another year, another day, another hour – but time runs dry. My advice? Die before you die.

Part One

1

Aadam ascended the basement stairs to meet his clients. Rounding the top his eyes fell on an overcast Wigmore Street, yet he still smarted at the natural light. Basements truly sucked. Outside a horn blew and some loose words were exchanged, but by the time he reached the doors all evidence was gone. Vehicles shunted forwards in batches, like sections on a caterpillar's body. Aadam smiled. First rain drops smacked into windows and his smile broadened. He observed the human stream, rippling as scarves got adjusted and brollies opened up. Aadam's heart did a little dance, for today he was immune – the short days and early nights, the cold that would only get colder and the rain that would not relent – today they couldn't touch him. For tomorrow, *tonight* ... the fasting would end and the feasting begin. All troubles would be put aside and the good things indulged in. This innocuous dying day, for Aadam, heralded renewal.

'Hi Sarah,' he said, smiling as he propped himself up by the front desk. The receptionist drew near, her aura light and pleasant. 'I'm expecting some people – from the Capital Actions project. Looks like they're late.' Absentmindedly he looked back outside.

'The Capital Actions project?' She straightened her spine, hands braced for action. 'Which meeting room are you in?'

'Oh, none – they were all gone.'

She looked alarmed and began checking the bookings.

'Relax,' he said. 'It's OK. We'll hold it right here.' He gestured towards the foyer. 'I'm going there now. Bring them over, would you?'

'Of course, Aadam,' she demurred.

'Oh, and buzz George once they've arrived. Some teas and things would be nice.'

He dropped onto the settee, upholstered to the ostentatious demands of a West End lobby. It squeaked as he adjusted, sinking slowly, one arm resting on fine leather and the other holding meeting notes. He checked his watch and planned the day's end: discuss the project, write up some notes and then straight home. He'd be in another world come this time tomorrow.

He looked up at a widescreen above the mock fireplace, constantly tuned into BBC news. The volume was off but there were subtitles as well as looping headlines: another American soldier had been killed in Iraq. His curiosity roused, Aadam nevertheless changed channel; he fancied a nibble of the story while he waited, but not when served up for the British palette. For this morsel, a dollop of American pathos would go down nicely. He kept flicking, looking for something more laissez faire, current affairs US-style, cut for the man on the street. He stopped on seeing some anchorman flirting with a weather-girl, the dainty love giggling dutifully. Meanwhile a banner flashed on-screen to present the next item, which Aadam reduced to: 'Would Eid herald an increase in terrorist activity, in the new colonies or the Free World?' *Bon Appetite* ... Sitting behind a front desk that resembled a Möbius strip, the anchorman introduced the debate, along with two pundits seated either side.

'*Sir, can we expect the lull in militant operations that we witnessed over Ramadan to now end, and end violently?*' Anchor threw the opening gambit to the spokesman from the Department of Homeland Security, who deftly ignored it.

'*Before we begin, I'd like to extend our deepest condolences to the family of Private Archer. We mourn every one of our departed servicemen and women, and hope that his loved ones are comforted in knowing that his death was not in vain.*' The spokesman looked back at Anchor who expertly took the baton.

'*Well I'm sure that all of us here as well as those watching at home, echo those earnest sentiments. Our thoughts and prayers are with Private Archer's family and friends.*' It was delivered with such decorum that when Anchor turned to the other pundit to ratify the consensus of the civilised, the man could only oblige with an

'Absolutely'. He paused just a little before affirming, though, and Aadam wondered whether he was thinking of the wedding party that the Americans had blown up, just the day before.

Prayers. Thoughts and prayers. Aadam breathed deeply and took a long look at Anchor. He wasn't young – definitely over forty – but he wore his age well: his shoulders were broad, his features firm and his muscles still defined. But if you looked hard enough, you could see so much more. Behind him was his wife: past her prime but way off menopausal and, crucially, still desirable. And to the right were his kids. There was giddy, young Jessica, full of energy and ideas, a bud just waiting to blossom. And Jake, that chip off the old block: working hard, thinking of the future and determined to stay on the team. Anchor was an anchor, the heart and soul of America. *But when did he actually last pray?* This morning before he put on his crisp, linen shirt? Last night as he kissed his children, fast asleep in their beds? Maybe it was at Thanksgiving, as he praised the Lord for his bounty. No? Still further back? And what of his thoughts? *A penny for your thoughts, Anchor.* Was he thinking about what he'd have for dinner or who'd win the game at the weekend? Maybe he was preoccupied with that girl from the typing-pool that he'd love to nail. Or maybe, just maybe, he was thinking of Private Archer's mother, sitting alone on her kitchen floor and clutching a picture of her son, aged five, blowing out the candles on his birthday cake. Maybe ... Human suffering in all its density, spirited away by civil words, technology and that fucking Möbius strip. Thoughts and prayers indeed, *ya cunt.*

'A penny for your thoughts?'

Aadam whipped around. His boss, George, was commanding the ground right in front and next to him stood two others. He grabbed the control and searched desperately for "mute" before bolting to attention. George introduced the senior member of the delegation, followed by a much younger guy who wore a distasteful expression.

Was I thinking out loud? He shot a second look at the younger chap whose curled lip remained. Panic infested him, freezing him to the spot. The thought was *too* terrible. But soon George was singing Aadam's praise and his generous smile and fatherly hand dismissed his fears. His boss gestured and the delegates took their seats, the delight in their plush surroundings evident.

'Thank you, Sarah,' said George pointedly, as the receptionist placed down tea and biscuits.

'*You're* Adam? But ... We've been speaking on the phone, right?' The younger guy, Stanley, looked confused. He wore a traditional pin-striped suit and, unusually for his age, carried it with a style that lent weight to his sneering.

'That's right – you're the trainee analyst, yes? Good to meet you.' Aadam forced a smile.

'What's it short for then?'

'What's that?'

'*Adam* – what's it short for?'

'Nothing.'

Stanley looked short changed.

'You seemed far away back there,' remarked Terry, the elder of the client party. He glanced Aadam's way but was busy getting comfortable, stirring sugar into his tea and eyeing up the biscuits.

'Err ... yeah, I was watching the news.' He looked for a reaction but Terry was pre-occupied with a custard cream.

'What's the latest then?'

Aadam jumped towards Stanley whose stare was arresting. 'What's that?'

'The news – what's the latest?'

'Errmm. Oh, another American soldier has been killed. Dunno the details.' He gestured dismissively towards the screen, a mute Anchor looking animated.

'I dunno what we're doing over there, eh?'

'Aha.'

'I mean, why try and help those who don't want to be helped? After all, you can take a horse to water ...'

'Right!' declared George and immediately the chatter stopped. 'Thank you for coming, gentlemen. As you know, we at Realogica are developing a new suite of products, specifically targeting investment boutiques such as yours.' He waved an open hand, like a Padré blessing his flock.

'Capital markets are changing, gentlemen, and at speed. The challenge for niche operators is to carve out expertise, shout about it and then sell it.' Aadam settled back, happy to listen to the preacher evangelise. Realogica had a lot of smooth talkers but no-one worked an audience like George. And for some reason – one that he still hadn't figured out – he'd taken him under his wing. George was now Chief Operating Officer, and he'd ensured that Aadam had been involved in every project that he truly cared about. Maximum exposure, maximum reward. There were others as good as him, *better* than him, but it's the breaks that count and George had ensured he'd got them.

'If there's movement on a key deal – anywhere, anytime, you need to know. Sure, everyone finds out eventually, but by the time young Stanley here is an experienced analyst, a difference of a minute will tell in millions. And that's where we can help.'

Despite the live show in front, Aadam was unable to ignore the one being played out on the widescreen.

'*Sir, the American people need to know. Is Iraq today a more dangerous place for our boys than it was yesterday, and if so, what steps are being taken to bolster their security whilst they protect this country?*'

Anchor was still on mute, with all his passion and no-nonsense gusto lost in the subtitles, but it mattered not: software he loved, watching George weave his magic he really loved, but *this* ... there was no word that stirred Aadam, like "Iraq".

'*Every day we're losing more of our young men out there,*' began the government spokesman, conceding the fact with almost moist eyes. '*But we're fighting the good fight,*' he continued, '*and this mission is not over until we've defeated the terrorists!*'

'Aadam?'

He turned sharply, with George's large frame snapping into focus.

'Sorry, George, I didn't quite catch that.' He felt the weight of his boss's widening eyes.

'Projections, Aadam – the Capital Actions system. When do you think it will be ready for a first pilot?'

'Well I need to sit down with one of you guys – perhaps yourself, Stanley – so I can capture your needs.' Stanley nodded tightly, like his movement was restricted. 'We already have most of the data. The question is in what form do you want it, and how do we push it through?'

'Any ideas?'

'Sure – I'm looking at an ETL solution.'

'ETL?' queried Terry.

'Extract, Transform, Load. There's a new platform that I fancy leveraging but ...'

'First pilot?' impressed George.

'Two months.'

'That's fine with me,' assured Terry, and George nodded his approval.

'... *but surely with your methods you are aggravating terrorism, rather than pacifying the situation?*'

The subtitles disappeared as soon as the sentence was complete, but for Aadam it was transcendent. What care was there for software in the face of such a question?

'... and we'd like you to second one of your analysts to us.'

'Depends for how long, really. And what you need him for?'

'We've adopted an agile approach here,' interjected Aadam, 'which means you get the final product in stages – and that makes your involvement more important.' Terry seemed impressed and a little lost. Perfect.

Anchor swivelled to usher Homeland Security back in but he was already there.

'*We gave peace a chance,*' he gestured boldly, holding his challenger's gaze. '*We gave peace a chance for ten years and we got 9/11 for our efforts. Well we aren't making that mistake a second time, Mister. America will never be seen as weak again!*'

9/11. 9-fucking-11. Would he live to see another day, Aadam wondered, when he wouldn't have to see, hear or read about someone, somewhere, still bleating on about it? So many lives touched, torched in an instant – and here was the young widow, heavily pregnant and reliving the exact moment she heard the news. And the mother being helped out of a hearse, on her way to bury her son. And then there was little Johnny, just way too young to understand. But Aadam wasn't feeling for them, for any of them – cause no-one was even counting the fallen, faceless wogs.

Aadam was visualising the film; the inevitable film about Private Archer – this Private Archer or some other Private Archer – that he'd find impossible to blot out when it came swaggering into town. He was picturing our hero lying in the dirt, in the desert, all alone. He was in pain but he was still struggling, though now it was hopeless: his life-blood was ebbing away. In his hand was a picture of Little Johnny and somewhere in the ether a string arrangement was playing, accompanied by someone who sounded like Enya. In life he looked dashing, but now, in death, he was bettering that: he was looking noble. Private Archer was breathing his last with dignity, and there wasn't a dry eye in the house. Despite the blood loss he'd taken on an ephemeral glow, no doubt a gift bestowed upon God's special children. And the Iraqis? Oh, they'd be there too. Shouting constantly and barking orders through twisted faces. And they'd drop dead like flies, accompanied by some sinister sounding Arab techno. No moms or Little Johnnies for them.

'... and it does look awful outside.' Terry turned back wistfully before consoling himself with one last custard cream. Following his gaze, Aadam saw that it was getting dark – the sun had finally set on the month of Ramazan, 2004. Hastily, he poured tea into his hitherto empty cup. Terry looked on, bemused.

'It'll be cold now.'

'Actually, I've been ... I prefer it like this.' He threw Terry a brief, big smile before beginning his clandestine break-fast.

'Right, we must be going.'

'We'll be in touch,' glowed George, shaking hands firmly. 'Aadam here will organise some sessions. They'd be most instructive for young Stanley.' Young Stanley looked unconvinced. George's baritone chuckle conducted the atmosphere and only Stanley snubbed the closing chorus.

Aadam switched off his workstation and checked the contents of his overcoat: phone, coin wallet, travelcard – he was good to go. Buttoning up, he marched swiftly towards the stairwell but, as he was about to ascend, George spotted him.

'Aadam.'

He jolted to a halt on the first step, cursing silently.

'Hi, George. I was just ...'

'I know – a minute of your time, please.'

He made his way to his boss's office, closing the door behind him.

'It's Eid tomorrow, isn't it?'

'Yes, George. That's right.'

'Spending the day with the family? Taking the wife out?' He was sounding pleasant but his gaze made Aadam nervous.

'Family tomorrow, George – I guess Nazneen and I will do something over the weekend.'

23

'Good, good. Do give her my regards.'

'I will,' he said, trying to mask a growing unease.

'How do you feel about working with Stanley?'

Aadam swallowed hard.

'Fine. I reckon I can capture everything within a week and then ...'

'He seemed hostile. You can handle him though, right?' Again, those scrutinising eyes.

'Sure.'

George moved towards the window and tweaked the blinds, revealing an empty pavement, a bare hedgerow and a dusk shroud.

'Do you know how long I've been here?' He paused for just a fraction before continuing. 'Twenty–seven years. I was the first employee who hadn't been to Oxbridge, apart from the tea lady. I'm from Hull myself, though the years down here have washed away my accent.'

Aadam made to respond but his throat caught.

'You won't know this, but when I was a boy, journalists interviewing politicians used to finish with something like: *"Minister, is there anything further you wish to say to a grateful nation?"* He gestured theatrically before turning to gauge the reaction. Mute and with his head down, Aadam gave few clues. George turned back to his view – nobody passed, nothing blew by – he might as well have been gazing at a still. He tweaked the blinds shut again but otherwise didn't move.

'These are difficult times, Aadam, especially for you – I can see that. But what the hell did you think you were doing back there?'

'Sorry, George – I'm not sure I ...'

'Gawping at the bloody widescreen, Aadam. Don't play the innocent with me.'

'No, of course not. I was just ...'

'*Just* nothing. You think the Iraq war has a place in this company? What if it was Terry that you'd put off instead of Stanley? You're damn lucky he was more interested in the bloody biscuits – otherwise we'd be nearly £1m worse off right now.'

'George, I didn't mean ...'

'I don't care. This is where you work. We don't pay you to be preoccupied with the War on Terror? Understood?'

'Absolutely. It'll never happen again.'

'You're damn right. I have my views and no doubt you have yours, but when you're here, stay focussed. You *will* stay focussed, OK?' He finally turned around, demanding a response.

'Of course, George. My work's very important to me.'

'I know it is, son, I know it is. And despite impressions to the contrary, this is an egalitarian country – you mustn't forget that. Don't waste your chance. You belong here.'

Aadam remained rooted to the spot – arms straight, head still down.

'*Eid Mubarak*, son.' And a speechless Aadam shook George's extended hand.

2

Right here, right now. This was his prize: just him and her. Meditating on the deliciousness of anticipation realised, he suddenly felt giddy. He took a step back to find the bed's edge, but hit the cabinet instead. Disorientated, he stalled. Seconds passed and the only movement was from his heel, slowly coming to rest on the carpet – sweat denying his foot purchase. Moisture around his buttocks coalesced, forming beads of sweat that trickled downwards, tickling his clammy skin. Finding this amusing he came to, allowing him to regain control – he wanted this to last.

He remembered how long he'd waited for this, this precious time. He had the whole evening with her, and he inhaled purposefully whilst holding the thought. Convinced once more of his mettle he looked at her through fresh eyes, drinking in her languid body. She was absolute perfection: trim waist, shapely thighs and buttocks that were tight, unblemished and fleshy, though not large. Her auburn hair was straight and past the shoulders in length with a few wisps resting on her chest, contouring the rise of her breasts. And her taut skin, though flushed with excitement, hinted at a Mediterranean heritage. Perfect tones.

Slowly and deliberately he sat on the bed, his eyes moving down to her hips – slim, but naturally so. She smiled at him, such a carefree smile, and all of a sudden he felt jealous. Jealous of her toned, svelte form, convincing himself that it hadn't been achieved but was merely a gift: a gift from the gods, from the lottery of conception. '*One should choose one's parents with great care,*' a Sri Lankan doctor had once jovially advised him. It was a cute line and it had stuck in his mind, but he didn't appreciate it at the time.

He snapped back, noticing his shallow breath, the product of wan thoughts. Inhaling deeply with intention his discipline again floundered, getting lost in harmonic motion, the gentle swaying of her hips. She was teasing him, looking him in the eyes and grinning as she moved in time to some music in the background, fingering the lace of her knickers. He gave up his battle with himself. He slumped back against the headboard, his body arched – one leg on the bed, the other dangling. He closed his eyes and felt semen working its way out – it was a pleasant sensation. There was a knock on the door and she was startled out of her idle play in front of the mirror. Jolted back into reality, she forgot her robe as she cantered to the door, which made the strapping plumber on the other side grin.

He shut his burning eyes and cursed. Pornography had come a long way in recent years, yet he had been flogged some rubbish from ten-odd years ago. He couldn't even get buying porn right. The film continued playing and the guttural exchanges in German between Bored Housewife and Plumber just cranked up his frustration.

'What you looking for?' the wide-boy pirate had asked him over the phone. Imtiaz was in the mood for a treat – no squinting at a low-quality stream on his laptop tonight; only a DVD would do.

'Oh, something modern, and American or British. No foreign stuff.' *This is a clinical, discreet business transaction*, he'd assured himself, and there was no need to become nervous – *just state what you want*.

'I'll be round in forty minutes,' assured wide-boy, and for the next seventy he paced his small flat, getting excited: a whole evening alone – him, a couple of drinks and some porn. He wandered from room to room, working himself into a state. Scenes from past movies flooded his mind and he began rubbing his penis from the pocket of his trousers. A steady trickle of pre-cum had begun leaking out and his pants were already damp.

'Proper stuff, this,' wide-boy declared confidently on arriving.

'Great, thanks,' muttered Imtiaz, and he handed over some notes before shutting and locking the door. He sprinted round to his bedroom and tore the DVD out of its plastic case. His mouth was parched but he dropped the thought, focusing solely on inserting the disc. Once in, (and it had taken a few seconds to steady his hand), it began playing ...

And there she is, alone. Bored. Considering herself in front of a mirror. There's some music in the background – anodyne, contrived – and her slim hips sashay in time. She undoes a clip and releases wave upon wave of auburn hair, flowing, undulating in slow motion. Adjusting her garter belt she puckers suggestively, mocking her absent lover.

Imtiaz was under a spell. Outside of space and time there was no distraction – just a focal point, a flickering flame on which to meditate. But then a *ding-dong* and the illusion was shattered – for him and for her – and she cantered to the door, forgetting to put her robe back on.

* * *

Ripped out of the moment, the weight of disappointment pinned him to the spot. *Water,* he eventually thought. *I need some water.* But for the moments it took to fill a glass his mind became a canvas; a smorgasbord of pornographic imagery. Standing at the sink he closed his eyes and saw nothing but flesh: pink flesh, splayed flesh, sweat, movement, rhythm, sighs and screams. His mind was saturated, scrambled, and he had to hold on to the edge for support whilst drinking.

Sounds from the running film interrupted his reverie, and as he walked back he glimpsed how this would make him feel. He'd pay back for this, and with interest. Mentally he'd be low, physically he'd feel sluggish, and this would last for days. The price was high, too high – all this had long stopped being a simple pleasure. And besides, Bored Housewives and Plumbers? *Oh purleese* ... Even he had more refined tastes. But then he was drowned out. First a whimper – speculative, contained, but then a howl – a low, prolonged shiver of animal satisfaction; a bolt of pain, washed away by pleasure. *No,* he ordered himself, *turn around, walk away. You can do this.* But inevitably ...

Imtiaz stood still, watching his TV screen with childlike wonder. She was perched on top of the washing machine, heels supported by corners. The plumber was bent down in front, pleasuring her with his tongue. Imtiaz's eyes bore into her, burning their way through. A feverish sweat precipitated on his brow, with every pore of his body open, begging to absorb – be absorbed – to dive into his TV. But still he hesitated, and dreamed – of walks in the park, hand-in-hand on a sunny day. Happiness ... It was still possible. *Was it still possible?* And of course tomorrow was Eid-al-Fitr, the festive day celebrating the end of Ramazan, and he was going to his mother's for the feast. Everyone would be there. So many people and it just got harder and harder – he had nothing to say. The thought made him shudder, but that was tomorrow – another day. And, as inevitable as it was, this was now, and there was no force strong enough to prevent him from indulging.

Imtiaz gazed at the Event Horizon. In front of him, nirvana: suspension of sorrow, extinction of self, immersion in bliss. And behind? A sad, lonely and simple man, with nothing to look forward to and no answers left. But still he hesitated, still he dreamed – *Switch it off. Change your life* ... But just then the plumber entered her – slowly, cautiously, measure-by-measure. She buckled, bringing herself a little closer and opening herself up wider to ease his passage. Imtiaz was powerless and conceded defeat. *The more I sink into fantasy, the further I get from reality.*

3

Salman was sitting alone in the *masjid's* main hall, enjoying the peace and quiet. Most of the congregation had now left to start their own celebrations, as would he eventually, but not for a while. His wife, his two kids, his parents – they'd all be expecting him home soon enough, but he could buy himself a little time. Well, either way, he was going to indulge.

He'd been hoping for a quiet Eid, just the immediate family, but then the whole thing had snowballed. First his brother Aadam had invited himself along, which he was OK with, but then his mother had gone and ruined the whole day.

'We're going to Arwa *Masi's* for Eid,' she'd declared nonchalantly a few days back. 'Pasha and Imtiaz are going to be there.' His heart had sunk. He'd protested but the damage had been done – there was no getting out of it. He liked his Aunty, his Arwa *Masi*, but her husband was a fool. And as for her sons, well ...

He and Pasha were once close, but the words of a wise man offered consolation: '*He who accords his wisdom to overcome his voraciousness is more elevated than the angels, and he who accords his voraciousness to overcome his wisdom, is lower than the animals.*' He felt vindicated. But he still couldn't stem the bitter memories from surfacing. Him and Pasha. School days. Their so-called happy days.

Sunday, Monday ...
trying the latest moves with two left feet.

Tuesday, Wednesday ...

stepping up and stepping out. Hanging loose, looking bored and being ... *COOOL* ...

Thursday, Friday ...

snub what you like and love what you hate. Staying out till 3am, drinking Plonk de Plonk.

Saturday ...

beers, birds and baltis. Lager, chicks, kebabs. Meat markets and cows. It was non-stop action with zero-participation. Salman was the Boy in the Bubble.

It was the best thing he did to break from that life. Leave the British to drown in their own swill. Salman felt privileged – saved. Unlike Pasha, still lost somewhere in that Saturday night, the bloody coconut. Brown on the outside and white on the inside. There really was nothing worse.

4

It was 5.51 am and Pasha was already awake. Even though the day due to break was a weekday, he wasn't going to the office. Not today. He knew this last night when he'd left his alarm off, but nevertheless here he lay, wide-awake, minutes from when it would ordinarily have rung. Damn his internal clock – he didn't know how to switch that one off. He'd always operated with Teutonic efficiency, which of course was a very British quality (if you follow). Thinking, though, about how his minions would fare in his absence, he wondered if that still applied to this generation. He mused on the point, letting his mind drift. *These people's great-great-grandparents built an empire.* They were once a disciplined people, the British. And now? Pasha concluded that it was a great time to be him; a great time to be alive. Such smug satisfaction ... Ibrahim Pasha Walayat – Pasha to his friends, Pasha to everyone. He'd always preferred his lush, Turkic, middle name, to his Arabic first name. No-one ever called him Ibrahim, except his mother.

Birds chirping outside distracted him and he turned to see how far into the dawn chorus they'd reached. The drawn curtains were opulent and thickly-set, but had the sun already risen there would have been light leaking in – and yet he lay in total darkness. There was still time. If he got out of bed now he could say his prayers on this auspicious day, this Eid morning, before the day broke – just as it was meant to be. He remained unmoved, though. At a practical level he wasn't even sure he could remember the recitations. And before starting he'd have to bathe, perform ablutions to cleanse the stains from his decadent life. This really was an increasingly difficult sell. Stretching under the warm duvet, tilting from the recovery position to lie virtually flat on his front, he settled on enjoying the morning in bed. His penis, trapped between himself and the mattress, burgeoned into an erection. He could have really done with his girlfriend right now. She wasn't by his side, though; not this morning. His lifestyle and the day to come were just too jarring. Feeling so healthy, however; so full-of-blood, he now regretted asking her to leave. He had an animal's urge to nuzzle up to her, to sink into her. He cursed his bad decision but was quickly consoling himself – her riches would be his again, and soon. He ran by the idea: sex as a prize, his prize for enduring Eid. Sold.

Contented once more, he opened his eyes ... The first shafts of light were breaking through – Eid-al-Fitr was nearly here. He suddenly thought of his long-deceased grandmother and remembered her getting all flustered one Eid morning, once upon a lifetime ago. 'So much for the woman of the house to do,' she would bemoan half-heartedly, whilst not begrudging her lot at all. That didn't stop her reciting the mantra, though, as if she were flicking prayer-beads out aloud.

And there he is, little Pasha, sitting in the kitchen of the family home in Karachi. His legs swing unimpeded under the seat, still too short to touch the ground. And he's watching this woman in wonderment. He doesn't know what to make of it, of any of it: this day, this strange country, his grandmother's fuss. He's fascinated by her, though, this round ball of a woman. She's rolling from room to room, arms gesturing here and there, and machine-gunning orders to daughters and daughters-in-law: '*Rashida, find that silver leaf ... You can fry those samosas now, Arwa. Sara, crush those cardamom seeds and lay out the sweetmeats. Where is that silver leaf?!*'

On being woken up he'd initially been grumpy, but now he's just plain mesmerised. He doesn't understand the live show that he's watching, but he's gripped. And besides, anytime his mummy or one of his aunties passes by, they make time to give him a taste of something, or tickle his tummy, or give him a kiss and a hug, enveloping his little face in their bosoms. He loves his mummy and he loves his granny, the grand-matriarch whom everyone else is afraid of. But now dawn is close to breaking and a sonorous cry cracks open in the distance. He's heard it before; they've all heard it before, but this time it stops Granny in her tracks. A tear rolls down her cheek. She approaches little Pasha, cups his face in her hands and tilts his head up gently.

'Do you know what that is, *Mere Chand*, my piece-of-the-moon? Do you know what he is saying?' He shakes his head and maintains his wide-eyed gaze. 'It's the *Azaan*, my son; the call to prayer, and he is proclaiming the Glory of Almighty God. Your father has taken you away from me, away from us all, and you will grow up in a strange land. But never forget who you are. Promise me that.'

Surprisingly his erection hadn't waned, though solely through the trapped blood, rather than mental or physical stimulation. He shifted slightly. The room was now as full of light as it would get, when filtered through those ostentatiously thick curtains. Morning had broken. It was too late to pray. Pasha felt neither shame nor satisfaction, yet a nascent grin remained on his face as he drifted back to sleep.

5

Health is a state of harmonious chemical balance, and maintaining that balance is key. Beyond diet and exercise, even thoughts and behaviours can disrupt the equilibrium, and thus Natural Law was prescribed: a design for physical, mental and spiritual harmony. Failure to adhere to Natural Law would and will harm us: physically or psychically.

And thus, through the kinks in our armour, the efficiencies of our bodies become compromised. Be it a restless mind or an angry disposition, a tendency towards obesity or sexual overindulgence, our bodies pay for weaknesses hard-coded into us at the moment of conception. First come the warning signs: loss of sleep, headaches, irregular bowel movements. Nature informs that all is not well and you either heed its gentle prod or tear up its message through allopathic drugs. Ignorance isn't bliss though – not when the shit-storm continues to brew, just out of sight. And one day maybe all those hamburgers you ate, or that hatred which you didn't even try to excise, or that broken-heart which you never quite managed to mend, will be the last straw. And what black-day will that herald? What misfortune will it precipitate? The growth of a cluster of deviant cells? But were you always in control? Can you be blamed for being so easily excitable, without even time to chew your food? Was it your fault that you were all alone, that you never found your soul mate? You never had that trump card to play, no curve ball in your pocket. Dinner for one can really destroy a person, but you didn't know that when you were young *and arrogant; only after the window had finally shut. But were you born arrogant, did you become arrogant or were you allowed to become arrogant? And when it's all over, will God wipe the tears from your eyes or will you stand and fall by your own account, without mitigation?*

Everyone must expect illness – after all, we are here to pay off debts. But whilst most of us are compromised, there are others whose protection is complete. They will enjoy good digestion and assimilation, eat moderately and be well built. And their steady minds will incline them towards sobriety, forgiveness and measured moves as opposed to fright, fight and flight. In mind and body they, amongst all, are best equipped. Like rice or wine, age becomes them, enhances them, whereas most cannot escape from withering under its assault. In Ayurveda, such a state is known as Tridosha.

Nazneen sat upright in bed, holding the book in her lap. Comfortable in her lotus position and with her back supported, she wrapped herself up in languor. The phone then rang, the shrill tone violating her quiet space, and with irritation she picked up.

'Happy Eid!' someone blurted out down the line. 'That is right, isn't it, Naz? That is the way you say it?'

'Oh hiya, Nikki! Wow, what a surprise! Not to hear from you, I mean. It's just today; I wasn't expecting to hear from you, today.' Nazneen winced. What a silly thing to say – way too honest. She gulped air as discreetly as possible. 'Oh and yeah, thanks girl – "Happy Eid" is fine.' They both giggled. 'But how did you know?'

'Know what, hun?'

Nazneen reached for the remote and, settling back once more, switched on the TV.

'About Eid. That today is Eid – you've never mentioned it before.'

Nikki fell silent as the TV sprang to life, and a scream of *Allah-u-Akbar!* boomed through the speakers, chased by a volley of gunfire. Nazneen pounced on the remote, assaulting the volume button. The footage ended and cut back to some studio, where a camera French-kissed a cartoon of a man, replete with fuzzy beard, glass eye and hook for hand. Rendered mute, however, he communicated more clearly. The camera adjusted, zooming in for porno detail, leaving the viewers in no doubt:

Eid, Islam, Muslims ... Mad Mullahs, Militants, Terrorists. Rabid, scathing, foaming at the mouth. Book burners, wife beaters, rag wearers. Suicide bombers and Jihad.

YOU LOVE LIFE; WE LOVE DEATH.

Who didn't know that today was Eid?

'Oh...' Nikki almost whispered. 'I think I heard it. Somewhere...'

Silence. Nazneen swallowed her rage, and her hatred for the West, and her hatred for the Muslims.

'Listen, Naz...'

'Yeah?'

'It's Charlie's second birthday soon.'

'A-ha.'

'Will you come?'

'Sure, Nikki, sure,' she exhaled, still trying to centre herself.

'Great! I've got loads of people coming, mostly from my pre-natal group – they're really nice but I don't know many of them too well. Will you come early, Naz? Help me out a bit?'

'No worries, girl. But I'm no good in the kitchen, OK? You can put me in charge of decorating!'

'I'll put you in charge of Charlie, more like! Honestly, where have you been? You've not seen him in ages. He's changing all the time. He's really big now and a lot more playful. He's a really happy little boy.'

Nazneen sank back under the still-warm duvet, seeking embryonic comfort. *Oh, the luxury!* She stretched her legs before bringing them back up, and the next moments were spent simply revelling under down, her legs affecting a half-hearted pedalling motion.

The phone rang again.

'A change of plan already, Nikki?' She spoke lightly and stretched to fill a glass of water.

'Hi, Nazneen.'

The tumbler slipped from her hand, the glass smacking into her knee as cold water splashed her thighs.

'Nazneen, it's Martin.'

Still no response.

'How did you get my number?' She gazed down at her soaked nightie and bed sheet, the warm pastel blue being devoured by a dark, expanding wetness.

'Remember Stefan? From uni? You bumped into him a while back. We still hang out together.' Her face soured. *Stefan, uni, Martin* ... Who the hell did these characters think they were, invading her space? And today of all days. 'I'm sorry about last time – when we met.'

She scoffed silently.

'You know my husband could have picked up.'

'So? We're friends, right? Old friends. It's OK to have a past, isn't it?'

'What makes you think you ever came up in conversation? And anyway, why call me? I thought you were only into "new experiences".'

She winced as she remembered – the last time they met, post-uni, after having split up.

'Please. I tried to explain. I wrote to you. I don't know if you ever got my letter.'

She got off the bed, threw the duvet on the floor and ripped the bed sheet off.

'What do you want, Martin?'

'Just five minutes ... To explain. That day when we met up – it was so disorientating.'

'Why? Because we weren't a couple anymore?' Cupping the portable to her ear she stomped over to the linen basket, slamming the sheets in.

'No. Dunno ... Maybe in part. It was just weird, meeting in London. And us both in suits!' He laughed nervously but found no echo. 'I'd just wanted to recapture. Remember. I hated this city when I first got here.'

'Really? You could've fooled me. I think the phrase you used was "Pleasure Dome".'

'Jesus, try and understand. This place is so ... anonymous. Back in Bournemouth, at uni – we mattered. In London I became just another monkey in a bloody suit. I was trying to be upbeat, let you know I was doing all right.'

Silence.

'I should go, Martin. I've actually got a lot on today. Speak another time, yeah?'

'You think I could ever forget you, Nazneen?'

And there was a sincerity in his voice that rattled her. She stayed silent.

'You ... you plague my thoughts.' He spat the words out like he was trying to exorcise demons. 'Remember Colorado? I keep thinking of that summer. Remember Red Rocks?'

She stood frozen at the end of the bed. On the wall above was a framed picture; her and Aadam on their wedding day.

'We went hiking there a few times. It was kind of innocuous, really. You've probably long forgotten. But just lately, Christ ... it keeps coming back to me.'

Red Rocks Park, Colorado. An infinite blue horizon, black as coal by night; red sandstone pillars, lacerating earth and sky. But it wasn't about the terrain, it wasn't about him and it wasn't even about her. It was them – Nazneen and Martin – their summer together.

'I never understood why we broke up,' he confessed, his voice wrenching. 'Why you walked away ... from me.'

She couldn't take her eyes off that photo. Aadam looked so ... *childlike*, his joy unrestrained. But Red Rocks – she hadn't forgotten either. Could never forget.

'I'm happily married, Martin.'

'I'm glad. Never change though. Promise me that. Keep my number, OK?' He hung up. Nazneen kept the phone clasped to her ear, the monotone signal rattling her skull.

6

It was mid-morning and Salman stood outside the *masjid,* mapping out the day ahead: home in thirty minutes, relax with the family for a couple of hours and then leave at one. They could get to Arwa *Masi's* a little late – it wasn't an issue. *Be in-control,* he ordered himself whilst inhaling greedily. *And don't worry about Pasha. It will be interesting, our reunion today.* He looked around with wide eyes, willing phantom demons to challenge him.

Just as he began walking the wind picked up. His jacket was unzipped and the currents fleeced him, the sudden cold wrap shocking his body. He did up his jacket and took a scarf out from a bag, quickly tying it around his neck. He thought he must look so strange: loose and long cream-coloured robes, a short black leather jacket and a multi-coloured, multi-striped scarf. He resented having to look so undignified.

The wind blew again, but now reinforced he leaned into it to make headway. He looked up to the heavens to see only dark clouds – not pregnant with rain; just a stillborn day. Roadside trees were stripped bare, their naked branches shivering with him. A ball of scrunched up newspaper rolled across the road before hitting the kerb. Stuck. Modern-day tumbleweed for the desert nation. Rain he could handle, snow he could handle – anything real he could handle. But all this just sapped his soul.

With hands buried in pockets and chin nuzzled under scarf, he began walking stoutly. Turning a corner, he hit the main thoroughfare. Twenty-five minutes down this one straight road and he'd be home.

An old, old lady crept out of a newsagent's up ahead. She was bent double and more shuffled than walked, her feet barely coming off the pavement with each step. Two young women pushing prams and chatting animatedly strode towards her. The lady was inching forwards almost perpendicular to reach the crossing, and the young mums manoeuvred smoothly around her, without even interrupting their chat. Neither even threw the hunched sack in the middle a glance as they breezed past.

There were roadworks up ahead, a section having been cordoned off for "Emergency Works". There was no activity, though, as all workers had downed tools for a break. Salman counted five: pouring hot drinks from flasks, reading the day's redtops and smoking fags. An attractive woman strode confidently by. With her head held high she wore her layers with style, despite the weather: all eyes locked onto her. Wolf whistles, some simian cackling and a few *all right darling!*s followed, which naturally she didn't respond to. Then Salman caught the attention of one of the workmen. The man gestured to his pals, making them aware of the latest entertainment to arrive.

'What's up, Osama? You fancy a piece o' that as well?' He was grinning broadly and willing Salman to meet his gaze.

'Yeah, don't blame you mate,' chipped in another. 'All that time stuck alone up there in them mountains – you must be gagging for it.' All five started to titter. *Don't look at them.*

'Oi, Ozzy!' began a third, raising his voice despite Salman now being alongside, 'You get cable up there?' *Don't look ...* 'No? You've probably not even knocked one off in yonks. No wonder you're so uptight, all this Jee-had and stuff.' They were all laughing openly.

'Tell ya what, Ozzy, the next one's yours, mate. On the house!'

'A gift from her Majesty!' was the final volley rolled off. All he could hear was unabashed laughter and he pictured them bent over in hysterics. He was relieved to finally be out of their range.

The wind picked up again, this time accompanied by rain. It wasn't a downpour but Salman's initial grit had now gone: torpor was setting into his mind, inertia in his body. He saw three Asian men pulling up the shutters of a shop front. It was a restaurant and he figured they were opening up early, especially for Eid. All three wore suits that, whilst not objectively pricey, were probably the best in their wardrobes. Ties were done up with the knots made neatly, and two of them had meticulously gelled and combed their hair. All in their Sunday Best, especially for Eid. *Just who do they think they are?*

Seeing a bus stop up ahead he decided to wait under the shelter. He figured that getting a bus now wouldn't save much time; in fact it might even make for a longer journey, but he just couldn't face the walk – not anymore. He veered underneath the roof and felt immediate relief, hearing the wind and rain batter tin and glass, instead of him. He looked down the road but no bus was on its way so he just stood there, foregoing the empty seats.

'Gosh, what a miserable day!'

He turned round, startled to see a woman smiling at him. She was heavily pregnant; late twenties, early thirties and with bags of groceries by her side, and a rosy glow to her cheeks.

'Yes, yes it is,' he replied tentatively, before considering his response to be somewhat effete. 'Sorry, I was miles away. You're right – it *is* a miserable day. I can't wait to get home.' The woman looked at him quizzically and he smiled with embarrassment.

'Get home?' she remarked. 'My day has only just begun! Do you work nights or something?' Salman smiled, feeling more relaxed. She was still catching her breath and her words were mixed in with puffs and pants. The supermarket was only nearby but in her condition and this weather, and all those bags, one could quickly get despondent. Yet here she was, wiping matted locks from her forehead and enjoying being alive. Salman thought of a robin in a snow-covered landscape, busily foraging for berries: winter cheer personified.

'No, no, I'm not working today. I've got the day off.' He tensed a little before continuing, 'I'm a Muslim and today is Eid. It's like our Christmas.' He paused, waiting, actually expecting to see a note of discomfort as he mentioned the M-word, but it didn't come. 'I've been at the mosque this morning and I'm going home now to celebrate with my family.'

'Oh, that's nice!' exclaimed the woman. Her eyes were bright and her face seemed full of genuine delight. Salman felt renewed – such an elixir, the milk of human kindness. 'Do you give presents to each other?'

'Yes, of course. And we have a feast and enjoy being together. It's exactly like Christmas, minus the drink and the Queen's Speech!' Salman revelled in his own joke.

'Ah, that's wonderful. How many children do you have?' She settled into one of the seats and looked up, her smile uncomplicated.

'I've got two – a boy and a girl. They're right little terrors.' He pictured his Taimur and Aaliyah and wanted to be home now more than anything. 'And you?'

'Oh, I've got just the one, young Emily,' and she opened up her handbag and prised a passport-sized photo from her wallet. She handed it to Salman who looked at a miniature version of the lady herself – all big smile, rosy cheeks and strawberry blonde hair.

'And another one on the way, I see,' he gestured merrily at her bump whilst handing the picture back.

'Yes, yes. Only one month to go now!' She caressed her stomach before breaking once more into that pinball smile. 'Emily has already said that she only wants a baby sister, and that if we bring home a boy she'll leave him outside at the bottom of the garden!' The two of them laughed, enjoying the innocence of a child. 'We have so much to look forward to, sometimes it makes you desperate for those whose futures are so bleak.'

'What do you mean?'

'Oh you know, what we're doing in Iraq. I feel almost guilty when I look at what I have – especially when my country is wrecking the futures of others.'

'Yes, it's a sad business,' offered Salman simply. He'd never discussed the issue with a non-Muslim and took a cautious line.

'It's more than sad,' she stressed. 'It's an absolute travesty. Did you know that Iraq is being forced to pay reparations – even post-Saddam? Is that not sick?'

'I didn't know that,' he said, still unsure how to react.

'No? Well it gets worse. A lot of that money is going to big business. People don't even have clean water and there are dogs eating corpses in the street, and yet Iraq is forced to handover money to American Express, Texaco and Toys-R-Us.'

Salman was in rapture. He'd never heard a British person speak like this. He looked at her, her face thoughtful, all that sunshine gone.

'You shouldn't feel guilty, my dear. If God has been generous to you in this life, then just thank Him and enjoy your bounty!'

'I'm not a believer. It's not that I definitely don't believe, more that I don't know or care. God isn't going to come down here and wave His magic wand. It's up to us, isn't it?'

'Hmm, hmm.' Salman wasn't listening, his mind having got stuck at the point where she said she didn't believe. He noticed a bus finally appear on the horizon.

'Tell me, what does your faith give you?' Trying to avoid the question, Salman stayed focused on the bus.

'It gives my life meaning.'

'But my life *has* meaning,' she retorted. 'I love my child and my partner and they love me. Isn't that enough?'

'I'm glad it is for you,' muttered Salman, cursing the bus's slow progress.

'So why do you need more?'

Salman turned sharply.

'Look, lady. Islam is Allah's gift for humanity, His final word. We're all bound by His commandments. If you choose to ignore them then that's your loss.' The bus pulled up. The front door opened and Salman bolted for it, but then he remembered her condition and all that heavy shopping. He hesitated but picked up a couple of bags. She expressed mild surprise and smiled awkwardly, but he avoided any eye contact. He let her in first and after paying for his ticket he followed behind. Laying the bags at her feet he sprung up to make for the upper deck.

'Well, have a happy Eid!' She spoke quickly before he was out of sight.

'We say *Eid Mubarak*, actually.' He glared, hissing his displeasure. He waited until she forcibly looked away before rounding the corner and going upstairs.

7

Imtiaz was cold. Finally in bed after exhausting the night's entertainment, he wrapped the duvet around himself tightly; a spent force entombed. On his side he brought his legs right up, his knees close to his chest. The position though was uncomfortable and he soon gave up, bringing his hands together in his lap. He had recently cum however and his too-thin semen had spread and begun drying off. His lap, therefore, was both cold and damp. *How can my cum be cold?*

The mercy of sleep beckoned, though, and accepting gratefully, he began sinking. As he went below the surface he took one last glimpse at the clock radio, establishing that it was 10.01 pm and that the radio was on low. And then ... nothing. He slipped into slumber gently, belying the frenzy of the day just done. Stillness. Stillness and quiet, or rather almost quiet. If you listened hard, you could just make out the radio, the broadcaster introducing the new show, but Imtiaz was no longer listening; gentle waves were lapping his shore. *Come, come my son,* the night beckoned. *Enter my waters and drift away.* Seduced, he sank, offering no resistance. He landed softly on the water's bed, and with arms crossed and legs tucked under he simply was: no eye movement, a minimum of brain activity. A mere babe in an incubator. *Heal me ...*

Then suddenly Imtiaz is rising. Propelled upwards by a force other than his own he looks up at the approaching surface. There are lights, big bright lights. And people – lots and lots of people. He breaks through and is met by a din. Such a din. But now Imtiaz is rising beyond the crowd; the noisy, passionate spectators. And the searing heat isn't going to distract him either. Or the tension, or the drama. For destiny is calling the Boys from Pakistan.

Imtiaz squats behind the stumps and claps his gloved hands together. 'Come on, Imran!' he shouts, but Imran is well out of earshot. He is busy instructing his men, marshalling those of his troops that are nearby. The match is tight, delicately poised, but the initiative is now shifting England's way. The Pakistan captain must engineer a change. Imran Khan gestures to the man standing about twenty yards deep, square of the wicket on the off side. *Pull further back*, he says with his hands. Inzy obeys, his eyes locked on his captain.

Cricket. Baseball for gods. Carried by the force of empire but adopted with relish by Indian princes, Pathan warriors and the sons of slaves. Now the time has come to teach the old master a lesson, and there's no better stage than the World Cup Final.

Imtiaz surveys the scene whilst his captain continues fine-tuning. He rocks his head back to look into the Melbourne sky at night, but is hit full-face by the massive light towers. There is no night inside the Melbourne Cricket Ground – the MCG is all lit up. The stadium is packed, every seat taken. There must be 85,000-plus in here. Most are Aussies and Imtiaz wonders who they'll be supporting. The home team was knocked out some time ago and now, as hosts, they have to entertain the Pakis and the Poms. Poor bastards ... The rest are Englishmen and Pakistanis, and Union Flags and Crescent Moons abound. The green-and-white is still flying, though not as proudly as it was – Fairbrother and Lamb are starting to take the game away. But as Imran had said in the dressing room, '*Don't forget, we fight like cornered tigers.*'

The volume in the stadium dims and Imtiaz looks up – the Great Khan has finished his instructions. Everyone is in position. In the company of his men, the captain is once again alone. He's walking away from the centre towards the boundary, the perimeter of the playing area. His walk is perfect, each step seeming measured. Four tiers of spectators home in on one man, releasing their emotions: awe, expectation, love and hate pour into the night sky.

Imran Khan turns back towards the playing arena: the eye of the storm. *Thud!* He gazes at the ball in his hand before looking up. Alan Lamb is staring straight back at him. Man takes on man within the team game. Imran can feel his heart pounding. His face is pulsating, his ears are pulsating. Waves of heat emanate off him. One last check to the left and one last check to the right – he sees several of his men dotted in a loose ring around the wicket. An ambush of tigers, just waiting to pounce. First in line is Imtiaz, the wicket keeper. He's already crouching down behind the stumps and is well back, maybe even twenty yards. *He's judged that well*, thinks Imran. *This is juicy Melbourne turf and I'm extracting a lot of lift. That Imtiaz is a good kid with a steady head. He'll go far.* From Imran to Fairbrother to Lamb to Imtiaz, there is almost a straight line. Bowler, batsman, batsman, wicket keeper. Pakistani, Englishman, Englishman, Pakistani. *Who is vulnerable now?* The slip fielders, taking their cue from the trusty Imtiaz, lock into position – a trap just waiting to be sprung. Slips one and two, gully, cover point, mid-wicket and square leg. Check. *Fee-fi-fo-fum, I smell the blood of an Englishman.* Imran begins running in. The noise inside the cauldron increases, the excited overspill of anticipation. With ball in hand he hits the crease and leaps into his delivery stride, an archer drawing back the bow ... *Whoosh!* Lamb has half-a-second to play with: he's got to judge height, angles, the bounce once the ball pitches as well as speed, but he's seen it all before. It's not quite child's play but it's well within his compass; he sights the ball early and sees it big. *Tonk!* Alan Lamb drives sweetly through the off-side. He hasn't adopted the classic position but has lazily let the ball come onto him, his head over its line all the while. Cock-sure ... The ball cuts through cover-point and gully before clattering into an advertising hoarding. An Aussie brewer is grateful for Lamb's shot selection. Four runs. It's the end of the thirty-fourth over and from here the Englishmen needn't sweat. Imran stands with hands on hips, watching his team chase air. It's a painful display and he's got to turn this around quickly. Panic arrives in the heart of the warrior. Meanwhile, Alan Lamb plumps his feathers and begins strutting around, chewing his gum with renewed gusto.

Imtiaz stands up. Not wanting to see a creeping dread in his team-mates' faces, or for them to detect the same in his, he surveys the grandstands, now rippling with Union Jacks. It looks magnificent. *This* is magnificent. He is here and this is as real as the sweat on his brow. Despite the situation he is alive like never before. He throws his head back and pulls his top away from his drenched chest. He's so hot.

Imtiaz tossed the quilt away, giving his body the chance to cool down. He was breathing through his mouth, his nasal passages having become congested. The virus entered several hours earlier and established itself inside his nose. It did as viruses do and multiplied and multiplied and multiplied again, leaving it ready to take off. And the destination? The throat? The ears? The sinus cavities in the bones of the head? Luckily it was detected and histamine was released. Blood flow to his nose increased and his nasal tissues swelled up. His core temperature was raised to stop the virus reproducing, but he was wrapped up too tightly, preventing his system from self-regulating. A message was thus dispatched to disentangle himself, and he duly obeyed.

All the while the radio had been on, broadcasting to dead ears. In the speed of his descent he'd forgotten to switch it off; all those jokes, snippets of punditry and sober news items had simply wafted off. News bulletins came and went. Sports roundups left Imtiaz unmoved. He didn't know it but Pakistan were actually preparing for a big game, the Platinum Jubilee match being held in the majestic Eden Gardens, Kolkata. He'd have been excited by that, had he known – Eid 2004 was promising to be a real cracker. The present could wait, though, for he was deep in the past. Glory beckoned. He could almost taste it, they all could – but a change was needed. Wickets were needed. This partnership between Fairbrother and Lamb had to be broken.

Drinks break. The crowd takes a breather, the players take a breather. A cart is wheeled onto the pitch and everyone grabs some refreshment. Fairbrother and Lamb meet in the middle, away from prying ears.

'Nice shot there, Lamby,' says Fairbrother, praising his partner's efforts. They greet by knocking fists, the batsman's high-five.

'Thanks, mate,' states Lamb, trying to sound underwhelmed, but Fairbrother doesn't buy it. Lamb's mid-wicket stance, all leant up against his bat, is close to a pose. He's chewing some gum, checking it all out and tripping his nuts off. Fairbrother meanwhile sees Wasim come in from the deep.

Wasim Akram. A legend, a natural-born leader, a prince among men. That's all to come, though, for tonight he's only twenty-five and a star-in-waiting. He strides with purpose over to his mentor, his gait graceful, fluid. Athletically built and tall, he looks down at Imran, whilst looking up to him. He sniffs the air, the night air – it's nowhere near damp but the day's heat has dissipated, even within the cauldron of the MCG. It's now humid. Perfect. He picks up the ball and inspects.

'I think I should come back for my second spell, Captain. What do you think?'

'It's a bit early. Let me bowl a couple more and keep rotating Ijaz and Sohail from the other end.'

Wasim isn't convinced.

'There's some moisture in the air now, Skipper. And look at this ball's condition ... I reckon I can get it to reverse swing from the Pavilion End.'

Imran looks his protégé in the eye. He's right – if these two keep going, the match could be all but finished in six overs. A cornered tiger always comes out fighting. Lamb is picking him off easily because he's not getting any movement, whereas this kid can talk to the ball, make it dance for him. Imran places the ball in Wasim's hand; he himself doesn't let go.

'Come on, Was,' he both commands and pleads. 'Do it for us. Get us some wickets.' Mission accepted.

The drinks cart is wheeled off and Fairbrother sees Wasim adjusting his run-up marker.

'Don't do anything flashy against Was, just see him off,' he warns Lamb.

'Let's not lose momentum. Look for five to six runs an over. And be sharp on the singles,' Lamb retorts, re-asserting his seniority in the partnership. Meanwhile, Imtiaz crouches down behind the stumps with Wasim turning round at the other end.

Imtiaz was getting cold. The virus's progress had been checked and his temperature had lowered. His chest, though, was still exposed and he was losing heat. He was nearly awake and nearly asleep and re-wrapped the duvet around himself. Facing the radio he lifted his groggy eyelids to check the time. 12.05. Then a word pierced his mental fug: Eid. '... *Tonight for most of our listeners is just another night. But for Muslims, not only in this country but worldwide, tonight marks the end of Ramadan, the annual month of fasting,*' the broadcaster began introducing the new item. '*And tomorrow is Eid, a day of celebration. However three years after 9/11, we have assembled a panel to discuss the issues facing Muslims, and Muslims in the West in particular. Can they respond to contemporary challenges whilst preserving their identity? Can they be loyal citizens in Britain and in Europe, or will their first allegiance always be towards the* Ummah, *the worldwide Muslim community? Over the course of the next hour we'll be putting these and other questions to our panel.'* Imtiaz drifted back to sleep.

'Ms Petiffer,' began the broadcaster and chairman of the debate, addressing his opening question to the journalist, the counsel for the prosecution. 'What do you see as the major challenges facing Muslims in Britain today?'

'Well, as a woman I'll begin with women's rights. Women in the West enjoy freedom: freedom to work and near-equality in the workplace, ownership over their bodies, their femininity and reproductive powers. And education is their birthright. Muslims here not only have to respect this in theory, but embrace it in practice. We should no longer accept their daughters being smuggled out of the country to be forced into marriage. And we must make it clear that there is no place for the importation of barbaric, feudal practices, such as so-called "honour killings".' Looking over the rim of his spectacles, the broadcaster turned to the Arab gentleman seated alongside.

'Dr Qasim?'

Dr Qasim gulped.

'Nobody is going to defend honour killings or forced marriages, least of all myself, but it is simply not an issue for the majority of Muslim women, in this country or elsewhere.'

'Are you saying these issues are unimportant?' the lady half-turned, exaggerating surprise. Possibly a slam-dunk coming up within one minute?

'No, I'm not saying they are unimportant. I'm saying that in the context of this discussion – the future of Muslims in Britain and Europe – it's irrelevant.' This was too easy – time to mop up.

'Well I find that incredible. Incredible and offensive. How can we accommodate a religion that has misogyny encoded into its very DNA?'

'Ms Pettifer, you misunderstand me. Forced marriages and honour killings are, of course, a stain on the cultures that perpetuate such practices. But it is simply inaccurate to maintain that this is part and parcel of the lot of a Muslim woman. To make out that they, as a rule, live under such threats, is simply incorrect.' Dr Iqbal Qasim felt emboldened and patted himself on the back. Nevertheless his trimmed beard was now almost completely grey and he looked tired.

'Oh come now, Dr Qasim, the lot of women under Islam is appalling. And we're not just talking about isolated incidents. How do you explain the Taliban? Yet another blip? And at what stage do the blips join up to paint the complete picture? You can draw a distinction between theory and practice only up to a point.'

'That's a valid argument is it not, Dr Qasim?' the broadcaster interrupted. 'You can't forever claim that the religion itself remain detached, wholly untainted by the way in which it is repeatedly practised.'

'Indeed,' impressed Ms Petiffer. 'Is the case of Amina Lawal merely another blip? Do you want to defend the stoning to death of women for adultery? Doesn't Sharia law show up Islam for what it really is?'

Dr Qasim made to speak but his throat was dry. When he went to sip some water, Ms Pettifer couldn't help but smile.

Wasim's first spell of bowling had been crucial, with him snaring Botham early on to take the first England wicket. He'd received a ball that bounced more than expected and caught the outside edge of his bat. And, positioned perfectly behind the stumps, Imtiaz took a regulation catch. *Out!* He never dropped those, did that scion of Pakistan. Ian Botham, an ageing lion with his dreams in tatters, walked off prematurely from the biggest stage of his life. And Aamir Sohail helped him on his way, taunting the Englishman: *'Hey Botham, send your mother-in-law in!'* No one had forgotten his remarks on returning from a tour to Pakistan, where he described the country as *'the kind of place to send your mother-in-law to, all expenses paid.'* It was no wonder that Wasim found an extra yard of pace for Ian Botham. But now he has to do it again. Unless he can take a wicket and separate Lamb and Fairbrother, it will have been a pyrrhic victory. Wasim begins running in.

'Have you heard of the Lord's Resistance Army of Uganda?' Dr Qasim asked rhetorically. 'The LRA, for your listeners, is a fanatical cult, whose "soldiers" in large part are merely abducted children. Their leader, Joseph Kony, is a self-declared prophet who wants Uganda to live by the laws of the Ten Commandments. Does any of this sound eerily familiar to you?'

'Answer the question!' came a sudden cry from the audience. 'Indeed', impressed Ms Petiffer, emboldened by the support. 'I put to you, again, does not Sharia law show up Islam in its true light?'

'There are over 1.5 billion people who consider themselves Muslim. It does not mean the same thing to all of them. The LRA recruited young boys and inducted them with unimaginable cruelty, forcing children to kill children. And so I feel obliged to ask, what should I take from this? What are its implications and how widely should they resonate? Sure it tells me something about the LRA, but what else?'

'Well, beyond this tragedy confirming that Uganda has yet to find peace, more than forty years after independence, there's little else to say.'

'Really? Charles Taylor, the warlord supreme of West Africa, was a lay preacher. Once when challenged about the blood on his hands he retorted, "*Jesus Christ was accused of being a murderer in his time*".'

'You are demonstrating nothing to us here, other than that Africa still has many obstacles to overcome.'

'Sure, but what part does religion, does Christianity, play in all this savagery? After all, in both cases the main protagonists claimed to be acting in Christ's name. Should I take their claim seriously? And before anyone thinks this is solely a black African problem, let us not forget that the Afrikaners were not simply card-carrying Christians who happened to be racist, but rather their religion was used to explicitly justify their theory of racial superiority. And moving on from Africa altogether, what should I make of Christ's holy warriors in Europe? Have you not heard of Milosevic or Radovan Karadzic?' Dr Qasim paused, this time genuinely expecting a response. None came forth. 'I'm counting quite a few "blips" now,' he commented with a wry smile. 'So can I too claim the right to paint my own picture? And can I apply it wherever I like? To a Catholic from the Philippines? To an Anglican in India? And as an Egyptian shall I slap it on the face of my Coptic brothers and sisters, and henceforth look upon them too with greater suspicion?'

Wasim bowls. He hits the deck hard and the ball tears into its flight path. It traces parabolas, the first from release point to pitching being close to a straight line, with the second arc being more discernible. His sense of urgency is apparent and the delivery is fast, but his aggression has not been controlled. The ball doesn't pitch in line with the stumps and it swings way too much. The umpire judges it wide and thus a bonus run is awarded to England. Wasim turns immediately.

He doesn't want to discuss anything and neither does he wish to dwell on a poor first delivery – he needs to think about the next five. This is make or break.

'Oh come on,' began Ms Petiffer, sounding too relaxed for Dr Qasim's liking. 'The madness in the Balkans was *ended* by the West, the Christian West, at a time when the Arab and Muslim world could only blow hot air. And your reductionist suggestions with your African examples are just laughable. Africa suffers from manifold problems, each complicating the other. Poverty, disease and corruption interweave to create a dark, dark shroud, covering much of that continent. To say that Christianity stands alongside that unholy trinity is in very poor taste. Frankly you surprise me.'

'I said nothing of the kind,' he stated. 'In fact, I agree. I was playing ... how do you say, Devil's Advocate. My point is that the Taliban say no more about Islam than the LRA do about Christianity. Can you accept that point?'

Second delivery, thirty-fifth over. Wasim slides the ball up his hip, removing any excess sweat. He begins running in. His expression tells of an introspection that belies his youth: countless millions are focused on him and Wasim is meditating. Gathering momentum smoothly he exchanges the ball from right to left hand. *Take aim ... Fire!* His coil and spring action is effortless, poetry in motion, and he releases the ball. He's looking to get it to dip in, pitch in line with off-stump and then move away late. It doesn't happen, though. Instead of altering its line and coming back into the batsman, the ball continues from off-stump to leg-stump. Fairbrother plays a classic on-drive. The batsmen run three and thus exchange ends. Alan Lamb will receive the next ball.

'Dr Qasim, you live in England. You live here and enjoy our freedoms – freedoms that were absent from your own country. Here you are free to come on the radio and criticise; criticise *us*. Criticise our country, our culture, our politics and our religion. And you can go back home and no agent from the state will be waiting for you in the shadows. And you can then visit your mosque and pray to whichever God you like. Why? Because we are free. The Christian and post-Christian world is overwhelmingly free, Dr Qasim, and the Islamic world is overwhelmingly enslaved. It is driven by basket-case regimes that suppress their own and foment envy, and a religion that foments hatred. The Taliban lie at the end of a very large wedge, and therefore the association between them and Islam hold, in a way in which that between the LRA and Christianity doesn't.' Ms Pettifer's nostrils flared and she looked at her accuser with wide, glaring eyes. With her greying-blonde hair Dr Qasim thought she looked like an aged Valkyrie.

Fifth ball, thirty-fifth over. Wasim's third and fourth deliveries were tight and Lamb was unable to score. He'll be looking for runs now. Wasim releases the ball with its seam, the six lines of stitching down its middle, angled slightly to the left. The rougher side is to the fore, with the smoother, more polished, side behind. The ball is travelling extremely fast and turbulence is created as air passes more quickly over the smooth side. The ball swings in. It pitches in line with off-stump but then changes line. Alan Lamb doesn't see this, though. He's shaping to play a textbook on-drive, waiting for the ball to come onto his legs, but instead it's hurtling towards his off-stump. Wasim hears ball shatter wood. Lamb hears the terrible sound too and he looks round to confirm the worst. One heart breaks, the other soars. 85,000 people erupt. Wasim screams with joy and pelts towards Imtiaz, who from behind the stumps was the first to see Lamb's defences breached. They meet in the middle and high-five before hugging, sheer relief the overriding emotion. Team-mates dash inwards and flock around but Wasim can't acknowledge any of them. Still hugging Imtiaz, he is more being held up by him than being embraced, such is the release of tension. '*What a great delivery*!' gushes the commentator. '*Left-arm round the wicket. Alan Lamb has been cleaned up. And perhaps so too have been England.*'

'Do you know how the Taliban came into being or who these puritanical fanatics are? They are the orphans of your proxy war with the Soviets. The leftovers from the international network of Islamic militants that the U.S. helped to create, train, finance and arm, to fight the Russians in Afghanistan. You lose the right to now take a step back, point an accusing finger and look upon us all with contempt.'

'Dr Qasim,' sighed Ms Pettifer, responding as if talking to a child. 'The West might indeed have armed the Taliban with weapons, but not with ideology. That was theirs to begin with. We didn't force their women to wear tents, with nothing but a mesh to look out onto the world from. We didn't ask them to amputate the limbs of thieves or to ban chess and kite-flying. We didn't require that they close down girls' schools and dismiss women from work, and we certainly didn't cajole them into executing heretics. Islamic fundamentalism is as old as Islam. It's a home-grown creation; nothing to do with us.'

Last ball of the thirty-fifth over. Lewis to receive. Wasim bowls, continuing from around the wicket. This time the ball pitches outside the off-stump but it's an in-swinger, a very fast in-swinger. It jags back and squeezes through a tiny gap to hit the top of leg stump. There's no such thing as an unplayable delivery, but that's as close as you'll get. Chris Lewis has been clean bowled. The celebrations repeat but this time Wasim keeps running, unable to contain his joy. England will continue to fight but realistically it's over. In two balls he's turned the game on its head. He finally stops running and his handsome face is beaming.

'Once I was talking to a friend, an English friend, about Iraq. Not the current crisis but rather about sanctions, and the after-effects of the first Gulf War. I remarked that just beforehand there was a growing problem of obesity amongst Iraq's youth; a product of too much comfortable living. Doctors at the time wrestled with ways to get the youngsters off their couches, knowing full well the toll a sedentary life would take on them in later years. Then I told my friend that after the first Gulf War, obesity rather dropped away as a priority. I mentioned that on top of malnutrition, doctors were suddenly having to deal with the after-effects of depleted uranium. That because of the weaponry the Anglo-Americans had used, the water table had become poisoned and the food chain affected. And I explained that the young were especially vulnerable, and that, as a consequence, cancers of the immune system and congenital abnormalities, previously never recorded, were now being observed with alarming regularity. And then I said that in today's Iraq, there are babies being born with no heads – literally no heads – and he laughed. He was holding his son at the time, cuddling his one-year old baby in his lap, and he burst out laughing. He's not some callous buffoon or a maniac; on the contrary he is an intelligent, decent man, who loves his family and works hard to provide for them. And yet he found the thought of headless Iraqi babies, well, funny.

Are you starting to see a connection yet, Ms Pettifer? None of us lives in a vacuum, my dear. We are all intimately connected.'

'Dr Qasim,' interjected the broadcaster. 'We haven't, unfortunately, got time for riddles. Can you please explicitly state what you mean?'

'I mean, sir, that hatred begets hatred.'

'Nope. That's not good enough,' dismissed Ms Pettifer. 'Your rather clumsy friend cannot help you deny the charge.'

Dr Qasim paused, shocked by the steel of the woman.

'The truth is that in your eyes we just don't count, and never have done. And the genius is you've carried your people with you, through Crusades old and new. No wonder you were convinced that your troops would be hailed as liberators; greeted with cheers and garlands, no less! And no wonder my friend found the thought of headless Iraqi babies funny. Our hatred for you doesn't come from envy, from Islam, or even from our innumerable tin-pot regimes: it's born out of your hatred for us.'

Fairbrother is holding up the party. Despite Wasim having inflicted serious wounds, England continue to fight. And with Fairbrother there, anything's possible. Minds need to be concentrated. Aaqib Javed delivers a quicker, skiddy ball that comes onto Fairbrother a fraction earlier than anticipated. He skies it, the ball going high up in the air without carrying. Only two men are nearby: Aaqib himself and Imtiaz. They both tear towards it, to the beat of 85,000 hearts in 85,000 mouths. But as the ball begins its descent Aaqib stops running – only Imtiaz can catch this one now. Constantly looking up past the rim of his floppy hat, Imtiaz cups his hands, slowing down slightly before the ball lands safely. Aaqib simply stands with arms aloft whereas Imtiaz continues running, wearing a big grin. Once again the stadium explodes into colour and noise. Spectators at the front of each tier bang the advertising hoardings in approval. The Aussies in the crowd, having been politely supporting both teams up until now, have finally thrown their weight behind Pakistan. Everyone loves a winner. It was a really well judged catch, and Imtiaz accepts everyone's praise without much fuss; he knows he's good.

'May I remind you, the both of you, that we are here to discuss the challenges facing Muslims, specifically here in the West?' the broadcaster reiterated in a desperate tone. 'We haven't much time left and I must ask you both to stick to the questions.'

'Absolutely,' began Ms Petiffer. 'And accordingly I would like to put to Dr Qasim that the greatest challenge facing British Muslims now, is how they respond to the War on Terror.' She was looking self-satisfied – mutual loathing filled the air. 'Leaving aside the politics of it all, of whether one agrees with the line taken by our government, one is obliged to live by the rule of law.'

'Without a doubt. Agreed.'

'So I ask you then, Dr Qasim, exactly how welcoming can we be towards Muslims, when according to MI5, London is saturated with sleeper cells of Islamic terrorists, just waiting to bring us to our knees? Do you know how frightened people are? I have friends who have stopped travelling on the Tube. I know others working in Canary Wharf or living nearby, who are thinking of moving for fear of being attacked. And you still want us to reach out to you?'

'Well I'm sure that if Iraqis can get on with their lives whilst Anglo-Americans drop 500-pound bombs on them, then you can keep your upper lip stiff. It is, after all, meant to be a very British quality.' Dr Qasim winced.

'Wow, that's a simply outrageous comment. Do you realise how hurt and offended British people were when they saw pictures of young Muslims in this country, rattling collection tins for Bin Laden?'

'Well it looks like they've finally called the nation's bluff, no?'

'Meaning?'

'Meaning they've been portrayed as fanatics for so long, they've at last descended into fanaticism.' Dr Qasim felt numb all over.

'So would you agree that the "challenges" are all but insurmountable? That Islam cannot co-exist here, in secular, pluralistic, democratic Britain?'

'I would say, Ms Petiffer, that theory and practice are often two different things. In theory Islam demands that adherents live loyally by their land, which is wherever they choose to make their homes. No buts, no exceptions. Furthermore one should work hard to contribute, so much so that others see you as an asset and would not want you to leave. None of this is new. This isn't a bolt-on, grudgingly applied to appease you; these are the immutable laws of Islam, of year-zero Islam. But as mentioned, theory and practice are so often very different. No one is listening anymore: not those kids, and not you. Entropy.'

The broadcaster cleared his throat.

'So in conclusion, Dr Qasim, would you say that Islam does or does not have anything to contribute to this country? Can it add positively to Britain's rich Greco-Roman and Judeo-Christian heritage?'

'Sir, I must tell you that however proud you rightly are of your heritage, your country today has little to do with either aforementioned axis. Socrates in his day would be what you now call a celebrity. A student of his, Alcibiades, often spoke of the extraordinary effect his words had on him. He once wrote that *"From the moment I hear him speak, I am smitten with a kind of sacred frenzy. And my heart jumps into my mouth and the tears start into my eyes."* Today throngs swoon similarly in front of TV personalities and pop-stars, people whose every move – indeed whose every word – is carefully crafted for them. Socrates demanded that his pupils look into themselves and transform their lives for the better. Celebrities ask you to buy products, which their accountants select for them to endorse. Therefore I say to you, sir, Ms Pettifer and listeners, that there are certain points between my world and yours at which I would politely decline any invitation to connect. However there are others – many, many others – where I'm crying out to be met half way. The rest is up to you.'

The match is over. Pakistan are the Cricket World Cup Champions of 1992. Despite some lusty blows struck by the remaining England batsmen, their contribution wasn't telling; just the last, proud stand of a dying animal. It was fitting that the final wicket fell to Imran – the closing act of a long, illustrious career. Ramiz took the catch, another running effort, and he almost took off as he kept on running. Imran the Leader just stood his ground, savouring the fruits of his life's work. Some fell to the earth and kissed the turf whilst others began dancing. The rest looked dazed, unable to absorb what they had just achieved.

As they make their way off the pitch, Imtiaz begins leading an impromptu *bhangra* jig. He is a great mover, is Imtiaz, one of that select band of men with natural rhythm. He steps in front of the whole team and begins dancing and singing: arms here, hips there. Some join in and others just watch, clapping and laughing. Imtiaz is such a joker, such an entertainer – everyone has fun when Imtiaz is around.

Outside the flat fireworks went off. First it was just one or two but soon there was a volley of bangs. Eid had begun.

Imran is handed the trophy; a crystal globe on a cubic base. The podium is hastily erected and dignitaries roll out from their executive boxes. Interviews are conducted and commiserations and congratulations offered liberally. Speeches are given and Wasim is made Man of the Match. At the precise moment that Imran holds aloft the trophy, fireworks are let off. The Melbourne sky becomes a riot of colours, exploding into the night. Imtiaz has of course seen fireworks before, but this was something else. He points one out to Wasim standing next to him, and the two friends savour the display. It's for them, all for them.

Bang! More fireworks. Fireworks inside, fireworks outside. Fantasy met reality. Imtiaz woke up.

8

'Ooh, ooh, ooh, ooh!' - The Nigerian takes to the pitch. He's coming on as substitute and being greeted by a chorus of monkey chants. It wasn't an uncommon experience for the player, or for English clubs in general, when competing in Europe.

The audio clip from the Santiago Bernabéu Stadium ended, and the broadcaster began interviewing the commentator from last night's game.

'Well, that's just utterly despicable,' roared the Englishman, his lungs stoked with outrage. 'Was it like that throughout the match?'

'In the first half we couldn't be sure,' began the Five Live chump. 'We got reports of some of the other black players already on the pitch being subjected to taunts, but we couldn't be certain ourselves. But when the Nigerian, Francis, came on in the second-half, the monkey chants could be heard from all around the ground. Why Francis should be singled out for the worst of the abuse, I don't know. It was just deplorable.' He was sounding both meek and aggressive, and in so doing was setting the mood for the item, the radio station, indeed the whole damn nation. Everyone fell into line, everyone knew their role: pundits and politicians queued up for a slice of the action, eager for the free brownie-points on offer. Pasha's nostrils flared. He hadn't got time for this. He loved his radio but today he only wanted a background noise, a wall of sound. Yet now it had penetrated his foreground and displaced his pre-occupation: Eid. Pasha was already late and playing catch-up, before he'd even started. He'd cursed himself on waking, when he turned to see that it was 8.30. It was far too late when he had to be at his mother's in London by 1.00. And that was just the time that everyone else would start arriving. He had planned on being the first one there, to have some time alone with her before the others arrived. *Why did I fall back asleep?*

A procession of the disgusted followed: the captain was interviewed and said it was shameful. The coach was angry, the sports minister appalled and everyone called for an enquiry. *The Spanish should do this, UEFA should do that.* The nation coalesced, unified by victim-hood. The previous night's commentator was wheeled out again and repeated his incomprehension as to why Francis got the brunt of the abuse. "Because he's the blackest of the black players, you dick," muttered Pasha, getting increasingly wound up.

Listeners' texts were read out: *I taped the game for my seven-year-old son, and had to tell him this morning that I couldn't let him watch it. He's in tears now. What should I say to him?*'

Pasha was close to throwing up. *Everyone has their blacks,* he mused, furiously retuning the radio. And the Spanish, being more traditional folk, had simply stuck to the tried-and-tested. The English, however, had moved on. What was their anthem, for when they played Turkey? *"Oh I'd rather be a Paki than a Turk, oh I'd rather be a Paki than a Turk, oh I'd rather be a Paki, rather be a Paki, rather be a Paki than a Turk."* Pasha considered the contrast in reaction ... *We're your niggers now.* But then again, the Pakis couldn't just throw their hands up in the air and play the uncomplicated victim. They had a responsibility, a part to play, and they blew it. *They? We?* Exactly who was he?

He slammed the radio down by the bathroom sink and patted his face dry with a towel. He'd just finished shaving and was stretching his face, making 'O's, appreciating the cool sensation on his cheeks. Pasha reached up for a bottle of aftershave. Resting it against the basin he began unscrewing the top, but in his haste it set off into a spin. It took clean off, bouncing on the basin's edge before coming to rest somewhere underneath the toilet. He cursed again and fell to his hands and knees, contorting himself within the space available. Unable to spot it he ran a couple of fingers along the toilet's base, where they met the thickly piled rug. He collected dust, pubic hair and toenail clippings, the assorted muck on his fingertips making his blood boil. He used to take so much care of this place when he first moved in, all those years ago. Then it was his pride and joy. It still was, but he just couldn't manage the domestic chores like he used to. It frustrated him, knowing that his standards had slipped. *Maybe I should get a maid*, he thought, without being convinced that it was the answer.

Sitting back on his heels his eyes swept across the rug, one of the set of mats that Imtiaz had bought him as a housewarming present. Functional but soulless, the rugs and his brother, he concluded neatly. Contempt was frothing in his stomach. Whilst the pile was still long, it had now lost its lift, its previous restitution, and it looked lank and lifeless. His face stayed spoilt as he considered the imminent prospect of his brother's company. What a dullard. And then there was Salman. *Fucking hell*. His innate effervescence, his once indefatigable *joie de vivre*, was dampening fast. It had become more vulnerable these days. *A sign of age*, he conceded, trying not to dwell on his fast approaching thirty–ninth birthday.

Predictably enough he soon found the top and he screwed it back on, without dispensing any of the Cool Water inside. This was expensive, quality stuff – to be applied only when in company. Female company. He felt sexy when he put this on, or rather it confirmed to him that he was sexy – big difference. Either way today was not such a day, and he reluctantly put it back, holding onto the bottle a moment longer than necessary. He needed to reassure himself, and the Cool Water, that normal service would be resumed soon.

9

Returning from Eid morning prayers, Aadam pulled up outside his house. Sighing deeply he decided to be gentle with himself – the day may indeed have just begun but the month gone by had been long. He was exhausted, but his fatigue ran deeper than the physical.

Outside an ill wind blew hollow, hitting discordant notes. Leaves rustled and tin cans rattled, protesting their violent displacement. Aadam adjusted the mirror ... His face bore a sobriety unbecoming of his thirty-two years. He rubbed his jaw line, trying to stimulate his pallid skin, but gave up: a massage was not the answer. Work, friends, London life – none of it really captured him any more. He'd drifted from a lot of people and others had drifted from him. He didn't like it, but anyway, Nazneen was it – his one silver lining.

He remembered when he first laid eyes on her – in a gym of all places – with her cranking up the pace on a treadmill. Her hair had been tied back in a simple ponytail, bobbing up and down, up and down, up and down ... And her skin shimmered with the hollow of her neck – a teardrop; hues dancing like sunshine on olive oil. He recalled sitting down on a nearby workbench, hunger tugging at his soul, and thanking the Lord for the miracle of lycra.

But that was yesteryear. He still loved her, of course, beyond question, but he felt like he was at war – in a state of standing revolution. He wanted to leave the country but his ideas were vague: difficult to share, reluctant to communicate. And besides, he was the man – this was his burden.

He turned towards his modest home. What had been a generously-sized four-bedroom, post-war, detached property had been converted into two less-than-generous flats. It was cramped and a bit rough round the edges, but it was theirs. He checked his watch. The day was still young; they could have a good couple of hours alone together, before they'd have to leave for Arwa Aunty's. It was time to have his furrowed brow smoothed out.

He walked delicately towards the front door, hoping that Nazneen hadn't spotted the car from their bedroom window. Inserting the key slowly, he measured its progress click-by-click, until fully in. Again there was precision in how he turned it, and he negotiated the resistance to minimise noise. Aadam pushed and the light door swung silently. He heard the muffled, tinny noise of the radio coming from the kitchen – the sound of home. Picking up some letters, he began climbing the stairs, distributing his weight so as to avoid creaking. *Which room was she in?* He could still hear the radio, so bereft of any other clues he headed for the kitchen.

She stood with her back to him. Jagjit Singh was singing, crying Ghalib's poetry, and Nazneen was evidently lost in the lament. Picture perfect. Wearing an old short-sleeved *shalwar kameez*, her pale wheaten arms shimmered under winter sunlight, streaming in through the window. He gently placed his belongings by the foot of the door and moved swiftly. Once upon her he pressed right up from behind, sweeping arms across her waist and torso. Tea spilt as she knocked a mug, buckling under the force.

'Hello beautiful,' whispered a voice by her ear. She inhaled greedily and twisted round.

'Aadam, don't ever do that again!' She half-screamed, half-coughed her protest and attempted a slap, but was encased in his embrace. His face was now buried in her neck, lips running against soft skin, his nose inhaling a delicate scent.

'Aadam, you really ... Don't do it again – it wasn't funny.'

He pulled away slightly, his arms still embracing her. Cupping her face, he kissed her on the third eye, his lips lingering. He gazed down, drinking in her royal features.

'Hello, beautiful,' he sighed again, wearing an almost pained expression. With eyes closed, his focus shifted: the feel of her breasts, the vibrations of her beating heart. His greedy hands swept over her, up to her warm, sticky-soft neck, touching, smearing lips, and then plummeting down, down to find the rise of her smooth curve. Nazneen made to protest but she was now giggling, declaring too easily that her resistance was fake. Easy prey. With her back to him, he squeezed with some force, nuzzling against her, working into her crevice. His hands dived underneath her tunic, negotiating their way around her layers. Done. Skin on skin. And then the doorbell rang.

'Leave it,' Nazneen immediately ordered, but an invisible cord had been snapped. The bell was no gentle *ding-dong*; no *excuse me*, but a heavy, monotonous drill. Forget simply hearing it; they actually felt it from where they stood. *But what should I do? Who can it be?* The postman? If so, the package could be important; work-related. Someone else? His brother? Had there had been a problem? He resisted the temptation until the bell rang a second time. Muttering something, he let go and hastily made his way out, deliberately avoiding the eye contact Nazneen was trying to make.

'*Eid Mubarak, Bhai!*' said Kishore on the doorstep, doing his best to sound full of festive cheer. Aadam looked his friend up and down, a big grin jarring with his appearance. This he wasn't expecting. Sensing his friend's alarm, Kishore began explaining, whilst Aadam bent down to play with Bina, Kishore's little girl. 'Kirti's away on a week-long conference so I decided to go out on the lash.'

'On a Monday frigging night? Bloody hell, Kishu, couldn't you at least wait until midweek? And anyway, what about this little one?' He spoke whilst unzipping the waterproof covering of the buggy.

'She's staying at her granny's so I decided to take advantage. I never bloody learn. I'm getting too old for this. I felt so rough this morning I phoned in sick. I was just moping around so I decided to go for a walk, help clear my head.'

'And then you picked up Bina from her *nani-ma's*?'

'Yeah, I needed quality time with my daughter. I work like a dog.'

'And pushing her around on a November morning whilst you nurse a hangover, counts as quality time?'

Kishore flinched.

'Look, I just needed to see my daughter, OK? I don't claim to be perfect.' He paused for a moment and looked genuinely vulnerable. 'Kirti's mum lives two streets away. It's sometimes a good thing but...'

'But mostly a bad thing. I know, *Bhai*, I know the score.' Aadam swept Bina up in his arms, having finally dealt with every zip, fastener and buckle. 'You been looking after Daddy, then?' he enquired of the little one, tickling her on the tummy. Bina beamed and nodded exaggeratedly, glowing at being made to feel so important.

'Anyway, let's not chat on the porch. It's freezing out here.' And, rubbing his hands, he moved to step into the flat.

'Whoa, one second Kishu. We're going to an Eid function shortly. You've picked a really bad day to turn up unannounced.'

'Come on, Aadam. Are you going right now? You don't look dressed. Just half an hour. I just want to get out of this cold, have a cup of *chai*. I've even brought the *chappu*,' he added, producing the day's newspaper from a pouch on the buggy. It was crisp and clearly unread. He must have bought it with this visit in mind. Aadam's will was relenting. 'What do you say, *Bhai*? Do you have any *chai masala*?' And he smiled a smile that said *help me out. I'm but a poor boy from a poor family,* which was untrue on both counts. Aadam held Kishore's gaze warmly, sharing an unspoken moment with his Hindu friend. Kishore completed that step.

Nazneen, thought Aadam. He hastened his climb, hoping to inform her before Kishore came into view. He entered the kitchen carrying Bina. Nazneen blinked hard, trying to control her reaction.

'Look who's here, darling. Kishore and Bina have popped by.' Aadam spoke louder than necessary and with an intonation more appropriate when talking to a child. She got up and tickled Bina on the calf before turning towards Kishore.

'Hi, Nazneen,' he said. 'Oh, and *Eid Mubarak*.'

'Thank you, Kishore.' She nodded stiffly before turning to Aadam, straining to maintain composure. 'Darling, we haven't got time for this. We've got to leave for your Aunty's soon.'

'I know that my dear, but I thought Kishore could stay a while – just half an hour. We'll go soon.'

Nazneen condemned him in silence, her eyes sparing him no mercy.

'I'm off out,' she offered simply. 'Your tea is cold.'

'Does it have *masala* in it?' asked Kishore.

'No.'

Aadam stood still and listened to her walk into the bedroom. There was silence before she came back out and cantered down the stairs. The front door shut with a bang.

10

Imtiaz woke abruptly. He'd been sleeping on his back and he rotated to face the clock radio – 1.36 am declared the luminous green dial, staring back impassively. His nose was blocked, his mouth bone dry. The pillow under his cheek felt cold, though instead it was damp; saliva dripping from the corner of his mouth. He felt so drained. The radio had been on all night but it wasn't the broadcaster that had woken him, but the fireworks. Fireworks? Of course: Eid. Dragging himself out of bed, he put his glasses on and shuffled to the window but his vantage point was not ideal. A thin fog hung in the air, but from his first floor flat it was irrelevant – he simply wasn't high up enough. He couldn't see anything but each rocket's last moments of life.

He lived in Watford, in a block of flats that backed onto the high street, but he couldn't see the life outside from where he was. A row of purposely-laid conifers separated the shops, pubs and restaurants from his residential complex, and he was just below their tops. He liked those trees. Tall, evergreen and dense of shrub, they did a surprisingly good job of blocking the sights, smells and sounds emanating from the world outside, providing an almost hermetic seal. It wasn't impenetrable, however, and on a Saturday night he could often hear the *boom-boom* being pumped out from Destiny's nightclub, just a short walk away. But this was early Tuesday morning and Watford's youth still had days of sobriety to endure, before *kismet* would once again come calling.

On this night it was the fireworks from the park nearby that had woken him, and he wondered how – from where he stood this was no extravagant display. In fact, "sparse" was the defining adjective. Rather than a festival of lights and sound being sprayed into the night sky, he'd seen four modest affairs in the last three minutes. It was as if each rocket was being launched with all the care, forethought and hesitancy of a homing pigeon. And they were clearly not expensive: instead of their last moments being an orgy of colour and noise, each whimpered along its final arc apologetically, before expiring. He really was staggered that this had woken him and made a mental note to buy some more Night Nurse; only alcohol and paracetamol would guarantee a deep sleep these days.

He remembered Eid from his childhood, recalling the almost surreal pleasure of that day. Couples – even jaded parents – had love in their eyes, and children were fussed over and made to feel so special. Imtiaz began drawing mental pictures: he could see little faces wrapped up against the cold, and sparkling eyes peeking out from under coat hoods. The sense in which a child became everyone's child, society's child, was a beautiful aspect of traditional culture and he took a surprising amount of comfort from acknowledging the fact. All on his own, though, the irony of his take on tradition soon made him uncomfortable; he couldn't even indulge in romanticising.

It had started to rain, no – spit gently – and he watched nascent droplets pitter-patter down, illuminated by the lamps accompanying every second tree along the boundary. The lamps straddled the entire perimeter, providing light where needed most along the parking bays. He felt tired and considered ending his window-side vigil, but he also knew he couldn't sleep without drinking something. A trip to the kitchen would be needed but right now that seemed too far. What to do? He felt sedated, numbed or, more accurately, lobotomised; he couldn't reach a decision. He eventually concluded he was comfortable enough, and so inertia settled the dilemma.

A heavy, low creaking noise came from outside, as the gates providing vehicular access slowly opened. A car waited for what seemed like an age before idling through and swinging into a bay directly under Imtiaz's gaze. Glad for the distraction and safe from being spotted, he followed the car as it ground to a halt, the gravel crunching satisfyingly under wheels. The whirr of the engine died along with the headlights and moments later his neighbour got out, exaggerating a shiver. Rubbing his hands, he jogged round to help his wife, emerging laden with bags. Imtiaz looked on in respectful silence as the man adjusted the scarf around his wife's neck. He was saying something, and although Imtiaz couldn't catch the exact words, his tone was encouraging and he wore a warm smile.

Imtiaz rubbed his heavy stomach. He hadn't eaten for several hours and yet it felt like a stone lay in his belly. His nose was blocked, his ears were blocked, all digestion had ceased and he was constipated. Combing his hair in the mirror this morning, he for the first time saw what he would look like as an old man; he'd lost all the gloss of youth. Forced to breathe through his mouth he felt his forehead. No, no temperature there, thank God. He was relieved to not be developing some acute condition. The generic symptoms of an accelerated ageing process he could cope with, but he didn't want to be coughing and sneezing. Not tomorrow, or rather not today – Eid would be tough enough. He'd lived alone for too long and slowly, slowly, the daily grind had worn him down. But the day to come would still bring the same questions. *Why no contact? What people were occupying his life? Was he busy? If so, then doing what?* He'd arrive at their banquet a beggar, feeling terribly exposed. But were they being too demanding? Probably not. For success to mean anything, there had to be losers. And he'd lost. But he couldn't explain that for him, just making it to the end of the day was achievement enough. To be fair, the astute ones had now figured that a line had been crossed. His aunties used to be playful, badgering him about not being married, but they'd since tired of such conversations. Tactful smiles, suspicious glances and forced, polite conversation had replaced the warmth with which they once approached him.

'Oh Imtiaz,' his Bilqis Aunty had cooed some years ago. 'There's this lovely girl from Manchester. I've seen her and she is so pretty – a real Urdu princess. You must meet her.' He never had done. He couldn't even remember why now. He'd always been her favourite, and the delight in those dark eyes as she'd sidled up to him that day touched him even now. She had looked at him like a mother would at her own son, as she tried to sell him this blue-chip daughter of Pakistan. What would he say to her later today? *How the hell had it come to this?* He remembered a moment of revelation.

Scouts. He was twelve, maybe thirteen, and the whole Pack had gone camping for the weekend. It was his first time away from home; away from Mum and her constant struggles and non-stop weeping. And

Dad – always grumbling about dinner and getting angry. Homework and helping and being a good boy. For one weekend the rules could be forgotten. For two whole days they were troopers, adventurers. *Men.* He wanted to be just like the older ones – tall, strong and wearing his gear like it was part of him. They came to rest and made bivouacs under fading light whilst the Scoutmaster assembled logs for a campfire. Night came and they were exposed under stars but for once Imtiaz had no fear. He was one of the gang. He felt it. He *knew* it. As they sat around the crackling logs, he felt free. His stained, grubby hands resembled those of everyone around. Even his clothes and boots were the same: soiled. Just like everyone else's.

One of the older boys returned to the campfire with a plastic bag, and a huge cheer rang round as he pulled out cans of beer. Along with all the younger ones Imtiaz wasn't allowed to drink, the Scoutmaster saw to that, but when the older lads started passing round some magazine, he didn't stop them. Some of them were getting really excited, turning the pages and pointing in disbelief. Sometimes they turned pages quickly and other times they just stood and stared, cooing with satisfaction before breaking again into excited shrills. *Just what was this magazine?* Imtiaz had no idea, but when one of the lads came up to show him, he was giddy with joy at being allowed in on the joke.

'Get a load of this, Imtiaz,' jollied the biggest scout in the pack, sitting down next to him like an elder brother. He'd long since forgotten his name but his legacy had lived on. After all, he'd opened up Pandora's Box.

None of us can recall our biggest "firsts" – our first step, our first word. The first time we smelled a rose in full bloom. These moments are for parents to treasure, to sustain them as dawn's fresh promise gets broken. But Imtiaz broke no promises – he was always such a good boy, always trying to make Mum happy but she was still sad. Always trying to spend more time with Pasha but he wasn't interested. And he kept working hard at school but he was forever stuck on C-. And he was starting to feel things. Things he didn't understand. He wanted to say something to the girls on the bus, but they didn't even see him. They were too busy giving attitude to the footy boys. Now *they* knew how to get the girls' attention. *How did they do that?* He'd ask but he wasn't part of their crowd.

But within a blink of an eye, none of that mattered. Lucy was here, smiling ever so sweetly whilst he stared at her, hypnotised by her shame.

Look at that, and *THAT!* This was the key, the one he didn't even know was missing.

And suddenly he's alone, alone with her. Her smile doesn't fade. And there is no more weepy Mum or angry Dad, or another C- from some bored teacher. No. Lucy's not ignoring him or demanding that he be special. Lucy is uncomplicated. She's the only one that makes sense, the only one that he can turn to. There is simply nothing as pleasurable as spending time with Lucy.

The weekend ends and he goes home, and whilst he talks excitedly about building a bivouac, he keeps Lucy a secret – they're already special friends. And soon Dad is shouting again and Mum is crying more and more, but it's no longer as bad because Lucy is always there. And the best part is she's got lots and lots of friends. Who cares about the girls on the bus now? *They can get lost 'cause none of them are as attractive as Lucy and her mates.*

Imtiaz is fifteen, sixteen and a lot of the boys have girlfriends. They hang out in the evenings and, experiment. *Sometimes he's invited and sometimes he goes, but he just can't find a way in. It's different from when they're in class. And the girls, they – they* frighten *him. It's just too difficult, too uncomfortable. And Imtiaz needs comfort. Lucy opens up her arms.*

Imtiaz is eighteen, nineteen and school's out. There's a big do, a final bash. The class of '90 together for one last time. The boys are all wearing tuxedos. They look like men. They are men. When the hell did that happen? *And the girls. Women. Young women. He's sat next to them for the last seven years but tonight they are unrecognisable. The disco lights flash, splashing whirligig colours onto a canvas of flesh, making them seem transcendent, other-worldly. Long legs, silk stockings, black high heels.* Click, click, clickety click. *Sunshine hair swishes on a crowded dance floor but Imtiaz has no courage. And besides, all the girls have a guy – the natural order of things. There's no room for a spare part.*

Pert bosoms strain against fine cloth and he turns away. But wherever he looks he's being taunted, mocked by a parade of riches that he'll never know. He catches Fiona's eye and she blanks him. He sat next to her for two years, during History. He helped her with the French Revolution. She's wearing an off-shoulder purple gown and she's put some glittery stuff on her chest and hair. She's with Graham as a slow number starts up. The lights dim and she sparkles. He watches them kiss. There's nothing romantic about it – like everyone they've both been drinking and Graham's hungry like the wolf. From where Imtiaz sits it looks like he is chewing her face. Yeah, he's chewing her and kneading her. Enjoying her. She's ten feet away and completely out of reach. He sees this clearly for the very first time and feels anger; resentment. Something's gone wrong – horribly wrong. Why is he so disconnected? It's too big a question and as he leaves that night he buries it. It'll be ten years before it resurfaces. On getting home he seeks solace in Lucy and her mates but the illusion is shattered – the relationship has lost its innocence. Over that summer he graduates in another sense, though – he discovers hardcore pornography. In truth, Lucy and her playmates had long since begun to lose their charms, but this ... oh yeah, THIS. And that goes in there and that goes in there and that goes in there and that goes in there. There was nothing else in God's good world to compete.

Imtiaz is twenty-two, twenty-three and he knows there's a problem. He has a big, big problem. He cares about zilch and only one thing in life excites him. But the more he thinks about it the more down he gets, and the more down he gets the more he needs a release. RELEEEAAASE. Take me to another place. And then the Internet arrives. All thought of escape is now futile.

Imtiaz is twenty-five, twenty-six, seven, eight, nine. He contemplates suicide. On the eve of his thirtieth birthday he believes there is only one way out. Mum, Dad, Pasha, work and friends – he has lost all meaningful contact. He now exists only in a bubble which he shares with Cindy, Sandy, Jenna and Mandy. He hates himself. He hates them more. But they've snuffed out his light and he needs them to see, to feel, to know he's alive. He just can't look away. Sometimes he tries. Days pass, a week, two weeks. But eventually, inexorably, Cindy pulls him back. She does things. She looks so ... Oh Sweet Jesus. He would sell his own soul to experience that, just once. Her tight body and pixie face, her groans and sighs and ups and downs. Oh Allah, please. But Jesus doesn't come and Allah doesn't come. He's stranded.

The fireworks had stopped. Exactly how long ago he wasn't sure but he now felt the chill in the air. His hands and feet were cold. Where has all my blood gone?

Turning away from the window he faced the black hole of his room, the sole light provided by the clock radio. He was only mildly surprised at how long he had spent doing absolutely nothing. Knowing that he could not sleep in he walked towards the kitchen with something approaching haste, determined to get a drink and end the day. He switched on the fluorescent light, staying by the entrance until it had reluctantly spluttered into life. He stood his ground, surveying the sight before him. The furnishings and equipment were all now old and the Formica top was chipped in several places, but everything was in order: no dishes piled high, no foul smells, no mess to clear up. He had learned to tread water admirably, but he wasn't sure if anyone considered stoicism a virtue any more. Walking to the sink, he filled the kettle before locating a jar of assorted herbal infusions and taking out one chamomile tea bag. Warm, soothing and sleep-inducing, he felt comforted by the very thought of the slightly sweet brew. He returned to his bedroom and climbed back into bed, sitting comfortably with outstretched legs. Lifting the saucer, he basked in the rising steam, caressing his face. He stirred lovingly, precisely: an act of worship. Squeezing the bag, he studied the last of the liquid fall through: the drops coalesced, looking thick; almost unctuous. He sipped. The tea was hot but he held a spoonful, letting it coat his throat. A healing syrup. So much pleasure from such a small thing. He closed his eyes, imbibing more this time, and felt the warmth from his trachea spread outwards, and his chest loosen. The desire to sleep was overwhelming him fast now, and taking a final gulp he let exhaustion draw a veil over the day. The radio was still on, but with the volume down low he curled up and drifted back to sleep. Rest. At last. For now.

11

Salman turned the key to his front door and warmth greeted him. He entered the hallway and touched the radiator – piping hot. No one was in sight, though muffled voices from the kitchen, along with the hiss of the pressure cooker, provided all the information needed. There was no place like home.

All of a sudden the living room door opened and his children tore out.

'Daddy, Daddy, Daddy!' screamed Aaliyah, running with arms raised.

'Daddy's home, Daddy's home!' shouted Taimur, holding up a model car. 'Look what Majid Uncle gave me!'

The boy looked so thrilled. Salman couldn't wait to give him his own Eid present. It was really from him and his wife but it was Salman who had chosen it. He cupped their chins, feeling their soft, soft skin, their tender baby fat. They were talking excitedly and he was listening, full of interest in their stories, but he was also a little lost. He was looking at the sparkle in their eyes, the ringlets in his daughter's hair which bounced along with her jerky movements. He was the richest man alive.

Walking into the kitchen, steam and heat assaulted him. He smarted at the change of environment but his kids flew past unaffected, making for their grandfather at the kitchen table. The old man was reading a newspaper and looked deep in concentration, but didn't mind being bothered by his grandson's toy car for probably the fiftieth time that day.

'You look cold, Salman,' his father observed. 'You should have taken your long coat.'

'You're right, Dad. I made a mistake.'

His mother and wife, both standing by the cooker and engrossed in some gossip, looked surprised to see him. It was a happy surprise, though, and Kahina squeezed past, pushing a chair in to reach her man.

'Ooh, you *are* cold,' she confirmed, wrapping arms around his neck and kissing him lightly on the lips.

Salman smiled. '*Eid Mubarak* to you, too!' he said, and his wife giggled.

'Was the *Masjid* full, son?' asked his mother. She was stirring an open pot, bubbling vigorously. It smelled great and he suddenly felt hungry.

'It was totally full,' he said. 'I had a good time, everyone was there. But why are you cooking? Aren't we going to Arwa *Masi's* soon?' Salman was hoping, praying that there'd been a change of plan.

'Yes, in about one and a half hours,' she suggested, turning towards the wall clock. 'But we'll not eat straight away so have something now.'

Salman looked at himself in the mirror. His father was right – he should have taken his long coat. He was still wearing his leather jacket and was studying his reflection. It wasn't that he was wet or cold or even somewhat dishevelled – it's just that he looked so damn absurd. *I should throw this away now*, he considered as he took it off. He turned back and made to adjust his turban but it was the one thing on him that wasn't out of place. Despite his parents being from Karachi, his strong features and broad shoulders told of a lineage from further north. He'd put kohl around his eyes and the blackness of the make-up contrasted his pale face. Black eyes, Pathan skin. He thought he looked like a *mujahid;* a warrior from history. His mind wandered to a more glorious past and he imagined himself as a companion of Babur, conquering *Hind* in the name of Allah.

'Don't worry, Salman, you're still a handsome man.'

He turned abruptly to see Kahina by the bedroom door, grinning widely. He felt angry but also somewhat silly, so said nothing. She walked towards him and held him and his negativity melted away. They kissed, but with no urgency, and sat down on the edge of the bed.

'You look troubled,' said Kahina, studying her husband's eyes, his pallor, his slight hunch.

'I'm OK.' His words were laboured. He closed his eyes and flopped backwards. 'I'm just a little tired.'

'Did something happen at the *masjid* today?'

'No, nothing like that. I had a nice time. It's just ... it's so miserable outside. It's good to be home.' His eyes remained shut as her hand caressed his jaw line; his neat beard bristled. She ran fingers through his hair before gripping a handful, giving it a gentle tug.

'Come on. Get out of these wet clothes and come back down. Have something to eat.'

'Ah, that's lovely.' Salman lingered over his first spoonful. His wife had just poured him a bowl of chickpea and potato soup, cooked just so. The chickpeas were tender; South Asian tender: boiled till they yielded to the slightest pressure, releasing their floury interior. Salman smacked his lips, appreciating the salty, astringent quality. He tucked in whilst his family read, played and talked around him. There was a small television in the corner and his father hushed everyone down on seeing pictures from Iraq.

'*Beta*, turn it up a little, huh?' Salman picked up the remote.

'*What can you tell us, Captain?*'

'*Well, sir, this is a militants' stronghold. We know that the city has become a beacon for terrorists, mostly foreign fighters, and we're ready for a final assault. We're gonna give this city back to its people.*'

'*So when does the action begin?*'

'*Well, sir, for obvious reasons I can't tell you exactly when, but soon. Very soon. We've been softening up the target for a while now. We're ready for action.*'

Husnain's fuse burst, drowning out the reporter.

'Did you hear that bloody fool?' he asked rhetorically. 'That soldier stands there and talks about "foreign fighters", without any sense of irony. I mean, he doesn't look like a typical Baghdadi to me. You know, Salman, language is so important.'

He nodded but otherwise didn't respond. He didn't have a clue what his father was on about but he loved it when his dad got all worked up.

'And all this talk about "softening up" targets. It's sounding more and more like some damn computer game. And what does it mean anyway, eh? They're blowing it all apart: homes, businesses, children's playgrounds. And they wonder why they're hated by us. How can they expect anything else?'

'Don't worry, Dad, they'll get nothing else from me,' said Salman, reducing the volume back to its previous level.

'Be careful, Boy.' Husnain leaned in and looked his son in the eye. 'It's your decision to live in this country but, whilst you do, live as a good citizen; a loyal citizen. Create good relations with your neighbours. Reach out to people.'

Salman thought about the lady at the bus stop and felt bad.

'You don't know what it's like out there, Dad.' He wanted to say so much but felt tongue-tied. He looked across to his own son and hoped that he would take more after his grandfather.

'It doesn't matter. You have to think of the future. *Their* future.' He gestured towards his grandchildren. Instinct told them not to act on their curiosity.

'Enough of this!' interrupted Bilqis, Salman's mother. 'Have you forgotten what day it is? This bloody war will still be here tomorrow – you can argue about it then.'

'Come on, let's start getting ready,' said Kahina, now carrying Aaliyah.

'That's a good idea,' Bilqis affirmed, noticing the time. 'Chop chop, everybody – we should leave soon.'

Salman took Taimur by the hand and the four of them left the kitchen.

'We should get ready too,' said Bilqis to her husband, putting a hand on his shoulder. He looked up at his wife and she thought he seemed scared. She was determined not to revive the conversation, though – at least not today.

'Right, have we got everything?' It was Salman's stock question on leaving the house, to whomever he was with. He and Kahina were holding various odds-and-sods, household things which they were returning. The kids however were more interested in what their grandfather was holding – shiny, wrapped up parcels.

'Can I see, can I see?' came Taimur's request for the umpteenth time, upon which Salman decided it was time to go.

They all squeezed into the old Ford Mondeo. His Mum had Aaliyah on her lap and Kahina held a slightly restless Taimur. Salman really wanted to get a new car, one of those people carriers, but he couldn't afford it. He sometimes felt inadequate. He breathed deeply, trying to shake off the cobwebs that were constantly settling over him. He turned back and four faces smiled his way and he felt better.

'OK, Dad?' he said, turning back to the front.

'Let's go, *Beta,*' encouraged Husnain, patting his boy on the knee. Salman turned the ignition and the engine kicked into life.

12

Pasha approached his BMW with wrapped presents in hand and a city-style overcoat draped over his forearm. He opened the boot and placed the presents carefully before catching his reflection in the rear screen. He felt he looked good: trousers, shirt, no tie. Top button undone. He'd considered wearing a suit, he'd considered wearing a *sherwani*, he'd considered wearing a lot of fucking things, but he'd settled on this. He was disappointed in having become so rattled. He'd visited his mother six months ago and he was fine then – in fact he'd looked forward to it. And he'd seen Imtiaz within the last year, and Aadam not long before, when he got married. But Salman he'd not seen in, well – it had been a long time. He'd never met his wife or children. He'd bought them presents especially.

Despite a poor start he could get there on time. Negotiating the M6 and M1 down to the tip of London would be easy; driving into the capital would be another matter though. *We'll see*, he thought, happy to enjoy the clear road ahead.

Pasha was cruising through the breezy roads of Cheshire. Trees and farm-fields flanked him on either side. A few minutes earlier, taking a short cut, he'd found himself approaching a group on horseback. He'd slowed right down and overtaken at a snail's pace, giving the horses as wide a berth as possible. As he passed, the lady in front gestured *thank you*, which he'd returned with the same good grace. He looked again at the fields. He'd be back in just twelve hours, and yet he felt a sadness more akin to a longer sojourn.

He'd never gone back to London; not to live, anyway. He'd left to go to university in Durham and fell instantly in love with its waterfront and quayside nightlife. How special was that? Sure, London had the best club scene, but Durham's was good enough and it had other stuff too. There he was just twenty minutes from the Yorkshire Moors. In summer, parts of it got covered in lavender and from certain peaks you could look out onto a sea of purple. He had it all: nightlife, fresh air and fresh people. Even back then, so soon after leaving home, London seemed a distant, fast imploding ghetto. He'd have made his own way, somehow, had he stayed on, but it would have been more difficult. He'd have had to consciously avoid the cliques, the petty small-minded mentalities. A friend once told him how the Asians in big city universities always initially stuck together. But then, after their first year, they broke up into huddles of Hindus, Muslims and Sikhs. What prats. He just didn't want to be surrounded by that. In Durham he was on his own but no one, virtually no one had an issue with his colour. He had prepared himself for prejudice, thinking not unreasonably that he'd experience problems, but the exact opposite transpired. People loved him. Sure, some of it was down to his relative exoticism, but what the hell – he had so many friends. Weekends were spent in the quayside bars or the Georgian theatre, where they always had live acts. They used to go on cruises on the Tees at term-end and do white-water rafting during the summer. London simply dissolved away.

Pasha accelerated smoothly through the 80s until he hit 90 mph. This part of the M6 was generally clear and he didn't expect any build up until reaching Birmingham. Cities, towns, places and people just swept by. Motorways were like portals; gateways connecting different worlds.

He thought about his girlfriend, Jenny, and felt bad about having chucked her out of his flat yesterday. *Their* flat. Oh what the fuck, he didn't have to pretend right now – it was his flat. Jenny was an easy girl. He enjoyed having her on his arm when out, and having her in his bed when in. And he liked tickling her when half-cut. The End. Their story deserved no sonnets.

He slipped from third lane to second, letting the flashing Porsche behind him go. The driver looked across fleetingly, his face defined by arrogance. Young Buck, Big Wheels. *That used to be me*, thought Pasha, and his mind wandered back to the night he and Jenny got together. It was nearly four years ago, when the two of them were working for the same company. It was a small concern, a start-up, one where all the staff chipped in wherever they could: as software architect Pasha often participated in sales, and the girl who answered the phone also cleaned the toilet.

One time they'd travelled to give a demonstration, and afterwards they were taken out to dinner by the client. Pasha was tired and had wanted to go home but it was all part of the package. Schmoozing. The sales manager was OK – very capable and thus useful as an associate, but too dull beyond those boundaries. Jim Althorp, though, as the humble northern boy made good, was a self-appointed philosopher-king.

The four of them had gone to a steak house and Pasha got annoyed with Jim right from the start. Before they sat down they had a drink by the bar and with a nod and a wink Jim said, "Get yourself one", to the bartender. Northern Soul. And once they were seated and the waitress had come over, he kept calling her 'pet', and made sure he had a chat with her before she began taking the orders. Needing immunity from the man's ways, Pasha began to drink.

When dinner arrived – huge servings of meat, vegetables and gravy – the waitress accidentally tipped Jim's plate as she placed it down, spilling some of the sauce. Full of embarrassment and apologies, she frantically began wiping the table. He gently grabbed her hand and said, 'It's OK, pet, no harm done. Our little secret, eh?' She walked away flustered but relieved, knowing her boss wouldn't find out about her accident with such a prominent local man. Once out of earshot Jim leaned forward towards Pasha, seated opposite him.

'It pays to be reasonable,' he commented with a wink. 'I'm a reasonable man.' Pasha refilled his glass as Jim began boasting about being some modern day Scrooge (post all the spooking). He went on about all the Tiny Tims that he'd helped and kept saying *we've* done this and *we've* done that, when what he really meant was *I*.

Sensing Pasha's growing frustration, Jenny stepped in, congratulating Jim on how expertly he'd handled the situation. Jim, of course, looked more than happy at the approval he got from the young lass.

'Harrison. Jenny Harrison. That's a fine Lancashire name,' he commented. 'Where are ya from, pet?'

'I'm a Formby girl, born and bred,' she said, knowing the information would go down well.

'Smashing,' said Jim, overjoyed to be in the company of his own. 'Are ya family still there?'

'Oh aye. We're Formby for generations, although me mum's from Heysham originally.' Dear old Jim could barely contain himself.

'Smashing, just smashing,' he repeated, his ample cheeks all ruddy. Refilling his glass he looked at Pasha and made to speak before swallowing his tongue. 'Smashing,' he muttered again, but with downcast eyes.

'It's OK, Jim,' said Pasha. 'You can ask me where I'm from as well. It's no problem.'

Jim stalled, unsure how to react. He looked hard at Pasha and drained his glass. 'I said nothing, son, not because I'm rude, but because no one is sure what they can and can't say anymore. We're all confused, in our own country.'

Mindful that he was here on business, Pasha let it go. Meanwhile he felt Jenny discreetly taking hold of his hand underneath the table. Jim's wisdom turned to the police, and how full of admiration he was for the Boys in Blue, but Pasha wasn't listening. Jenny was squeezing his hand a little and had turned to face him, holding his gaze reassuringly. She was no beauty, but she looked so tender, wearing that gentle smile. He felt real warmth, though the alcohol in his bloodstream was making him horny, too. He stared into her northern face and at her pink lipstick. He wanted to taste those bubble-gum pink lips.

Alone in his hotel room, Pasha felt exhausted. He splashed his face over the sink before examining himself in the mirror. Water dripped off his smooth, glistening skin. Glistening brown skin. Brown skin stretched over Semitic features. He smiled.

The room bell went and he wondered who the hell it was. *Jim,* he concluded, and he braced himself: either an apology or a lynching was coming. He opened the door to find Jenny on the other side. She'd changed into a nightdress but hadn't taken off her make-up. She welcomed herself in, a drunk, playful grin on her face.

'Hi, Pasha,' she said, pressing a palm on his chest as she breezed past. He closed the door, bemused, and turned to see that she was sitting on his bed.

'Get us a drink, Pasha. Wine would be good but anything will do.' Feeling a little awkward he turned away, towards the mini-bar. 'Listen, I'm sorry about Jim. Him getting all aggro with you like that.'

Pasha was crouched down and inspecting the mini-bar contents. 'Why are *you* sorry? Anyway, to be honest, he had a point.'

'What do you mean?'

He handed her a glass of red. 'Oh, nothing. I can't blame the Jims of this world for falling out of love with us, that's all.'

She looked uncertain and changed the conversation. 'So are you married, then?'

'No.'

She sipped generously and laughed. 'Don't look so nervous. I'm not about to propose!' He smiled and sat down beside her, and which point she flopped backwards and closed her eyes. 'You're different to other paki lads.'

'Different 'good' or different 'bad'?' he asked, trying to shake off her casual use of 'paki'. She'd clearly had more to drink than he had realised.

'Different ... good!' They tittered at her hesitation.

'So are you going to get yourself a nice Pakistani bride?'

Pasha was irritated by the question. 'Why? Do you know any?'

'Not many down my way, I'm afraid. Just us local girls. We've got more ... spirit.' And with her eyes still shut she nestled up closer. Her hands were by her sides whilst she absent-mindedly opened and closed her legs, with the soles of her feet remaining together. Little butterfly wings. *Flutter flutter, come taste my nectar.* He considered just chucking her out and going to sleep, or fucking her first before chucking her out and going to sleep. Nip-and-tuck. Her head moved gently from side-to-side, as if she was listening to some tune. But there was no music. This was easy, too easy, and a surge of anger bolted through him. For a moment he was close to hitting her and he was relieved he hadn't done so. Still looking down, he curbed his disdain – he couldn't hate her, this salt-of-the-earth British girl. British women: they didn't have the *élan* of the Italians, the femininity of the French or the sheer native beauty of the Spanish. No. But they had a rawness, a baseness, a kind of prostitute-quality that really worked for him. He leaned in to touch her hair and, feeling his weight, her smile widened. He ran a finger over her bubble-gum pink lips and her butterfly wings re-opened. He moved on top, pinning her, and kissed her with hunger. Enjoying her firmness he bit her neck, holding a fold of skin and flesh in his teeth, inhaling her cheap, stale perfume. Pasha's mist descended. He sprang up, pushing her pliable legs to either side and smoothed his thumb over her knickers. He moved slowly from outer to inner labia, and then clitoral hood – mapping her out through silk. He could tease himself no longer. Pulling down her lace, he descended – bubble-gum pink to bubble-gum pink. And instantly he recoiled. She stank. She was giggling and for a second time he came close to violence, but again he pulled back. He studied her ethnic features, her blotchy pink arms and her pink, pink skin. Indissoluble pink. Jim Pink. Jenny opened her eyes and clasping his tie, pulled him onto her.

'Love me, Pasha,' she said. And they'd been together ever since.

He'd reached the outskirts of west London. A mortal dread gripped him. He looked around like a wide-eyed tourist who, expecting to see pinstriped suits and bowler hats *à la Mary Poppins*, could instead barely see a white face. Into the heartlands he went: a *sari* shop passed him on his left and a Middle-Eastern grocer's on his right. Five minutes later he came up to the Lahori Kebab House, which he remembered well. He'd loved it there, being a regular throughout his teens. Part of him wanted to rush in and say *I'm back!*, but most of him didn't. A woman wearing what could only be described as a tent crossed the road. Her face was covered and Pasha genuinely wondered if she could see where she was going. Turning a corner into Elmstead Avenue, he saw two Asian kids kicking a ball. One wore a polo shirt which declared that he was *Proud to be Pakistani*. It didn't say *Proud to be British* or *Proud to be British Pakistani*; just *Proud to be Pakistani*. And there he was – number forty-five. Home.

13

Aadam carried two steaming mugs of tea into the living room. Bina was sitting on the floor, focused on defacing some magazine. Kishore sat slumped on the settee. His eyes were shut and he looked pale, and Aadam considered just letting him rest a while.

'Tea's up, bro,' he soon announced loudly, and Kishore jolted awake before gratefully accepting the mug.

'Oh man, that's better. That hit the spot.' He sighed on sipping, the ginger biting his throat. 'Nazneen will be OK, right?' Kishore quickly refocused without waiting for a response, and picked up the TV remote.

'Oh sure, I'll sort things out.' With newspaper in hand Aadam settled by the dining table, trying to brush the incident off. Deep down, though, he was shaken; upset that she'd walked out. He'd really chosen badly in letting his friend trump her.

'*Eid Mubarak!*' came the cry from the box. On the screen was a sea of Muslims at prayer. They were all dressed in white and going into *sujud,* moving down from standing. To prostrate themselves. Prostrate themselves before God. Before Allah. Together. Muslims to the left, Muslims to the right: an unending sea of Muslims. Kishore changed channels. Britney Spears appeared and Bina's head turned. She watched open-mouthed as the attractive girl went through a series of interesting moves. Daddy was watching open mouthed too.

You wanna look at me? Look all you want, baby. I'm so young, I'm so fine. You like my hair, my Little Bo Peep plaits? And the rest of me? Do you like my shirt, my school shirt done up like that, all turned up like it's a crop-top? I think crop-tops are sooo cool. My stomach's nice and smooth, huh? I know you like me in my uniform. When you're off to work tomorrow, will you think of me when you see all those schoolgirls on the streets? Their skirts are short but not as short as mine. Here, let me turn around. Look at my behind. No, REALLY look at my behind. Isn't that the peachiest peach you've ever seen? Can you imagine? Are you imagining? You are, aren't you? That's OK, I won't tell. Hit Me Baby, One More Time.

'Britney Spears is fucking hot, man,' blustered Kishore, releasing a shiver as blood flowed to his extremities.

'Yeah, but she's not a patch on that Christina woman. That girl's so dirty, it's a compliment.'

'Filthy and cute, man, filthy and cute,' came the refrain in unison as the pair burst out laughing.

'Hey, look at this!' said Kishore as the next video started. His eyes were wide and his smile pure, and Aadam couldn't help but catch his friend's excitement.

It was the Spice Girls, a bunch of has-beens looking so eager in their *Wannabe* days. 'That one was Posh Spice, right?'

'Yeah, I think so,' said Aadam, and they watched the pretty little thing slink across the set. *Pow!* Another of the gang introduced her identikit identity to the world with a high-kick: Sporty Spice, and they both grinned, warming to the theme. A third member took her turn, beckoning the viewers towards her before running away. The frigging tease.

'And this one? Who the hell was this one?'

'Oh I don't know,' sighed Aadam, losing interest in the guessing game. 'Make-an-old-man-very-happy, Spice?' Kishore began laughing but stopped. Aadam was still fixed on the screen, an easy contempt spoiling his face.

'You know, Kishu.'

'What's that?'

'The worlds of pop and porn have a lot in common.'

'How's that, then?'

'They both need a constant supply of fresh meat.' Aadam went back to the newspaper, leaving Kishore to channel surf alone.

'Mother of God!' said Aadam. With head down he continued reading, though, and Kishore let it go.

'For fuck's sake!' he spat shortly afterwards. He looked up and Kishore gestured for detail, whilst still watching TV.

'Get this. There's this article here on the rewriting of history in Indian schools. They've reprinted this question, from some state's elementary maths exam: "If one *kar sevak* can destroy four mosques, how many *kar sevaks* will be required to destroy twenty mosques?" I mean, what the fuck is going on? Can you imagine being a little Muslim boy and sitting that paper, and coming across that question? How would you feel?'

He looked at Kishore who stared back but said nothing.

'Well? How the fuck would you feel?'

'Five.'

'What?'

'The answer's five.'

Kishore kept on staring and Aadam turned away. He went into the kitchen, leaving Kishore sitting alone in silence, stung by his own venom.

'Hey, *Bhai*, you seen *"Devdas"* yet? That Aishwarya Rai – God, now that's a woman!' After a minute Kishore had followed Aadam into the kitchen and found him over the sink, rinsing some dishes. He put an arm on his shoulder, tenderly.

'No, Kishu. Actually, I saw five minutes the other night. One of Nazneen's friends brought it along. I got bored pretty quickly.' He moved to stack plates, deliberately brushing off Kishore's hand.

'Really? But that Aishwarya Rai – come on, man...'

'For God's sake, why is everyone so gaga about her?'

'Cause she's a stunning beauty – why else?'

'Oh come on, there are plenty of others just as classy.'

'No, no. Not in her league. She's stand-out.'

'Yeah? Course you know why she really does stand out.'

'Go on.'

'"Cause she doesn't look Indian.'

'What?'

'Aishwarya Rai *is* attractive, but you Indians have only gone so dizzy cause she doesn't look like a bloody Indian.'

'What the fuck? You don't know what you're talking about – India is a huge place, one billion people. Not everyone has dark brown skin. There are so many looks: Tamils, Goans, Bengalis, Gujaratis, Punjabis. None of them look the same.'

'Too right they don't. And Aishwarya Rai's appeal is precisely that she looks like none of them.'

'Oh fuck off,' Kishore spat, turning his head away. Aadam laughed.

'You know I'm right. Look at the crop of current actresses. Sure, they're all beautiful, but that's not the point. Their features, Kishu: very fair skin, green eyes. What does it say about India that the idea of feminine beauty excludes ninety per cent of the nation's women, on ethnic grounds alone?'

'You tell me, then?' asked Kishore; *dared* Kishore. He was looking Aadam full in the face, just willing him to throw one more insult.

'Look, *Bhai*, let's not fight. We've known each other too long. It's an interesting observation, that's all I'm saying. Draw your own conclusions.' Aadam stacked the last of the dishes and Kishore stepped back, sorrow reshaping his features.

'What's happening to us?' his voice was breaking, suddenly soft. He sounded defeated.

'Perhaps we're just getting old, Kishu,' Aadam replied, knowing full well that age had nothing to do with it.

Aadam closed the front door and went back upstairs. From his bedroom window he watched Kishore trundle down the street until out of sight, pushing Bina in her buggy. He never looked back, not even once. Aadam wondered if Bina would have any Muslim friends when she grew up.

14

Nazneen drove, the heat of her rage bleeding into space. Her burning eyes sought not to separate the innocent from the guilty; her tongue flickered only to taste revenge. She'd really wanted, *needed* him, to confirm, cement, eliminate all doubt: Husband and Wife – till death us do part. *How can he prefer to spend time with that idiot, rather than be with me?* Her mind reeled at the insult, unable to get a handle. *What kind of man is he?* But this cold November day remained unimpressed: the pallid sky did not stir with her dark thoughts, and no passer-by shrank back in dread. Impotence returned her to the present.

Choking back tears she took a sharp turn, attracting a horn plus a volley of abuse. *Why didn't I see this side of him earlier? Why was I so hasty?* A dancing Scooby Doo air freshener fell onto her lap, the stickiness of the base all gone. Without slowing down she picked it up. *Scooby Doo.* They were together when Aadam had bought it. Halfords, some Saturday afternoon. *How the hell has it come to this, spending Saturdays in Halfords?* He'd liked it straight away. *Funny, quirky, cute*, he'd said. She'd said it was stupid, childish. He bought it anyway, along with an in-car coat-hanger or *travel valet*, as he'd called it, without any sense of humour or even noticing that she didn't want to be in fucking Halfords on a fucking Saturday. It was on his list, he'd said. He had to get it, he'd said, so he could cross it off. *THE GUY MADE LISTS.* Surely he should have declared such anal-retentiveness, prior to marriage? Did this not constitute breach of contract or something? *Must get in-car coat hanger. CHECK. Must get car air freshener. CHECK. Must make wife cum...* Forgot to put that on your list, eh? EH?? *YOU RETARD. I'LL SHOW YOU SCOOBY FUCKING DOO.* She took another loose, fast turn into a residential street. She was eyeing the Scooby Doo repeatedly, pouring hate into Aadam by proxy. A boy was crossing the road. She didn't see him. She still didn't see him. She saw him ... She floored the brake pedal and tyres screeched on biting tarmac. The car stalled. The wail of burning rubber crescendoed then died. The boy was standing, his hand on the bonnet. He was staring straight at Nazneen but not really seeing her, his face framed by shock. Voices rushed in. Foreign tongues. It woke him and he banged on the bonnet, his look suddenly aggressive. Nazneen was frozen. There was a bang on her window and she jumped to her side: another lad was gesturing wildly, also shouting in a foreign tongue. A third lad, tall and sinewy, rushed in. He kicked the driver-side door and tried to open it. Nazneen was yet to respond – no words, no action, no gesture. The oldest lad spat and translucent dribble slid slowly downwards, leaving a mucus trail. A woman approached, pushing a buggy. She barked and the three lads reluctantly moved on, each holding a stare. Nazneen darted nervously from one to the other before the woman shouted from up close. A portion of her face was obscured by the sliding spittle. She was wearing a flowing burkha which even covered her hands, and when she banged the window the sound was dampened.

'I'm sorry,' Nazneen finally spluttered, but there was no look of forgiveness in those spittle-veiled eyes.

She turned the ignition and the car jolted as the engine revved. Scooby Doo promptly toppled over on the dashboard, his fixed grin now seeming sinister. She remembered when they first met, in the gym of all places: her and the skinny Asian guy, sitting on a bench and watching her on a treadmill. He thought he was being discreet, the silly sod. Still, he at least had the guts to follow after her, and he seemed kind of all right. Cute. A cute boy. But six weeks earlier she'd been with Martin. *Martin.* Their dates were certainly different: Aadam liked holding hands in Kew Gardens; Martin liked taking her to Sandbanks harbour after dark, finding an unlocked yacht and soiling a millionaire's bed sheets. But all that ended so suddenly. Sure, it was all her doing, but still – his absence left such a hole. And she felt unsteady, unbalanced, in need of anchoring.

She remembered when Aadam proposed. A beautiful summer's day. Hyde Park. They'd lunched under glorious sunshine; the air unburdened, soft, and lilting with notes of freshly cut grass. He talked and she'd listened, his words caressing, reassuring. They'd taken shade under a large tree, him up against the trunk and her inside him. And he was wrapping her; her arms, her legs, her whole being encased by him. And his touch: delicate, restrained, thumbs exploring, lips brushing skin. And it did nothing for her. Absolutely nothing. She'd wanted it to – part of her was desperate to get swept away, to have faith in his quiet yearning. But as Aadam caressed her, like a blind man trying to make sense of a masterpiece, she couldn't stop thinking of Martin, always making her forget the world. But Aadam was so, *decent*. And smart, responsible and driven. *And Muslim*. Whereas Martin was ... The very promise of summer lay in his smile but summer had to end, right? *Only today, forget tomorrow*, he'd often say. This was all there was for him: seeing it, tasting it, touching it. This strange gift, this sliver of time. This Life. She'd started to dislike the very things that she'd first found so exciting. Because it wasn't just about today, was it? But for him there would never be anything else – just this bizarre gift. The banquet was prepared and there was no need to fast, only feast. But then Ramazan came and suddenly she *did* want to fast. She hadn't previously – not the year before or two years before, or indeed ever. But that year she did. A voice deep inside, whispering secrets. And she heard, she understood, but she didn't obey; *couldn't* obey. After all, what words could explain that the feast couldn't go on? And so she walked out, finding excuses, but she never lost her jungle instinct. But Aadam had no edge, no hunger. *Where was the maniac inside?* She couldn't remember the last time he'd been reckless, thrown the dice, been spontaneous. Sex was OK, but he had no ... *animal*. Whereas Martin *was* animal. Raw, unrefined, moving on instinct. *Oh Martin, me and Martin. I wanna go back. Take me, take me away to Red Rocks, Colorado.*

Martin. *Yeah. He'll be back in our room by now*, she thought.

They came out here on a working holiday, at the end of their first year at uni. Whilst everyone else was downing Snakebite and Black and bopping along to *Dancing Queen* for the three-hundredth time, Martin and Nazneen headed off to Keystone, Colorado. Three whole months to work and play like never before. They'd found employment at a lakeside resort, Martin joining the landscape gardening team and Nazneen becoming a maid. She wasn't exactly thrilled to be handling industrial-strength toilet cleaner daily, especially when Martin got to do fun things like plant trees, but it was only for a few hours a day. And then they'd go swimming and canoeing, or ride mountain bikes up and down the surrounding foothills. And when time allowed they'd take trips out to Red Rocks Mountain Park, along the eastern slope of the Rockies. With its Mars-like geology it hypnotised, as they hiked through rifts and creeks, surrounded by 400-foot red sandstone monoliths formed 290 million years ago. *What does such time mean?* Nazneen once pondered as they gazed across the Great Plains, spread out under a vast blue sky. They'd be going back there today – one last time.

Nazneen finishes off the last room on her rota and heads back to the village, where all the seasonal workers stay. She's disappointed to find that Martin isn't back yet, and so busies herself by putting together whatever food is left for their final meal in their summer digs. She peers into the fridge and inspects the few scattered items suspiciously. The milk has gone off and the salad is now way beyond limp, but the quiche looks good and she opens the last can of beans to accompany it. As she does she hears a group of Americans arriving next door. A gaggle of excited voices compete to be heard over each other, and Nazneen struggles to latch onto the conversation. But soon she picks up the thread. Of course. The snow's coming. They're here for the winter, replacing the Brits who came for the summer, and the talk is about only one thing: "Aspen are predicting a big one this year. Yeah, I hear the slopes of Powderhorn are already getting white." *Powderhorn, Beaver Creek, Copper Mountain and Arapahoe Basin. Nazneen has never been to any of these places, but just the names make her tingle. Colorado was too good. She resolves to come back one day, and in winter. Arapahoe Basin – that sounds the most exciting. She'll hang out there. One day.*

    Nazneen puts out a couple of plates and some cutlery, and chides herself for becoming wistful. Have I forgotten the last three months already? Never. *Tomorrow they pack up, put on an extra layer, and begin the long journey home. But for the rest of today, tonight, well this is her High Noon, and the gods will worship at her altar.*

Part Two

O wad some Pow'r the giftie gie us
To see oursels as others see us

ROBERT BURNS

15

Arwa Walayat swung open her front door. Her first-born, Ibrahim Pasha Walayat was standing on the porch, his hand still on the doorbell. For a second, mother and son simply gazed at each other. Her first thought? *My Ibrahim, my son.* And her second? *He has some grey in his hair now. He's wasted his youth.*

Pasha thought his mother looked even smaller than before. Her billowing scarf covered her head and shoulders and hung loose, momentarily hiding the peeling Minnie Mouse motif on her apron. Her smile was tender, full of yearning – and her face and head seemed shrunken, her body amorphous. He was convinced that Death had been claiming her by stealth for years, rather than extinguishing her in an instant. He couldn't remember a time when she wasn't busy, slowly dying. Pasha fell into his mum's arms.

'Ibrahim, my Ibrahim,' she said softly, smoothing his head with her hands. He stood a good foot taller but it looked so natural. *'Ibrahim, my Ibrahim.'* Those words, that name, her voice. Pasha didn't say anything, couldn't say anything; he was trembling in her embrace.

Pasha was delighted to learn that he was, after all, the first to arrive. He'd made great time in travelling down and hadn't hit even one patch of traffic. After fetching presents, his attention was caught by noise from the living room: the sounds of a Bollywood movie gate-crashing his welcome home. He entered and was greeted by an enduring image: his father in front of the telly, doped up on his drug of choice – Hindi movies, Hindi songs, Hindi life. Pasha looked at the screen and wondered how a nation with such a proud intellectual history as India, could be responsible for such a thing.

'Oh hello, son!' his father exclaimed rather weakly, prising himself out from his favourite chair. He was smiling and extending his arms but Pasha knew it was a little bit put on. It's not that he wasn't happy to see his son, it's just that his viewing pleasure had been disturbed. All Zakir Walayat really needed from life was pretty girls on the box, jangling their bits to a Hindi soundtrack. Seeing his father now, though, so clearly an old man, he for the first time found it amusing.

* * *

Pasha stirred a vat of soup.

'Keep it constant, *Beta*, or it will burn at the bottom.' He was thirty-eight years old and his mother was still calling him *child*.

'Sure, Mum,' he replied with a measured tone, not wanting to make a thing of it. He was stirring slowly, making a spiral from outside in. It smelled nice but was hardly traditional.

'What was the traffic like, *Beta*?'

'Fine, very smooth. But what's in this soup?'

'Leek and potato. I got the recipe from a magazine.' Arwa went to the adjoining utility room and returned with an A4-sized folder, which Pasha instantly recognised. She opened it at the last page to show her son the cut-out recipe. She smiled, clearly wanting his approval. Pasha put a hand on her shoulder. He wanted to tell her that this is Eid, and that leek and potato soup wasn't appropriate, and that she should have realised it wouldn't work with the menu as a whole. Instead he just left his hand on her shoulder.

Not having seen the folder for so long, Pasha began flicking backwards through the plastic leaves. It had all been lovingly preserved, so much so that when he reached a recipe near the front – a magazine cut-out dated 1970 – it was in very good condition. He carefully removed it and held it up close. The colours had faded and the paper felt a little brittle, but it was still intact. On it was a recipe for chocolate cake, with a big picture accompanying the text, the font of which Pasha thought was now dated. But what really interested him was a small photo attached to the corner, which he lifted out from under a paperclip. It was of him and his mum in the back garden on this very same house. He was standing behind a stall on top of which a chocolate cake was perched, bearing three lit candles, and his excited little face was just making it over them. His mum was kneeling down beside him, holding him, and wearing the very same apron as today – he recognised the Minnie Mouse. Pasha was shocked; shocked to see what his mother looked like as a young woman. He just couldn't see any relation between the person in the photo and the one standing next to him. He was unable to project from lustreless grey hair to the shiny locks that once crowned the same head. Or transpose firm skin onto the same frame, and thus visualise the finer features that time had taken away. And his mum was only sixty-three, not eighty-five – it really shouldn't have been that hard. But he couldn't do it. She looked so beautiful, holding her Birthday Boy. He clenched his jaw and silently put the photo back.

Returning to the vat of soup, he considered the effort involved in all this preparation. His mum would have been working on the feast for days whilst his father did a little work, played solitaire on the computer and watched Zee TV. *She's getting too old for this.* Stirring once more, his mum continued talking, her rabbiting voice exhibiting excitement plus a few nerves. He noticed that she'd even written a menu, stuck up on the refrigerator: apparently the soup was for starters. He was relieved that he didn't pick her up on the leek and potato thing.

'*Beta*, can you fetch me some saffron?' Arwa asked. Knowing where everything was, Pasha got a chair to reach for the cupboard above the microwave. It was one of the bigger ones, boasting real depth, width and height. Peering in he saw seven, eight, no nine tall plastic containers, all filled with different kinds of pulses. He was initially bemused. *Why is Mum's kitchen so well stocked?* As if she regularly cooked for six. But deep down he knew that she wanted to cook for six; that cooking for six would make her life bright. But he also knew she'd die before any of those containers needed refilling.

'What was the traffic like, *Beta*?' Arwa Walayat absent-mindedly asked again. Pasha said nothing at all.

16

Husband and Wife – till death us do part...

Married couples never unsettled Pasha. On the contrary, they only ever rubberstamped his choices: love one person forever? Commitment? He wasn't that stupid. But looking at this couple, standing together on his mother's porch ... He was wearing a *sherwani*, a long coat-like garment. It was wrapping his slim frame tightly and fell to just below knee-length. She was wearing a turquoise *shalwar kameez*, one cut to a modern fashion. The *shalwar* was fitted, falling into a gentle bell-bottom around the ankles, and the *kameez* hypnotised, delicate fractals bleeding colour. She had a long scarf draped around her neck, one end of which she held gracefully with a bent arm, the length falling before being taken up by her wrist. The effect was so delightfully feminine it made Pasha uncomfortable. But it wasn't their clothes or their youth, her beauty or the pride in his smile; they just looked so natural together. Jenny flashed in his mind but he shook off the thought. *It's too late now.* Pasha caught the woman's eyes and she smiled. He immediately looked away.

... God, this is awkward. I squeeze Aadam's hand tight and give Pasha my best, fake smile. Actually, he's looking quite a bit older than I remember. When was it that we last met? Oh, I don't know. Pasha looks away quickly, like he's embarrassed. Good. I can use that. Allah, what are we doing here? We could have had a lovely day together, at home.

Aadam steps into the house and I reluctantly let go. The two of them hug and I feel a bit naked, left on the porch. I tuck away some imaginary stray strands of hair. I've never liked Aadam's family.

98

Actually, no. What I mean is I've never been comfortable with them; not truly at home. They're lovely people, mostly, but ... how can I explain. I love Pakistanis, I love *being* Pakistani, but I hate Pakis, I guess. One man who is definitely no Paki, though, is Pasha. Now *there's* a man who knows what to do. But then I catch his eye for a second time, this time over Aadam's shoulder, and *again* he looks away. That old confidence. He's definitely looking a lot older. Oh boy, this is going to be a long day.

'You're looking good, son,' says Pasha, before playfully slapping Aadam on the cheek. And so he does. And that's *me*, that is. That's *my* work – *my* patience, *my* encouragement and *my* love. Not that anyone from his damn family has ever acknowledged that. I've made a man out of the half-baked boy they gave me. It would be nice if I got some credit for it sometimes. But I won't hold my breath. Aadam accepts the compliment graciously, without seeming overawed. I must say, my man's carrying himself well. I feel proud to be with him – despite his mistake earlier with that damn Indian. I should've stayed mad at him for longer. I giggle, and finally Pasha acknowledges that I'm still standing in the porch, like some spare part.

'Come in, come in!' he beckons with a generous smile, reaching out a hand. 'Lovely to see you again, Nazneen,' and he pecks me on the cheek. He holds my eyes for no longer than politeness dictates.

'Thanks Pasha, lovely to see you too,' I reply, but we both know we're merely being polite. I don't think he's the type to feel offended, though. After all, I'm just his cousin's wife, and he barely even knows his cousin. Plus, I'm looking damn fine today, even if I do say so myself, and I can see that that's making things more difficult for him. Not that that would have fazed Pasha from a few years back. You can tell that in a man, you know, just from a look. That confidence, from knowing exactly what buttons to press – it's either there or it's not. Most men don't have it, though most can pretend, especially if they're drunk. I can't believe I used to run with that crowd. Seems like a lifetime ago.

Hearing all the commotion, Arwa Aunty and Zakir Uncle make their way to the front door. I watch Aunty effortlessly breeze past Uncle, arms aloft on seeing her sister's son.

'Come in, *Beta*, come in!' she beckons, before grabbing Aadam by the cheeks and forcibly lowering him to kiss his forehead. Honestly, it's like me, Uncle and Pasha aren't even there! Poor Aadam starts to blush but for Aunty it's all just natural. The others laugh and I laugh along with them. You see, this is what I mean. This is what being Pakistani is about. Love or hate, we do both with more conviction. We don't do PR or pragmatism – we're very simple people.

'Welcome, Aadam,' says Uncle, and the pair shake hands. I start to feel like I'm being ignored, again, and Aadam draws close as if about to introduce me, but there's no need. Aunty now grabs *me* and pulls me down, to plant another kiss of unblemished love.

'Welcome, Nazneen, welcome *Beti.*' She smiles, and as I look in her eyes I see the purest love of all: a mother's love. I melt and feel humbled. Love – it disarms you like nothing else. God, I better watch myself today. I don't want to walk out of here a damn Paki ... Aunty's knowing eyes follow Aadam's arm, still lingering around my waist.

'You're looking good *yaar*, Aadam!' Her eyes dance as she comments before turning squarely to me. 'You've put some flesh on my boy's bones, *che na?*' Her observation is matter-of-fact and she's bemused when everyone starts laughing again. I too can't help giggling and turn to Aadam, all flushed with embarrassment. *Oh Arwa Aunty.* Aadam plants a kiss on my cheek before turning back and smiling broadly, like the victor that he is. I give Aunty the dutiful-beautiful-wifey smile that she wants, whilst inwardly remembering how bitterly me and Aadam argued only hours earlier. No one would guess, eh? The thing that had pissed me off was ... Actually there were lots of things, but mainly, I hate to see him being so wet. I mean why put Kishore above me? I know he wouldn't even have wanted to. It's such a turn off. Martin would never have done that. *Oh, Martin* ... I like a man to know what he's doing. Always. That's the first rule and Aadam breaks it too often. And for what? To not look bad in front of his Indian mate? I don't mind Indians but I hate it when some Pakistanis get all dewy-eyed about them. I believe in having good relations with everyone, including that lot, but they shouldn't have any special place. Maybe things were different for our parents, when all brown people were new over here, but those days are long gone. Indians have worked hard to earn their place in Britain, and good luck to them. But Aadam has to realise not only that our fate has gone the other way, but that if anyone's enjoying seeing us drown in our own shit, it's the bloody Indians. He's invested too much in being Asian, in being brown, and it's a stupid badge to wear. I can only tell him so much. One day it's gonna really hurt him.

I breathe deeply, clearing angry thoughts. I turn to my man, whose hand I'm still holding. And there it is, as always – there's a look in those eyes that some women spend a whole lifetime searching for. He raises my hand and kisses it, with Aunty still looking on approvingly. Picture perfect. I really should be more grateful than I am. Happier than I am. I *am* happy, but ... happier.

Despite having opened the door, I notice Pasha is now standing some distance away. He's got this lost look on his face. He has shuffled backwards and is now watching us like some spectator. He feels ... he feels ... I really don't know what he feels.

17

Imtiaz pulled the door to his flat firmly shut and turned to go. His long overcoat flared and spiralled as he about-turned, like a Dervish, whirling to a rhythm. But his coat was black and Imtiaz was no Seeker. He moved swiftly, with concerted anonymity and no small pinch of fear, like Count Dracula through the streets of Old London Town, forced out of his chambers to face harsh daylight. The air was sharp and there was frost on the ground, and his warm breath rode briefly on the cold; burnt-out smoke from an extinguished flame.

He approached a newsagent's and, removing his glasses, forcibly kept his head down. Even before adulthood he was alive to the top shelf: shooting a look, stealing a moment; a micro-second's indulgence in the greatest pleasure made known to him. But something inside was now speaking and Imtiaz understood – this simply couldn't go on. But this battle – *God, please.* How could he keep on fighting, every damn moment? *There is just no respite.* Amongst the small cards in the newsagent's window advertising plumbers, cleaners and rooms to let, there were ones selling other services: *Massage, LOCAL – different girls everyday.* And another, bright pink and decorated with glitter and coloured hearts. *Massage – Come relax with our girls. Young hands for your body.* He fondled his mobile in his coat pocket, dreaming of young hands tending to his needs. And in front of the personal ads stood all the day's papers, including ... She looked about nineteen: wet, wavy brunette hair, falling onto bare shoulders. A low-cut white halter-top, a smooth white belly. And next to her, another. Bee-stung lips being bitten nervously, coyly, as a living doll made to pull her knickers down, her thumbs hooked under black lace. Some man somewhere would get to tug at that bow, undo that wrapping, *play with that doll*. The thought clouded his mind, disconnecting him from himself – from Eid, from where he had to go today, from where even he stood. Absentmindedly he fiddled with his penis through his coat pocket. A few people passed by and, feeling self-conscious, he swiftly moved on.

Eid. Family get-togethers. So many people checking him out, judging him. He'd been there before but it only got harder. He was trying to remember the last time he saw Aadam or Salman. What the hell was he going to say? *'As-salaam-u alaiykum, Salman Bhai. Are you well? And the Good Lady, and the kids? Who, me? No I'm not married. No, I have no one in mind. Work? Actually my job's a dead-end, but that's OK 'cause I'm a dead-end. No, no hobbies. No, no friends. Sport? Hahaha! Actually, I don't mind working up a bit of a sweat on my own, if ya knowhatimean. Rubbing myself whilst watching dirty women doing filthy things – know you of any greater pleasure, Salman Bhai?'*

He was nearing the train station but first he had to get past the public phone booth with its interior covered in tart cards. *Keep your head down, Imtiaz. Don't look up, don't look* – he looked. It was such a sight. *Behold, Original Man – Original Sin.* A platter of lovelies, all serving themselves up. *How the hell is he not to look?* He entered the Tardis and was instantly transported. There was no world beyond.

'Now is the winter of my discontent', he cried in silence, his voice echoing in his head. *'Discontent, Imtiaz?'* winked the brunette. *'Taste my apple – it'll change your life.'* Imtiaz dithered, unable to look, unable to not look.

'Stop dithering!' commanded the blonde, before purring: *'Take me – I'll open your eyes.'* She hissed; her lithe, long body ready to wrap itself around him, the very thought liquefying him with lust.

'No!' he beseeched suddenly, crumpling up a tart card in each hand. He staggered out, just desperate to make it onto the train and out of harm's way. *Fight, God Damn You, fight.* He saw a girl. She was crossing the road and heading towards him. She reached the pavement and was only a few feet in front, and Imtiaz was pulled into her slipstream. It was a cold November day and she was not scantily dressed, wearing a flowing, loose skirt, falling just below the knees. Imtiaz locked onto her petite, toned calf muscles, rippling gently under bronzed skin. She walked into the station and joined the queue for tickets, allowing him to nestle up behind. Her hair was tied back, simply, efficiently, and Imtiaz gloried in blonde streaks, meshed in with darker strands. She was wearing an off-the-shoulder top, light blue and fluffy, and a clear bra strap made the smallest of indents into her young flesh. He stood perfectly still, filling his lungs with her scent – notes of lavender, a hint of rose, and he wanted to rip her apart and feast. A loose cable dangled within, thrashing around violently, shocking him at random points. Waiting on the platform, he stood near her but not too close – his expertise judging a safe distance. He planned to get on the same carriage but as the train pulled in, something inside – some *shame* – made him walk along and embark elsewhere. Before taking his seat he checked his immediate surroundings – a man with a young boy and an old couple, comfortably of pensionable age. Relieved, he sat down.

The train trundled through drab suburbia, dominated by a seemingly unending chain of terraced houses. The little boy, though, was more vocal in his appreciation and was constantly tearing his dad away from his newspaper.

'Daddy what's on top of that house?'

'It's a chimney.'

'What's a chimney for, Daddy?'

'It's to let smoke out.'

'Where does the smoke come from, Daddy?'

And so it went on, with almost no respite. And at no point did the man look tired or annoyed with his son, or shout at him, or tell him to be quiet. Holding his son gently, the father readjusted the boy's glasses as he pointed to something else. Imtiaz wanted to cry. He was never the boy in such a scene, and he knew he'd never be the father either. He looked away, feeling like he was violating the beauty of it all, merely by watching. *I'm not a freak, I know I'm not – I'm just in need of some company.*

18

Everyone's adjourned to the living room, apart from Aunty, who has returned to what I guess is her spiritual home in the kitchen. Uncle is by himself on a three-seater sofa, which rests up against the length of the room. Pasha is opposite by the TV in the corner and me and Aadam are on a two-seater, just in front of the bay windows. A large coffee table dominates the centre – No Man's Land. Uncle, Aadam and Pasha start chatting.

'*It's been a long time. What are you doing these days? Is the money good?*'

It's a set-piece affair and pretty boring stuff but I still want to join in, only I can't think of anything to say. Aadam pats my knee. Somehow we're sitting right up against each other. It's like the sides of our thighs, arms and shoulders have been super-glued together, no doubt 'cause I've shuffled up closer and closer. *Why am I feeling so vulnerable?* I don't like this. I really don't like being this needy; not even with Aadam. Especially with Aadam. His love, it's ... I just need room to breathe. I don't like being disarmed.

I'm starting to resent having to make an effort, on today of all days. I mean, it's just wrong. And there's more to come – Aadam's parents, his brother Salman and his own family will all be on their way. And Pasha has a brother, too, I think. Aadam did tell me his name but I can't remember. He came to our wedding, apparently. Bit of a weirdo, so they say. Happy families, eh?

Ebb and flow, ebb and flow. I wish I was by the seaside, right now. *Nadi ki nare.* I could watch waves lapping a shoreline forever.

Sometimes you see God when you least expect it. I said that to Martin once and he gave me the strangest look, like he suddenly didn't know who I was. And he was right. We'd gone to Bournemouth after our finals; a week of sun, sea and ... yeah ... But in truth, the end for us had been building for a year, since I went home the summer before and my granny died. I hadn't seen her since I was a little girl and in truth she didn't even exist for me, but through her death we reconnected.

Me and Martin got together midway through our first year and stayed together until right at the end – until I saw God on Bournemouth beach. I didn't go looking for Him, honest. But I couldn't deny Him any longer. Don't get me wrong – I didn't go 'hallelujah!' or some Muslim equivalent and pick up a tambourine. I can't stomach religious people. Virtually all of them: dry, sterile, joyless drones going through the motions of some superstitious ritual. Ask any of them 'why?' and they'll look at you like you're disadvantaged, or just plain evil. At uni there were only two groups who I avoided – the Muslims and the Asians, especially the Indians. I loved the British. I loved their attitude, their joie de vivre. I found them so open, so free. It was easy to leave all that Asian crap behind. God, it's like it was just yesterday. Twenty was just the best age to be. It was so intoxicating, having your whole life stretched out in front. I remember everything: being in a club and surrounded by sound, lights, glow and sweat; your head spinning, your body spinning, your heart spinning. Wine, and being horny. I loved getting ready for a night out and feeling like I could crush the world. For a time, no stranger looked me straight in the eye: women turned away in envy and men were scrambled by lust. They say that a woman has nine-tenths of desire. I've never found a man who could keep up, least of all Aadam...

The Indians were really no different to the British, except they smeared everything in this brown veneer. As if being brown ever meant anything. And that's what I loved about the British – 'cause whoever you were and wherever you were from, it really didn't matter. Grab a drink, grab a girl – anyone could join in. I reckon the British and the Muslims are the truest of internationalists.

It wasn't until I was twenty-two and on that beach in Bournemouth, though, that I realised I couldn't be twenty forever. And it scared me, I can tell you. But then I remembered my granny. I don't think she was ever twenty.

I'd gone home after the second year for the summer holidays; I just missed Mum and Dad, I guess. But then within a week of me getting back, my gran died. I hadn't seen her in nearly ten years and neither had my mum. Pakistan had ceased to exist for us. For the first few days I felt vaguely sad but mostly just awkward. I had a distinct lack of any real emotion. Mum was of course devastated, but ... Anyway, a few days later I found myself tidying up and stumbled across some really old photos. Dad had lots of hair and trendy specs and Mum had a beehive! But it was the pictures of Gran that stopped me dead. She just wouldn't leave my mind after that. In every picture, she just looked so ... ethereal. I doubt if she ever did a single thing in her whole life, just for herself. And I couldn't stop thinking about that 'cause I'd started at this summer placement, and I saw all these people, in their mid-twenties, thirties, hell even forty-plus, still trying to act like kids. And I couldn't figure out which was worse: trying to be twenty forever or never being twenty even once.

Summer ended and I went back to uni but I just couldn't see things the same. We'd all spent the last two years utterly devoted to ourselves, but now it just didn't seem right. The nights out and the nights in; when someone got pissed and did something stupid everyone still found it funny – but I no longer did. I'd never before questioned who I was or where I belonged. People went on about racism and all that stuff but, honestly, I was British. I'd never felt out of place – or rather, I'd never been made to feel out of place. They could have used me for a damn poster campaign. This was my soil and I was of them. And then I saw the world through my own eyes.

Ramazan. It'd barely even registered with me before, but in that final year, I suddenly wanted to experience it: abstinence, discipline, inner peace. I wanted to cherish a glass of water. I wanted to witness the crack of dawn and search for the crescent in the night sky. But no one would understand. Martin – my beautiful boy, my savage man. He wouldn't understand. He would *never* understand because it wasn't the month of Ramazan; it was the month of February, and it couldn't be both. And I'd have to choose. But Martin made the stars dance for me and I just couldn't. Until I saw God on Bournemouth beach.

Aunty comes into the living room, bearing a tray of tea and biscuits. She places it down and gestures to me to pour from the pot. She asks Aadam where everyone else is: his parents and brother, and seems concerned that they're not here yet. He says he'll call but realises he's forgotten his phone.

'Have you brought your mobile, Nazneen?' he asks as I'm handing tea to Uncle.

'*Jee haan,*' I reply with my back to him, and he opens up my purse and rummages around, before finding my dinky handset.

'Great, thanks,' he mutters as he leaves the room.

'*Arre wah!*' remarks Aunty. 'In my day husband never ask for nothing, and wife always beg for everything!' She makes her point in broken English which instantly makes me chuckle. Women like Aunty seldom venture into English, and when they do it's because they *really* want to be heard. I'm guessing that it's Uncle to whom a message is being delivered here, and given that he's not responding, but is instead examining his biscuits with an undue intensity, I reckon he's received it loud and clear. And so *yes*, Aunty, Aadam is a thoughtful, considerate and caring husband. And I'm sorry that Uncle wasn't the same. I'm sorry that he never asked for your opinions or showed concern for your moods. Did he take care to warm you up? I bet he never hesitated to sail his boat, on rocky shores. Haha! Actually, Aadam's OK in that department, but he's no way near as good as Martin was. I remember my first experiences, finding it almost scary, being worked on like that. But I got to enjoy it; *really* enjoy it. I wish Aadam's appetite was bigger. I miss being ... *plundered*. Martin made me feel like a rag doll. *Oh, Martin.* Colorado seems so far away. I'd give anything to go back, to Red Rocks.

Lying on her front, she turns the page of a news magazine opened up on her pillow. She fiddles with her ponytail whilst skim reading. Nope, nothing interesting there*, and distractedly pulls on some bubble gum, teasing out a length.*

'Martin, Martin. Where the hell are you?'

It's been half an hour since she got back to the village and she's getting impatient. The quiche is on the table; the sun is approaching its peak. She needs to sear these memories. Destiny requires that he seal her High Noon.

She turns another page and a sentence grabs her by the throat: "Islam succeeded where Christianity failed, in shackling man's power of reasoning." *Suddenly she's no longer there. Keystone with its beautiful lake, the Rockies, even the beyond cool, Arapahoe Basin. Gone.* "Arab countries have no cultural disposition for scientific and industrial takeoff. Alas, these societies cannot make a brick, let alone a microchip." *And Martin, who alone in the whole world makes her eyes catch fire. Vanished.* "They are historically doomed to inferiority." *Friends, classmates, party pals and roommates – did they ever really exist?* "Yet now the West finds itself challenged from the outside by a militant, atavistic force, driven by a hatred of all Western political thought. The notion of co-existing peacefully is more our notion than theirs."

She feels ... a bite on her behind. She turns sharply.

'Martin!'

'Dinner's ready,' he murmurs, his eyes feasting on her rear.

'Oye!' she squeals. 'I've been waiting ages for you. Where the hell have you been?'

'Working up an appetite.' He speaks without inflection, like it were a simple truth. He crouches down onto her calves, locking her into position. He is yet to actually look her in the eye. He kneads her rump before gripping firmly; she can feel the heat from his spread hands transferring into her. He really does look hungry, *she accepts, with a woman's satisfaction.*

Hysterical laughter breaks out in the adjacent room, bringing Martin back to planet Earth.

'Those guys from Leeds have left, have they?'

'Yeah, must have. This lot only moved in an hour or so ago. Americans.'

'Don't tell me, the snow's coming!' *He pulls a funny face and drones in slightly mocking tones. Nazneen giggles and makes to turn fully round, but he still has her locked tight.*

'Hey, get off!' she protests with another squeal, despite loving his weight on her.

He doesn't budge but rather just sits back, smoothing his hands over her buttocks and hamstrings. She twists round further and they smile in silent mutual appreciation.

'There's some food left – some quiche. Let's have it and go. Red Rocks, remember?'

He says nothing but rather looks back at her buttocks, like he were considering his options.

'Hey there's time for that later!' she squeals for the umpteenth time, unaware that she'll never be such a girlie girl again. Finally he lets go and as she sits up, he notices the magazine on her pillow.

'What are you reading?' he asks casually. She snaps back and shuts it before flinging it off the bed.

'Nothing. Just killing time; waiting for you.' She smiles assuredly.
'Shouldn't we do some packing?' she adds, keen to change the subject.

'What? Now?' Don't worry about it, Naz,' he says whilst surveying the mess in the room. 'You can do it tomorrow.' She stares at him, not without rebuke.

'You? I meant we'll do it tomorrow.'

He winks and smiles and she knows his contribution will at best be a token gesture. But she doesn't mind; there's no point pretending that she minds.

The last time I ever saw Martin was nearly a year after we graduated. I'd started my traineeship by then and we met up in central London after work. He was seeing someone – in fact, the third different girl since we'd left uni. I asked him why, after all we'd been together for over two years. He said there was nothing like "new experiences", like that first taste of something. I really loved him, you know, like I don't think I've loved ever again. He was so handsome. No, more beautiful than handsome. He had such fine features, my stomach used to do somersaults just thinking about him. You can only feel that once in your life, I reckon. But what me and Aadam have is better than love. It's real. Aadam's very grounded. You get that in Muslim men, or in any religious man, really. They're more real. Realistic. You'd find the same in a Christian man too, but Christianity's dying, so it's irrelevant.

I stopped drinking some time ago now. I just grew more uncomfortable with it. I do miss wine though, sometimes. Floating away. I've started listening to *Qawwalis*. I swear there's God in that music. *Moula mere Moula*. And I just need to see 'cause I know He's there. Buried underneath all the politics and dead ceremony, there's Truth. I just know it. *Inshallah*, one day my eyes will open. *Ya Ali Madad.*

19

He'd only wanted to urinate but Pasha had been inside the toilet for ten minutes. Contemplating on his haunches, he marvelled at how nothing in this house had changed: no new carpet, no lick of paint. Actually, that wasn't quite true – the cooker was almost new and there was a microwave in the kitchen now. But in terms of furniture, optional extras, things that make a house a home ... Still, he had to concede, it'd all been very well maintained. In fact the occupants looked more moth-eaten than the things around him.

The temperature dropped. An object. Form. Taking shape. Pasha blinked rapidly and checked to his left and right. He was alone in the bathroom with his wet reflection staring back at him. *How long have I been standing in front of this mirror?* A sense of alarm gripped him but it was fleeting. *I look fine,* he reassured himself. He stepped out with renewed confidence and strode animatedly to the top of the staircase but then stopped dead. Salman was looking up at him. He was standing by the opened front door and, like Pasha, appeared stunned. A couple of children darted past, the young boy sounding excited, but Salman didn't move. More adults arrived behind him and he was shaken out of his stasis. The effect rippled out and Pasha re-started his descent, quick-stepping down with his gaze locked to the floor. They stood face-to-face. *What the fuck is appropriate here?* Aadam and Nazneen came out of the living room, each with one of Salman's children in tow. Pasha heard the kitchen door open and knew his mother would soon be conducting the melee. Salman extended a hand. Pasha ignored it and hugged him, and for the second time since arriving he was holding back tears. Arriving at the scene, Arwa was delighted.

'*Arre* Ibrahim, let me hug my sister's boy now,' she chided her son playfully. The two men parted, feeling a little embarrassed. There was no time to dwell on it, though, as Arwa pounced on her prey, kissing him on both cheeks and openly admiring his sturdy physique. Everyone laughed – the air was pleasant and light. The sisters Arwa and Bilqis embraced next and the whole gang moved on from the porch. Zakir made a beeline for the living room but, to his dismay, everyone followed his wife into the kitchen and from there to the adjacent breakfast room. Zakir grudgingly fell into line.

Greetings continued streaming forth. The brothers, Salman and Aadam, exchanged a few mock punches and Zakir and Husnain, the two elder statesmen, shook hands diplomatically. Husnain gulped, bracing himself for the company of his contemporary. He shot a look at his wife and her sister, the two of them already gossiping greedily. He knew he'd not separate them all day. The boys, too, would all be together and the idea of spending time with Kahina or Nazneen was a non-starter. Apart from his grandchildren, that left Zakir, who had already begun talking about the takeover of some accountancy firm. Husnain sighed. But at that moment he heard the excited voices of his boys. It looked like Pasha had made some joke; one which had tickled Aadam pink. He was bent double in laughter and Pasha was patting Salman on the chest: the joke was clearly at his stern elder son's expense but he was looking relaxed and taking it well. Husnain felt better already. He was determined to enjoy the day; by proxy if he had to. Imtiaz's absence suddenly registered but no one else had mentioned him, so he said nothing.

Taimur was looking for attention. He had brought a toy car along and was trying to show it off. 'Look, Aadam *Kaka,* look!' he said, holding the toy up for his uncle to inspect.

'Not now, *Beta,*' commanded his dad but Taimur continued appealing.

'Wow, look at this!' said Aadam, unable to dismiss the child. Taimur was made up. 'Is it your favourite? Look, Pasha Uncle, look at Taimur's car!'

'This is super cool!' exclaimed the new uncle, taking hold of the boy around the shoulders.

'But hey,' said Aadam. 'I think we can do better than this!'

'What do you mean?' asked Taimur, trying to keep his excitement in check.

'Well, I like your car,' Aadam began, his words slow and melodic, 'but Aadam *Kaka* has an even better toy to give his favourite nephew.'

'Eid presents, yeah!'

'Not now,' half-protested Salman, admonishing his brother with a look.

'Nonsense! Now's as good a time as any.' And he walked off before returning with Nazneen, who now held a couple of presents.

'Let me see, let me see!' beseeched Taimur, as he ran up to his Aunty.

'Patience, child,' she said, pressing his head to her body. Patience, though, was not a child's virtue and he tugged at her forearm, leading her back into the breakfast room. Pulling out a chair, he popped onto it, buttocks on heels. Everyone gathered round, rejoicing in children opening presents on Eid day. Nazneen knelt down besides Taimur, holding up a rectangular box.

'Can you guess what it is?' she asked the boy teasingly but with encouragement. She was hoping he'd take it and give it a rattle but he was having none of it. He began picking at the wrapping, not wanting to engage in the little game she'd set up.

'Be patient,' scolded Kahina but Taimur was getting frustrated and, not wanting to spoil the moment, Nazneen handed him the box.

'*Eid Mubarak, Beta,*' she said, and hugged and kissed him. Without replying he tore into the wrapping to reveal a toy gun. Taimur squealed, overjoyed. Salman winced.

'Thank you, Aunty!' He smiled and hugged Nazneen shyly before freeing the gun from its packaging. Aaliyah picked up the discarded box and began waving the cardboard absent-mindedly.

'I, too, have some presents,' announced Pasha by the kitchen door, all of a sudden laden with goodies. Everyone turned with surprise, having missed him discretely slipping out. He marched towards the breakfast table, revelling under the spotlight before handing a parcel to a speculative Aaliyah. She held the box out for her mummy to take without removing her eyes from the strange man.

'Thanks, Pasha,' said Kahina warmly, and he twisted his head to gesture *no problem*. Meanwhile, Taimur was frozen: the second box that the uncle held was huge and it *must* be for him. The uncle placed it down right in front. *It is for him!* Uncle patted him gently and said something, making the grown ups laugh, but Taimur wasn't listening. Rather he knelt to get an aerial view, just trying to take in its sheer size.

'Come on, son,' encouraged Pasha and he made to un-wrap the paper.

'*I* want to do it,' the boy immediately protested and he began unpeeling his gift.

'*I wonder what it is! Isn't it big? Aren't you a lucky boy?*' came random comments from around the table. And then there it was: the wrapping was lying in strips all around and Taimur was the proud owner of a brand new *Scalextric* set.

'You know, son, you always wanted one of these,' remarked Arwa.

'Too right, and you went and got me a bloody train set instead!' Everyone laughed aloud – except Salman.

'Really? *Now* you tell me!' said Zakir. 'Your mother assured me you wanted that train set. But you played with it for so long.'

'Yes, yes I did,' remembered Pasha. 'But I really wanted one of these.' He tapped the box and laughter again rang round. Pasha smiled without restraint and at last looked like he was home. Salman thought this must be the most excited his son had ever been, but he also knew he'd played no part in it. Too many emotions competed to grip him – none were positive, none settled.

'Mummy, Mummy look!' the young boy said, finally finding his voice.

'You've got one more present left to receive, son,' announced Salman, clearing his throat. The boy threw a beaming smile to his daddy. Young Taimur placed his gun on top of his *Scalextric* set before propping himself back up on his heels. *Daddy's present will be the best of all!* Kahina braced herself.

'Now, son, Ramazan is Allah's month and when you become a man you will fast just like Daddy. You understand?'

'Yes, Daddy,' came the chirrupy response.

'Good boy. *Eid Mubarak*, my dear Son,' and he kissed his firstborn tenderly and handed him his present. It was small but heavy, and without further ado, Taimur began tearing into the last wrapping of the day. It was a book, one with an exquisitely embroidered and padded hardcover. There was calligraphic writing on the front in a language which Taimur couldn't read, but nevertheless recognised. For Salman this was a key moment in his young boy's life – the day he was gifted his very own Qur'an. It signified the first step of his journey, his life's journey. Soon his father would begin overseeing his religious education, and then he'd be able to understand God's instruction for him. But Taimur didn't see it that way: he knew what to do with the gun and he knew how to play with the *Scalextric*, but what fun was he meant to get from the Holy Book? His father, knelt down beside him, was watching his response. He'd seen his son jump for joy over his other presents and he desperately wanted to see happiness on his face now. After all, he'd spent so long choosing it, selecting just the right one. Taimur started to cry. Utterly shocked, Salman was unable to compute the reaction. He looked up at his wife, dad and brother, but they too looked frozen and offered no clue. Then he looked at Pasha. *Is he smiling?* Salman slapped his son on the face. The boy started bawling and with burning eyes he turned to his mother. Kahina shot her husband a look and lead Taimur out of the kitchen. Awkwardness descended like a pall.

'You stupid boy!' Bilqis thundered, breaking the silence. Salman was still kneeling by the now vacant chair. He walked right out, slamming the front door shut. The only movement was from Aadam who stepped towards his wife, placing an arm around her shoulders.

'That stupid boy!' Bilqis repeated, fury punctuating her words.

'He didn't mean it, *Bahen*, my sister. He must be feeling terrible right now,' said Arwa, but Bilqis was having none of it.

'Well he bloody well ought to be.'

Hearing his wife fume, Husnain rubbed his weary head, worry and shame competing to bring him down.

'I'll go and talk to him,' said Pasha, and the sound of the front door closing again signalled the end of the drama.

'Come, Husnain, let's go into the living room,' said Zakir, and reluctantly he followed him out to receive the balm of telly.

'You know what everyone needs?' suggested Nazneen.

'What, *Beti*?'

'Tea! A nice cup of tea.'

'That's a good idea,' said Arwa with a sigh, and she turned with effort towards the kettle.

'No, no, I mean *proper* tea. Spiced tea – cooked tea. Do you have any *chai masala*, Aunty?'

'Actually I don't, child. I'm sorry.'

'Don't worry, I can make you up some.'

And with that Nazneen went to the cupboards, searching for the five or six whole spices that are essential to such a mixture. Arwa and Bilqis exchanged looks. Despite Nazneen entering the family two years ago they remained unconvinced by her, this fancy career girl. Bilqis could hear her son playing with Aaliyah in the corridor and felt it was time Aadam had a child of his own. Nazneen measured out different spices on a plate before tipping the lot into a blender. Individual seeds quickly merged into a powder, and pressing the plastic lid down she looked up at her mother-in-law, wearing a satisfied grin. *It's OK, girl. I'm impressed*, Bilqis thought. *But what else do you know?* Oblivious to the sceptical eyes, Nazneen began making the tea.

20

Pasha looked down the thin, shared driveway of his parents' house. The front garden was tiny – a small square lawn with a regular bush fencing two sides. There was an arrangement of flowering shrubs in the middle. Of course, there was no colourful display on this mid-November afternoon; only bare branches exposing barren earth.

There was no sign of Salman. He walked to the pavement and looked down the road and saw a big figure trying to look small in a beat-up car. His first thought was one of surprise; that Salman owned such a banger. *Didn't he study accountancy at uni? Wasn't his old man an accountant, too?* He approached the driver-side door cautiously. If Salman had seen him he hadn't reacted – he remained perfectly still. His eyes were shut and his chest rose evenly and deeply. For all the world it looked like he was sleeping. But then Pasha noticed a tear roll down. His nose also ran and he wiped the back of his hand underneath. Pasha remembered the two of them kicking a ball about on this very street, and marvelled at how life could get so fucked up. Gently, he tapped the window.

Allah, why did I hit him? *Why*? I didn't want to come here today. Why couldn't we have spent Eid at home, just us? Look at them, these ... he's ruined my day, my special day. Does Eid mean anything to him? That *na-paak*. I should have put my foot down; said something. But Mum treats me like a damn child. She'd treat me with greater respect if I earned more. I have tried, though. I've always tried, but this damn country won't let me win. *Allah*, I shouldn't have hit him. K*nock knock*.

Oh God, what is he ... 'I'll be in in a minute, Pasha.' I look up briefly and force a smile. 'Please – go back inside.'

I'm looking dead ahead. I don't want to see him again. He's not saying anything but he's not moving, either. *Go, you swine.*

'Please, Pasha. I just need a few minutes.'

'Let me in, Salman. It's bloody freezing out here!'

I close my eyes and wish ... wish I could wish things away. Like in that kids' film. Click your heels together, three times. I look up and he's smiling, smiling at me, *the swine*. And against my best efforts, I smile back. I've lost – again. I stretch and open the passenger-side door. Pasha hops round like he's walking on hot coals before jumping in. I just can't bear to look. I can hear the silence. I'm sat in my freezing car with my one-time cousin/brother/enemy, and now complete stranger. I want to go home.

Pasha rubs his hands together. 'Put the heating on, Salman!'

I slowly turn to him. We study each other. He's so familiar and yet a complete alien. It's really uncomfortable. *Allah* ... I remember us playing football together on this very street. We were kids, then – ten, maybe eleven. I bet he's forgotten all that. I can't believe this is the same person. They say Allah guides whom He wants to guide.

'I can't. The battery's really weak. I don't want to risk the car not starting when we leave.'

'Well, then get a better car!' Pasha punches me lightly on the arm. 'I know how much you accountants earn!'

I really don't know what to say. You know I'd always hoped that one day I'd get my revenge. Because he cut me loose when I really needed a friend, after he'd found his wings and I was still searching for my feet.

'I'm a Passport Control Officer at Heathrow Airport,' I say, matter-of-factly. I see Pasha bite his lower lip. Silence.

'But you studied accountancy, right?' He looks at me curiously but with concern.

'Yeah.' I don't feel like elaborating. Pasha shifts in his seat.

'You know I've been thinking about you constantly, these last few days.'

I raise my eyebrows but say nothing. He keeps looking at me, expectantly. He's willing me to give him something, anything, but I'm no longer finding it difficult to ignore him. Eventually he sighs and shapes to get out but some reflex makes me turn. Instantly he stops.

I'm on a roller coaster: brotherhood, distance, love, repulsion. But above all, compulsion. I just can't stop myself.

'I've been thinking about you, too. Do you know how long it's been?'

'Too long,' sighs Pasha, rubbing his temples. I feel his frustration, wishing things were different but knowing they never will be.

'Are you married?' Pasha stiffens at my question. I'll take that as a *no*, then.

'I have a girlfriend – a partner.' He adds that last part quickly, almost like a correction.

'Why don't you just marry her?'

'She's English,' he replies stiffly. He's staring like he's expecting some big reaction but I'm not sure if that's meant to be surprise, awe or disappointment. In truth, all three emotions shoot through me, but I'll not let on to any of that.

'So what? Kahina's Tunisian.'

'Kahina's Muslim, though – her nationality's irrelevant.'

Again he braces himself for some reaction, but it's too cold, he's not worth it, it's Eid and I just can't be bothered.

'I never entered accountancy in the end. I never got my foot in the door. I guess my face didn't fit. I'm glad now, though. It's not a clean living – usury, entertaining clients. Not clean. What do *you* do?'

'Oh, I'm in software. Look, it's not important.'

'Oh but it is. You just made my son happier than I ever have. How do you think that makes me feel?' I face him squarely and can see he's stunned. I am, too. I can't believe I just said that. But it is why we are both out here, in my freezing old car.

'I had no idea. Salman, I'm sorry.' And he looks it, he really does. But there's no way I'm letting this guy in.

'Don't you think I'd have bought him something expensive if I could have?'

'But it's not about the cost, Salman. Taimur's a kid. Don't you remember being that young? Would you have appreciated receiving a Qur'an as an Eid present, when you were eight?'

He's right. *NO*. He's wrong.

'It's everything to do with the cost. Kids want so much now. I'm trying to give him some deeper values. The British only worship money. Money, drink and sex.' I catch Pasha's eye and he looks horrified. I guess it's an uphill struggle for both of us, trying not to hate each other.

'Salman, I'm sorry. I can only say it so many times. I bought the presents with good will. I'd never seen your children before.' Again, sincerity. He's not making it easy for me.

'I should have been seeing *your* children today, too.' Pasha looks down into his lap. He looks lost, almost apologetic. I've not seen that look in him before, ever – not as a boy, not as a teenager, and not as a young man. That was what marked him out – total self-confidence. Sitting this close to him, I notice some grey in his hair. I have grey in mine, too. More than him, but I don't mind, not really. But I bet he does. I bet he minds a whole lot. Maybe my day of justice will still come.

21

Life is bland. Mostly. Days come and go and we buy comfort and sell ourselves. And then come the spikes. Extreme highs and lows puncture the cocoon, heightening senses, precipitating thought. Remember meeting that dear old friend after such a long time? Wasn't it just like the taste of Christmas Past, mellowed in oak? More often, though, you end up being force-fed some home-brewed hooch that leaves you half-blind and bleeding from every orifice.

Imtiaz had arrived. Out of everyone he lived the closest, yet he was nearly two hours late. He was just inside by the front door and was trying to take his shoes off. Their black-dyed leather was well worn and the laces utterly frayed; he fumbled in undoing the knot.

'Good to see you again, Imtiaz. How are you, *Bhai*?' asked Salman. Instinct, though, made him look away even as he greeted him. Imtiaz smiled weakly and muttered in response. A motionless Pasha was there too as Imtiaz continued wrestling with his shoes. The sleeves of his overcoat rode up as he picked at the knot, exposing thin wrists with skin wrapped tightly over bone.

'You're looking well,' commented Salman moronically. Pasha looked at him aghast before glancing back at his brother, hoping he hadn't provoked a reaction. He hadn't. Quitting whilst he was only just slightly behind, Salman about-turned and scuttled off; the two brothers were left on their own. Finally, Imtiaz stood up.

'Hi, Pasha.'

His face carried no expression at all, yet Pasha knew he was mortified.

'Are you well?' he asked, falling into the same trap as Salman. He bit his lower lip as the brothers embraced loosely.

Leading him into the kitchen, Pasha recomposed himself.

'Guess who is here, Mum?' He attempted a fanfare before briskly walking through and planting himself at the breakfast table, next to Salman. The two exchanged looks. Imtiaz stood alone, stranded by the kitchen door. His head was lowered in an attempt to hide under his baseball cap, yet a thin film of sweat was still evident – his skin glistened with dis-ease.

Aaliyah and Taimur stopped and stared. Nazneen and Bilqis turned away. Arwa looked full of shame.

'Hi, Mum,' he said blandly. His mother embraced him tightly but he barely reciprocated. Watching on, Bilqis remembered him as a little boy. He was always such a frightened child, always holding onto his mother, tagging behind on her apron strings. She was filled with sadness. *This boy just never stopped being frightened.*

'Hello, Aunty,' he peeped, a tremor in his voice.

'Why are you wearing this thing indoors?' She admonished him and swiftly removed his cap without seeming interested in a response. His head of hair resembled a sea storm: overgrown clumps lashed into random, frenzied shapes. Bilqis smarted at the display before running a hand through.

'And what is this, eh?' Her serious eyes bore no hint of remorse. 'No time for a haircut? No time to wash or comb?' She darted from one eye to the other, looking for some sign of life. Pity soon pulled her back. She kissed him on the third eye. His body was bent awkwardly and he tried smiling but it came out all distorted. She kissed him again and abruptly let go, moving swiftly to inspect the bubbling dishes. Imtiaz moved on.

'Good to see you again,' said Aadam with a handshake. 'This is my wife,' he jollied, those words accompanied as always by an unfailing pride.

'Hello, Imtiaz,' Nazneen smiled and held out a cup of tea. 'You look like you could do with this.' He responded to her brightness and accepted the drink gratefully. Taimur now held his toy car up to the strange man and Imtiaz reacted with delight. He was re-introduced to Kahina by Salman, them having met before, and then he tried to pick up Aaliyah but she screamed and writhed away in protest. Everyone laughed. His father and Husnain re-entered the kitchen and the coldest of greetings between Imtiaz and Zakir followed.

Pasha felt shaken. He couldn't take his eyes off him when he had first entered. His body had lost all structure, its definition distorted. His arms and legs had wasted away but bizarrely he'd also acquired a belly. And his face, too, was puffy but it was the total lack of expression that was the starkest feature: dead eyes peering out from a live but rotting carcass. The extra fat on his face (certainly more so than he could remember) had taken the edge off him as "him", blurring his features. He looked somewhat androgynous, amorphous. He had searched for the right adjective or phrase, and after dismissing "dishevelled" and "unattractive", had settled on "cartoon ugly".

But now he felt ashamed. This was his brother. He recalled that incident when Kahina had given him Aaliyah to hold. The little girl had shrilled and squirmed in protest until her mother simply had to take her back. Everyone had laughed; even Imtiaz himself had laughed, but he wasn't stupid. His brother was absorbing insult after insult with an animal's tolerance, and he was fully aware. Pasha hung his head.

22

"Your task is not to seek for love, but merely to seek and find all the barriers within yourself that you have built against it."

JALALUDDIN RUMI

Mother...

I'll never risk reading a magazine in this house again. I flick back to the front cover, curious to see what bizarre periodical has made its way into the Walayat household. *Sufi Psychology*, it says. Jeez. It's not what *I* pick up from the "special interest" section at *my* local newsagents ... haha ... But it's not really funny, is it. God. If I were a dog they'd put me down. I remember someone from work once blustering about a stag-do to Amsterdam that they'd been on, and how their top-shelf magazines put us Brits to shame. Now, I'll admit to having enjoyed more than the odd copy of *Mayfair* or *Men's World,* but over there they cut right to the chase: *Fist Cunt* and *Choco & Piss* are two titles that I pretended not to hear, but which were seared instantly into my mind. I mean, just how messed up can a person get? I ain't claiming to be no saint, but if I found myself next to someone browsing the latest issue of *Choco & Piss,* even I'd be running for the hills. I'm scared. I really am. I don't want to descend any further down this pit. I desperately need help.

I toss the magazine onto the coffee table and collapse back. I inhale greedily, trying to work out what the hell to do next: dinner's close to being served but it ain't ready yet. Five, ten, maybe fifteen minutes to go. *Please, God, just get me through this day.* I'm on my own in the living room but then my Old Man enters. *Oh God, please.*

'Oh, I'm starving!' my father jollies, taking his favourite seat. He's on good form today, I tell you. 'What's to come first?' he bellows with good humour, clearly expecting to be served on hand-and-foot. I'm guessing the question's aimed at my mum, but she's in the kitchen and no reply comes forth. He smiles at us nonetheless from across the coffee table, kind of flashy, and I wink back. *That's right, ya cunt. Start as ya mean to go on, I say.* He rubs his hands with glee, clearly picking up none of the poison in my eyes.

The breakfast table was too small to fit everyone so we decided to eat in the living room. Well, when I say *we* decided, I mean Pasha decided. He's rolled his sleeves up today, and no mistake. He's really getting stuck in, helping Mum and that. I should too, but ... it's the looks, those looks I get – seeing that same expression in everyone's face. It just freezes me over. I need to just sit here, recover a bit. I'm relieved all the introductions are over.

It's still only me and me Old Man who have taken up positions. Everyone else is doing something useful, I guess. Still, Daddy Dear is now providing me with some entertainment, and I watch him plump up some cushions. He turns back round, a satisfied grin on his mug. Someone, I can't remember who, but someone once said that Hell was being locked up in a room full of your friends, forever. That's startlingly close to the mark, you know. I think it was Socrates. Daddy Dear now switches on the telly and stretches out a tartan-patterned blanket over his legs before cleaning his teeth with a toothpick. Or was it Dustin Hoffman? Look at him, just look. Right now he wants for nothing. I envy the cunt, truly I do. I wish a tartan blanket and some good telly was enough to warm *my* cockles. I shake my head, marvelling at the insanity of it all. I mean, just what the hell are we all doing here, on this *miserable* planet?

This is far from ideal. Dad's sorted with his telly, but what about me? I consider my options: all that comes to mind is going into the kitchen but I'm not convinced. It's gonna take some serious effort to get out of this seat. Thankfully Pasha provides a welcome distraction as he enters briskly, carrying a stack of plates. But just then Salman's little boy runs in and tears past him, shrieking all excitedly. He knocks Pasha's hip and elbow as he screams through, his little arms all over the place. Pasha has to quickly readjust to secure his cargo and in doing so he pretty much saves Eid. I shit you not – I swear by everything that I know about my father that if that crockery had slipped from his hands and fallen, or hit the edge of the coffee table and chipped it, he'd have gone nuts. The fucker would have freaked. *Imtiaz, why are there crumbs on my carpet? Pasha, what are these stains?* We were pure petrified of him. My abiding memory of growing up in this house is of mum, me and Pasha forever tip-toeing around his moods. We tidied up like possessed people. Now Aadam appears and young Taimur starts running round the coffee table. Aadam's growling and trying to make like some ogre-type character, and the boy is going pure mental. He takes a step towards Taimur who shrieks again, but whilst the act's working on the boy, I can't help but chuckle to myself: he's just too skinny to make it work. Aadam takes another Frankenstein step and the boy simply cannot contain himself; he jumps up onto the sofa next to my father, grabbing his jumper by the shoulder. I tell you though, it's good to see the little lad all lively again. I heard what went on just before I got here. Boy, am I glad I missed that. My father sees none of the wider context, though, and flinches, and I know exactly why – 'cause he doesn't like this sort of play. Play where nice sofas get jumped up and down on, and during which plates and the like could get broken. The barely ten-stone Aadam takes another stiff stride and Taimur pulls more tightly at my father's jumper as he tries to squeeze in behind. My old man tries to shake him off but the boy is oblivious. Now *this* is interesting. Poor daddy is now stony faced and his frustrated eyes catch mine for the briefest flicker; I give him another wink. No smile from him this time, though – he just looks straight back down. *Not so full of festive cheer now, eh? What's upset you, Daddy Dear? The little boy jumping up and down on your nice sofa? Him pulling the stitching on your jumper? It looks new, that does. I've certainly not seen it before.* I allow myself a luxurious stretch before sitting up straight, eager to see how this is going to play out. *And look! Yes!* There's a faint smudge where the boy has been pawing at the jumper with his greasy mitts. The little bugger, eh? He must have been eating chocolate and he's not washed his hands! *No son of yours would have been so careless, huh? A brown smudge on your nice new cream jumper.* Aadam takes another stride towards the now-delirious Taimur who, in his desperation to squeeze in behind my father, elbows him in the side of the face. Suddenly he grabs the boy firmly and for a second I'm sure he's gonna whack him. *He's* probably sure he's gonna whack him, too, but he comes to his senses just in time.

'Aadam – stop fooling around!' my father orders sharply, and he plonks the boy down beside him. And, just like that, it's over. The boy looks relieved – saved, even – and Aadam acknowledges that his tomfoolery was misplaced. Meanwhile, Pasha places the pile of crockery down and begins whipping Aadam with a tea towel. He yelps and everyone laughs, including my old man. I feel short changed.

I'm thirsty. It's my nerves, no doubt, but I feel the need to be holding a cup of something. I'd love some herbal tea right now but I doubt my mum's got any. Pasha's gone back to the kitchen and Aadam's disappeared with the young'un, and so it's back to just me and the Old Man. God, this is dire. I look around for another distraction, anything, but no one else comes in and nothing happens. I turn back to my father, quietly watching TV. He looks pretty pathetic, I have to say. Actually, most people do, watching telly alone – gormless, at best. He flicks channels for a bit before settling on some American sitcom which he doesn't seem all that interested in. Crap telly pisses him off more than it does most people. I think he's forgotten that I'm still in the room. I'm now watching him like some fly on the wall. Despite myself, I feel hurt. I wonder what a fly on *my* wall would have made of what *I* was watching last night. God, I hate myself. I get up to get that drink.

I enter the kitchen and all conversation stops. I mean, it's just for a second – less than that, even – but everyone has to readjust to my presence. It's as if I'm some walking contaminant, polluting the space around me. Everyone is in here apart from Salman and his folks, who are upstairs praying, I guess. Aadam is at one end of the kitchen table with the kids and Pasha is at the other, ladling soup into bowls. My mum, Kahina and Nazneen *were* by the stove, but no sooner had I entered than the girls moved away. I'm a fucking dispersant.

They both give us this stock weak smile and Nazneen says, mouse-like, '*You all right, Imtiaz?*' but it's more of a nervous tick than a question. I am the anti-Midas – everything I touch turns to shit.

'Do you want something, *Beta*?' says my mum, and she comes up to us and rubs my back. I stand still and let her dispense her affection but frankly I'm more comfortable with the girls' revulsion.

'Do you have any herbal teas?' I ask, hoping she'll now stop touching me.

'I do,' she says, to my surprise, and moves towards the cupboards. 'Your father buys this peppermint *chai*.' She takes it out and holds it up but I'm not persuaded.

'Nah,' I say. 'It's OK. I'll just have some warm water.'

'Isn't that what old people drink?' pipes up Aadam. I try and think of some quick riposte but nothing comes to mind. He's probably right anyway, and that makes me more uneasy. I glance over at Pasha who looks busy counting bowls, but he's over-doing it; he's deliberately avoiding me and I don't know why. I catch Nazneen shoot Aadam a look that says *you shouldn't make fun of the spasmo like that*. I just pick up the kettle and start filling it. With my gaze locked onto the pouring water, I think of Nazneen. Now, that's an attractive girl. Objectively so, but I personally wouldn't go for her type. Isn't that weird? I think my buttons only get pressed now by 2D tarts rather than anything or anyone real. Plus she's Asian. I don't think I've ever been turned on by an Asian girl. Some of these modern Indian actresses are really beautiful; I've seen a couple of films. But where is demure Asian beauty compared to English girls' *brazenness*? I only go for dirty white chicks, like in last night's film. *Feeding disease on her hands and knees. In this satellite town she takes me down ...* Water pours out of the full kettle, the rushing water hitting the sink. I rapidly twist the tap five, six times, until it's off. I stand for a second, pressing my sweaty palm against my feverish brow. *God, how do I stop this?* This day is not getting any easier.

Finally we're eating. Me Old Man's seated where he's been pretty much firmly rooted for the past thirty-five years, and everyone else has found some space dotted around – on the sofas, the chairs and even on the floor. I'm sitting across the coffee table, where I was previously, and Pasha's next to me. Mum and young Taimur are on the three-seater with my father. I must say, that boy's got a lovely, bright face – full of joy. I think he must be relishing us all eating together and him not being separated from the adults. Husnain Uncle and Bilqis Aunty are on the two-seater in front of the bay windows, with Aadam and Nazneen on the floor right in front of them. Meanwhile, Salman, Kahina and Aaliyah make up the cutest trio on the floor, pretty much in front of me. Little Aaliyah looks up, still cautiously taking in the unfamiliar surroundings. I catch her staring at Pasha next to me with as grave an expression as a three-year-old can have. I click my fingers and give her a big smile but her sombre little face doesn't lift. She seems unimpressed by my efforts and soon switches back to simply staring at my brother. Only Husnain Uncle, who now waves and calls out her name, elicits a smile. She happily waves back to her granddad but gives no indication that she'll go to him. I guess there's no way she's moving from her daddy's lap right now.

First up was leek and potato soup. My father had looked at it suspiciously but, to his surprise (and, I have to say, mine too), it turned out to be damn good. A perfect starter for a cold day. Mum's ears were pricked up for all the satisfied *ooohs* and *aaahs* that came generously from all around. She looked really, really happy. And I felt happy for her. Next came a golden-coloured sweet dish made of carrots, followed by samosas and other savouries. After that, stomachs were patted, breaks taken and legs stretched in preparation for the *biryani*; the main course. Jokes were cracked and laughter rang around the room as tales of old were retold.

'Remember when we went to Leicester for the first time in '73, and we got lost on the way up?' recalls my father.

'*Acha*, and we stopped off at that service station to ask the way,' Aunty adds. Everyone knows what's coming next, like when watching a classic comedy.

'Yeah, and we asked the lady, "are we heading the right way for *Lesester?*" And she looks at us like we're mad, so we repeat, "*Lesester*". It took ages for her to work out that we meant Leicester, and for *us* to realise that the place was pronounced *Lester*, and not *Lesester*!' Everyone bursts out laughing. Taimur and Aaliyah titter too, on seeing all the grown-ups having so much fun.

'Bloody English language,' splutters Uncle through a coughing fit. He'd been taking a sip of something as the punchline was delivered and some of it had gone down the wrong track. He's patting his chest and trying to calm down, but the giggles are still bubbling up. 'Why the hell do they spell it "Leicester"?'

'Too right!' booms my Old Man in agreement. 'It's not as if we didn't have enough to cope with when we first arrived.'

'You know, I had the same problem,' Kahina adds, 'but Salman really helped me.' The proud husband pecks his wife on the cheek, making sure not to tip the plate resting on his outstretched legs. The others look on adoringly as Aaliyah plays with the food on her mummy's lap.

'You know, I can remember that trip,' begins Salman. 'In fact, it's just about my first memory. How old was I then, Mum?'

'Oh, you must have been four or five,' says Aunty, a little unsure.

'No, you were five,' says Uncle. 'I remember it well. You had just had your birthday. Pasha, you were there too,' he adds, drawing a nod but no comment from my brother. 'And Imtiaz, you were just a baby then. You couldn't even have had your first birthday.'

Everyone now flits a look at me. Bugger. I wasn't expecting that. I can't think of anything to add to the conversation, so I too just nod. It occurs to me how irrelevant me and Pasha are to this gathering. I wonder if he's thinking the same.

'Ooh, Imtiaz!' cooes Bilqis Aunty all of a sudden, her hands clasped for emphasis. 'You were *such* a cute baby.' She looks at me with beaming eyes before seeing the irony in what she's just said. There's now total silence and I'm barely able to breathe.

'Hey!' exclaims Pasha, clapping his hands twice. 'Let's get that *biryani!*' And he jumps up and ushers Mum to do the same, and the two of them head off to the kitchen. More approvals are aired and the background hum returns. *Thank you, Pasha. Thank you, Bhai.* I watch Nazneen play with some crusty bits on her plate whilst Aadam pats her stomach. I'm so far away from my dreams.

Soon we are eating again, all appetites having been restored at the first smell of the royal dish.

'*Wah,* Aunty, this is magnificent. Really.' The praise finds echoes once more and Mum accepts it all graciously. Her week-long efforts have all been worthwhile and I can see she's feeling wonderful. I wish I could have brought her more joy.

'Ramazan was tough this year, though,' says Salman to the floor, by way of starting a new conversation.

'Too right, bro,' agrees Aadam. 'It gets harder every year.'

'Oh come on guys, it's not that bad,' says Nazneen. 'I told my boss, all my workmates knew – it really wasn't an issue. I missed going to the gym and a few other things, but Ramazan has its own rhythm. You've got to get into it.'

Amazing. I never took that girl as the religious type. Neither Aadam nor Salman comes back with anything and no one else offers up any other Ramazan-related experiences. The thread is prematurely cut.

'You know, I spoke to my sister this morning, in Karachi,' Uncle mentions cheerily.

'Really?' asks Salman. 'When was that?'

'You were still at the *masjid,* son,' he explains. 'You know I haven't gone back in a long time now. It's high time. See Karachi again.'

'That's a great idea, Dad,' says Aadam.

'It's amazing, you know,' pipes up Pasha. 'I've grown up in the shadow of that country and yet I've only been once, when I was really young. You should have taken us more often, Dad.' Pasha looks across to our father, whose head is down with his focus on his food. He's chewing rapidly and I can hear his signature *clomp clomp* quite clearly. For some reason the food in his mouth has never reached his back teeth, and so they've always just clanked together to produce a dull sound. *Clomp clomp clomp.* It used to drive me and Pasha mad when we were kids; it was our own little joke. I smile and Pasha turns to me, also smiling. His face lifts and his eyes dance as they hold mine. He pats my knee gently and leaves his hand there. I feel *alive*.

Daddy Dear finally speaks without looking up from his plate: 'I brought you here to become an Englishman, son; not a Pakistani. Not even I'm a Pakistani any more.' He continues eating. The comment detonates around the room whilst Daddy innocently sucks on a bone. No one is quite sure how to follow that up. Pasha eventually changes tack.

'You know, Uncle, if you decide to go, let me know. I'll come with you.'

'Sure, *Beta*. Sure, son,' he assures with a sage nod.

'I'd just like to say,' begins our father, finally making eye contact. 'It's wonderful to be surrounded by my family today.' Briefly, he turns to everyone as he completes his little speech. 'Eid Mubarak, all. *Eid Mubarak*.' We all reciprocate in chorus and I see Dad kiss Mum in what is an unexpected show of affection. Clearly surprised too, Mum nevertheless responds positively to her husband's advance. Affection is infectious and soon Uncle and Aunty and Aadam and Nazneen, are also exchanging hugs and kisses. Knowing that we are somewhat out of the loop here, Pasha and I exchange pained, forced smiles. He removes his hand from my knee. Salman looks towards his son and pats his lap, at which point Taimur springs up from the sofa and darts towards his father. Husnain Uncle looks on contentedly as his first-born and his family reaffirm their love for each other. These sorts of riches you just cannot buy.

23

That was a really nice dinner. Dear Arwa Aunty looks across and smiles and I smile back. Bless her. She looks so thrilled. She's a lovely, simple woman – a homemaker. *Homemaker.* You don't hear that word so often any more.

Aadam's rifling through some scraps on my plate, seeing if there's anything worth pilfering. I tap his hand to gently berate but he ploughs on with his explorations. Watching on, Aunty beams more widely still and I know what she's thinking. *Aah, such a lovely couple,* but I'm getting tired of this show now. I know Aadam's loving it – all this, this *validation* – but if it was just me and him, at home, I wouldn't be getting the same attention. He's not even doing it deliberately, but there's a performance going on here and I'm not sure I want to continue acting. I need attention, affection and passion. And Aadam needs to know that we're on the best Gas Payment Plan. *No.* I'm being unfair. I glance across. My hubby's so happy, chatting animatedly to his dad and uncle. I feel all warm, seeing him like this. He's not boring. He used to have a lot more to give but he expends so much just staying afloat.

I should be like Aunty: a homemaker, making lots of nice food for everyone to enjoy. Like my friend, Nikki, with her chubby little Charlie and a happy hubby to make a home for. I have half of that already and Aadam would love it if I fell pregnant. I could become like my grandma: a matriarch. Like Mary, daughter of Imran, wife of Yousuf and mother of Jesus Christ. That's half the problem in this country: men have forgotten how to be men and women have forgotten how to be women.

I should be more satisfied. *What's wrong with me?* But inside, deep inside, *I want someone to spill blood, just for my pleasure.*

'I am not a number, I am a free man!' screams Martin, with arms aloft and head thrown skyward. The sun beats down, bleached-white and unimpressed; the parched red Colorado earth continues to bake. He collapses in mock exhaustion, prompting Nazneen to rush in, clapping excitedly.

'That was great, Martin! You should try out for Drama Soc. next year.'

'Thank you, Number Two,' he replies tersely, still in character.

'OK, OK Number Six,' she obliges with a sigh. She holds out a hand, encouraging him to stand. He takes it but pulls her down instead, making her yelp as she tumbles onto his chest.

'Come on, let's go. We can rest at the top,' she suggests, playing with the buttons on his polo shirt. Martin surveys the remainder of their route: a winding path snaking around this pancake basin, taking them up to the Trading Post – the crest of a colossal sandstone fissure, demarcating nothing less than World's End.

Winding up an increasingly steep grade, the approach becomes ever more stark. To the right the vista is beautiful and familiar: valleys and meadows, low shrubbery and tall evergreens; the occasional bird flying to or fro its nest. But to the left: an endless barren crust, interrupted only by red sandstone boils. Layered in variegated shades, the pillars point with crooked fingers, accusing the intense blue Colorado sky of some unknown crime. Nazneen looks down with relief, glad to be out of the basin. A deafening silence hung in that amphitheatre, challenged only by echoes from the Ancients – along the trails carved out by the Pioneers, at the sacred boulders around which Native Americans once prayed, and inside cliff dwellings where prehistoric man sought shelter. She stands on a precipice, with nothing separating her from a two-hundred-foot fall. Intermittently, a jutting rock-face or a solitary tree guards the path's edge, but mostly there is nothing. Just a vertical drop into an alien oblivion.

24

'So do any of you boys still follow the cricket?' Pasha glanced around, a hopeful look on his face. Everyone was finished eating and were fully done-for, appetites having not so much been pacified as beaten into the ground. Zakir actually looked in pain; by way of distraction he picked up the remote and began channel hopping.

'You know Pakistan and India are playing each other, either today or tomorrow,' he commented absent-mindedly.

'Really?' responded an excited chorus.

'*Yaar,*' Zakir continued. 'There is this one-off match, celebrating the Indian cricket board's 75th anniversary – 1929-2004. They've been advertising it all week.' He stopped channel-surfing on finding a nature programme. There was a huge, scary spider with hair closer to bristles, stealthily crossing some jungle floor. The background music added to the scene, giving Mr Spider a gravitas that he was blissfully unaware of. All looked on, easily drawn in.

'Well?' repeated Pasha.

'Well what?' asked Aadam idly, his attention on the spider.

'*The Boys* man, *The Boys*. Pakistan cricket...'

'They've gone downhill,' said Salman.

'True enough,' agreed Aadam. 'But do you remember '92? What a year!'

'Oh God, wasn't it just?' said Pasha, delighted that everyone was warming to his theme. 'The two Ws – Wasim and Waqar. They were awesome that year.'

'Yeah. Wasim, man, Wasim.' All turned to Imtiaz, astonished to see him come to life. 'It's not been the same since Wasim retired.' And with that he sank back into his seat, leaving the others stunned at his first voluntary contribution of the day. The conversation stopped dead.

'That was a lovely dinner, Aunty,' said Kahina.

'Hmm, the *halwa*, the *biryani;* it was all spectacular,' enthused Nazneen, and a final round of praise followed.

'Come, let's clear these plates,' Bilqis suggested, and with that the women, along with Husnain, got up. The four boys and Zakir, however, remained rooted to their spots: hairy-scary spider after hairy-scary spider followed, providing ample distraction. But Pasha was still thinking about the cricket.

'So, what did you make of all that "Zimbabwe" business?'

'Which bit?' asked Salman. 'England not wanting to go there or England not wanting them over here?'

'Either. The issue's the same: should a cricket tour be cancelled on moral grounds?'

'What moral grounds?' snapped Aadam.

'Well it's an open-and-shut case,' baited Pasha. 'Mugabe's a Bond-style villain. All his crimes have been well-documented.'

'Wrong! Maybe his recent crimes; not his older ones.'

'Such as?'

'Have you heard of Matabeleland?' Aadam glanced around. 'It's a province in Zimbabwe that Mugabe attacked ages ago. He killed loads of people there.'

'Why did he do that?'

'There was a rebellion against his rule, something like that. But anyway, his own people were killed on his orders. The thing is, no-one was getting vexed about playing cricket with Zimbabwe after that.'

'OK,' said Pasha, reclining in regal fashion, 'but that doesn't make a boycott now, wrong.'

'No, but it makes it hypocritical. Whatever the British say, they only really got worked up when Mugabe began bullying a handful of white farmers.'

'So you don't think there should be a boycott? There are severe food shortages there. How can you engage in something as trivial as cricket?' Pasha picked out a toothpick and began cleaning his teeth with royal pleasure.

'Look, this land issue – it's all hot air. The British just see pictures of their own under the cosh and get upset. I can understand that. But they should look at the facts.'

'Which are?' butted in Salman.

'Which are that Mugabe is basically right about land reform. The white farmers can't hog all the best land forever. Cancel a cricket tour on moral grounds? I'll expect every tour to here to be cancelled between now and Kingdom Come.'

'OK, calm down,' said Pasha. 'We're just talking, just having a civilised chat.'

Aadam leaned back, a little embarrassed.

'I never knew you were so feisty!' Pasha laughed but Aadam turned away, refusing to play the joker.

The phone rang and Imtiaz got up.

'Hello?'

Pasha looked for clues before Imtiaz opened the living room door. 'Mum!' The others in the room resumed idle chat. With hand cupped over the receiver he called out again – 'Mum!' Still no sign of Arwa. '*Mum!*' Finally she waddled in, her face beaming and full of import. *Mum, Mother, Ma, Mata* – for all of us, our first word. And from that very first utterance, it means so much. *I'm small, I'm lost. Please protect me, please love me.*

Mum. How sacred the sound.

Imtiaz really hated that fucking word. He handed the receiver over and wandered through to the kitchen. Arwa began talking animatedly and soon the others got up and followed.

Pasha was handed some peppermint tea.

'Here you go,' said Bilqis, thrusting a mug at him.

'What's this?' He looked into it suspiciously.

'It's good for you. Drink it.' There was no hint of invitation or suggestion in her voice and Pasha was left wondering just what it'd take to stop being treated like a little boy.

He trundled over to the breakfast table where the others were already sitting; Nazneen was wiping dry some huge glass tray and Kahina was filling the dishwasher with solution. She shut the door and the machine hummed into life.

'Right!' she announced, 'I'm going upstairs to pray.'

Salman checked the wall clock. 'Isn't it late for *asr*?'

'Yes, a little, but you can still say it. Your father is doing so right now.'

'I'll join you,' said Bilqis, and the two of them left.

There was still a huge pile of dishes on the worktop and, on her own, Nazneen continued wiping. She looked across at the boys who were slouched around the table, chewing the fat. *Typical,* she thought to herself, and then she caught Pasha staring at her.

'So, Pasha,' she said, startling him as he turned away sheepishly. 'Why didn't you bring your girlfriend along?' Pasha squeezed his mug and gazed down.

'This is an Eid celebration, and she's not a Muslim.' He took a measured sip.

'So? *We* celebrate Christmas. All she had to do was come down and eat a meal with us. It's not exactly hardcore, is it?'

'We're not married, Nazneen.'

'Then marry her,' she suggested, inspecting the shine on a glass platter. 'Islam isn't some parochial concern. It's a global culture – an alternative global culture.' She scratched away at some dried-on dirt.

'Really? In case you haven't noticed we're not exactly flavour of the month right now. Have you not heard of Osama Bin Laden?'

'But that's not Islam,' said Aadam. 'He has nothing to do with us.'

'Well, don't tell me. Explain that to the rest of the damn nation.' He raked a hand through his hair and it stayed ruffled. 'Why the hell would Jenny want to join our club? In fact, why would I want to stay in it?'

Nazneen placed hands on hips.

'OK, Pasha, forget it.' She picked up another dish.

'Oh no you don't – you can't drop the subject like that...' She continued wiping, her attention on her work. 'Don't you think you're being hypocritical?'

'And how's that?'

'Well, you're standing there and talking big about Islam, yet look at how you're dressed. Your *shalwaar* is not exactly cut to an Islamic design.'

'Careful,' said Aadam. 'That's my wife.'

'Exactly! And according to all your priests, her finery is for *your* eyes only.'

'I'm not dressed immodestly.'

'Are you sure?' Pasha's expression couldn't hide a faint grin. 'I don't think you are either, but your costume is fitted. I can make out the shape of your hips and thighs...'

'Pasha!' Aadam stared, the veins on his thin neck bulging.

'He's right,' said Salman. Pasha grinned.

'Oh come on, *Bhai*,' Aadam protested. 'Kahina isn't covered up right now.'

'True, but she wears a headscarf whenever she goes out. Nazneen doesn't cover up at all.' She slammed a dish down onto the worktop.

'I may be a Muslim but I'm also a woman. I'm also a feminist.'

Salman chuckled.

'A headscarf *is* feminist,' he said confidently.

'And how do you figure that one out?'

'Because it's a great–' He stopped, like he was searching for the right word. 'It gives women the chance ... I mean to be seen not just in terms of their body.'

'That's bollocks,' barked Pasha, propping himself up. 'I don't go around with a hard-on all the time. You must be some sort of sicko!' He looked Salman up and down, distaste fomenting on his lips. He waited for a riposte but surprisingly it was Imtiaz who piped up. Seated amongst everyone, he had started watching the small TV. The volume was off but he had nevertheless begun laughing. Everyone looked at him open-mouthed. It was a *Carry On* movie, and some doctor was looking aghast as a young Barbara Windsor virtually exposed herself.

'Turn it up,' said Nazneen, finally taking a seat, and Imtiaz gladly obliged. Kenneth Williams appeared and in no time he was going, '*Ooh Matron!*' It was irresistible stuff and they all started laughing.

'Looks like *Carry On, Doctor*, right?' Pasha's voice was gentle, his eyes once more soft.

'Yeah, must be,' said Aadam, his head twisted to face the TV. 'You know I remember watching this for the first time. The thing is, I can distinctly remember that scene – when Barbara Windsor exposes herself. I think that was my first sexual awakening.' He started tittering.

'Oh, dude!' exclaimed Pasha, wincing. 'That's disgusting! You once got turned on by Barbara Windsor!'

'You didn't have to tell us that, *Bhai*,' said Salman, eager to join in. A fresh round of laughter broke out and they let it linger.

'It looks so dated now, though,' added Nazneen wistfully.

'Yeah but it's still funny, right? This stuff is eternal.' Pasha didn't take his eyes off the screen. Everyone was focused on Matron, who had just intruded in on the action; she was not looking pleased with all with the chaos she was finding.

'Maybe. I'd like to think so. There's a kind of innocence to it.'

The doctor continued his examination of an impressively-fronted Ms Windsor, and he was close to blowing a fuse.

'Bawdy.'

'What?' Aadam lazily turned towards his wife.

'The word for this stuff is "bawdy".' She drained the last from a cup of tea and inspected the other mugs around the table.

'Wow, that's a great word.'

'Exactly,' she said whilst collecting the empties. 'And that's why it's dated – because it just doesn't work any more.'

'Oh, come on,' protested Pasha as Nazneen headed for the sink. 'There's always room for a bit of slap and tickle.'

'I wish! Bawdy only works, though, where there are taboos; not when everything's on tap.'

Imtiaz looked around. Sensing another debate about to break out, he decided to quit. Silently, without any protest, he walked out of the kitchen. The others exchanged awkward looks. He closed the door and silence descended around the table.

'What's wrong with Imtiaz?' asked Salman of Pasha.

'Oh, *Bhai,*' he groaned. 'What's right with him?'

25

'How do you play this?' asked Taimur. He looked up at the strange man, his father's cousin. Imtiaz was inspecting a pawn.

He'd gone upstairs into what was once his bedroom. He had no particular need to go there, just a curiosity to see what it was like now. Was it being used? If so, in what way? He entered to find Kahina praying. Aaliyah was lying down on the bed, his old bed, with Taimur sitting crouched upon it. His head was resting on one hand with the other idly flicking the pages of some book. The little chap looked bored.

Imtiaz had quickly apologised but Kahina gestured him in, mid-recitation. Taimur looked up, hopeful for some attention. He went over and the boy eagerly showed him the book: an ancient General Sciences textbook from his own schooldays. *Where on Earth did he fish this out from?* He'd hated school; the sheer impotence of not being good at anything. He couldn't kick a ball, couldn't impress in the classroom, couldn't chat up girls – he was emasculated even before puberty. His mum used to sit with him night after night, tirelessly trying to spark something within him. He recalled the two of them on the floor of this very bedroom, his school books all laid out and her gentle encouragement with sums; her enthusiasm for spelling and grammar, and her loving concern slowly morphing into frustration, then desperation and, finally, anger. Because he didn't get any of it. He wanted to go back; try harder; make his mum proud.

He caught the breath of sadness and refocused, taking hold of the book. Taimur sidled up to him eagerly and smiled. A pure smile, a child's smile. He held the boy loosely and began talking, explaining a few things about some of the pictures. The boy pointed randomly and asked questions – that sunshine an ever-permanent fixture. Aaliyah, too, now made her presence known by poking the book from underneath. The cherub clearly wanted some attention and her bright, mischievous eyes looked to catch his. Imtiaz touched a ringlet, smoothing the hairs with his thumb. He was caught off-guard – a teardrop falling, exploding on the page. He tickled the girl on her tummy and she let out a shrill giggle and grabbed his hand.

Tickle me again, those sparkling eyes said.

How did I miss out on all this? He closed the book and put it on the floor and, as he did so, he noticed his old chess set. There was a fitted wardrobe taking up most of the length opposite, and a chess set sat up on one of the exposed shelves. It was fully set up, waiting for a game to start. A flashback, a question at a pub quiz from many years ago. *Where does the game of chess originate from?*

'Persia. Ancient Persia,' he'd answered with confidence, before some Indian snapped back: 'It's Indian, not Iranian. *Indian!*' History – how so very important. He was standing right next to the board and remembering how he, and Pasha before him, used to play chess with their father. It's weird, remembering something positive that they all shared. This set had not been used for ten years, maybe longer. He picked up the board and held it carefully, returning to the bed. It was a really magnificent set, the board and pieces carved out of solid wood, depicting characters from the African plains. Imtiaz inspected a pawn, lovingly etched to make a Masai Warrior. It was so intricate – the ear lobes were long and the face chiselled, and the warrior was holding a spear.

'How do you play this?' asked Taimur, looking fascinated.

'Ask me next time,' Imtiaz replied, not altogether convinced that there would be a next time. He put the piece back down and Taimur looked a little disappointed.

'You're a natural with kids,' said Kahina. Imtiaz jumped to see her smiling with approval.

'Thanks,' he muttered, unable to stop his eyes from dropping. 'You have beautiful children.' He looked back towards Taimur and ruffled his hair. Kahina began folding her prayer mat and removing her scarf, all the while looking at Imtiaz.

'You know, it's not too late...'

Too late for what? he was about to ask, but he knew. He knew. He made to say something then stopped. Picking up the chessboard, he walked over to the shelf. He placed it and felt stranded.

'I, err, I should see what the others are up to.'

'It's not too late, Imtiaz.' Her words were clear, enunciated slowly. Her gaze was not letting him go.

'Look, Kahina, this is Eid.'

'Why do you live on your own? It's not healthy.'

He looked around. Both Taimur and Aaliyah were now watching him, transfixed.

'I'm going to be thirty-five soon. It *is* too late. I don't know what to do.' His head was bowed.

'You're wrong. It's never too late. We can help you; help you find someone.' She approached him and he was actually trembling. She cupped the palm of her hand around his neck; he naturally leant into her touch. She looked up at him, concern in her eyes – he didn't understand her concern. Her hand was soft and warm. He couldn't recall when he was last touched by another and began whimpering.

26

'Oh, God...' sighed Sarah Miles's character in White Mischief, *whilst looking out from her colonial mansion onto clear blue African skies, '... it's another fucking beautiful day.' And with that she promptly shot herself. She was the Summer Grinch.*

It's the height of fashion to hate the winter, but for some it's the summer that gets them down: tanned, over-exposed bodies, pavements pounded by exposed feet. Horns blaring. All those little bottles of water and arrogant sunglasses. The relentless optimism of it all. Summer just magnifies the dashed hope of a better life; one that never arrives. Where the love and laughter, festivals and fun, and long weekends with al-fresco meals? Bring on September and October, the glowing embers, the sobriety of an autumn wardrobe. Oh the relief when the hubris of summer is over, when the tyranny of the sunny day can be put to rest.

'Come on, Aadam!' beckoned Salman, a little impatiently.

'I'm coming, I'm coming,' he blustered from upstairs. The four boys had decided to go out. There was no particular agenda; just a desire to grab some fresh air and walk around. Pasha's idea. He stood by the opened front door with Salman and Imtiaz, ready for the off. Aadam, meanwhile, had gone upstairs to change.

'You look fine. Why do you want to take your *sherwani* off?' his brother had asked with annoyance as he'd scurried off.

Aadam descended the stairs taking quick, light steps; Nazneen was close behind.

'Here, put this on,' she suggested, handing him a scarf. He looked flustered and took it quickly. Pasha looked on with a grin and read the slogan on Aadam's t-shirt: *There are 10 kinds of people in the world: those that understand binary, and those that don't.*

Frigging geek, said his silent smirk. Aadam turned to his brother who was shaking his head in solemn disapproval. *Jeans and a denim jacket. Wah!* Salman would never consider changing out of his long robes. He looked like the chief of some International Jihadi Movement, Northolt Branch.

'Right!' stamped Aadam, shaking off all the negative attention. He returned the compliment by checking out Pasha, who looked every bit the slippery salesman: shiny belt holding up pleated trousers; linen shirt, top bottom undone. His polished shoes were a tan brown and screamed *middle-aged!* Apart from the shoes, though, it was all just a bit too flash for a man pushing forty. Pasha smiled his salesman's smile and Aadam was reluctant to smile back, lest his teeth be taken for deposit. Instinctively, the pair play-fought as they staggered out of the front door, soon relaxing into arms around shoulders. Salman followed close behind, sniffing the air and looking like he meant business. Imtiaz brought up the rear. His baseball cap was back on and he was wearing his long, expansive coat under which to hide: he was the Summer Grinch. Nazneen joined Kahina by the door and together they watched their men.

'Isn't he the most beautiful, ugly man you've ever seen?' Nazneen remarked joyfully.

There was a definite chill in the air when they left, past four o'clock. 16th November 2004 was, indeed, a bleak day. And the light of the day was dying. Eid would soon be over. They walked briskly to generate warmth as much as anything, and within fifteen minutes they were in the Parade with all humanity teaming around. School kids were everywhere, looking nonchalant in their uniforms. As they passed the entrance to the Tube station they saw a Muslim man entering with a packed rucksack on his back.

'There's Britain's first suicide bomber,' Pasha stated devilishly.

'You what?' said a blindsided Salman.

'Well, we're constantly being told that it's a matter of *when* and not *if*, for Al-Qaeda striking Britain, right? The Spanish and Australians have already been punished for siding with the Americans, so presumably it'll be our turn next. So how would you feel?' Salman looked thoughtful, like he was mulling over his options. Pasha continued. 'Imagine seeing a woman on the telly, a woman who was on the same train – the same carriage, even – giving her personal testimony. *The train was jam-packed. I nearly got on at the same entrance as him but it was impossible, so I moved along and a few minutes later I heard a scream of* Allah-u-Akbar, *then there was this huge bang, this explosion. The train came to a shuddering halt. The lights went out. I heard people screaming. There was lots of screaming. I fell down, someone fell on top of me.* How would you feel?'

'What do you expect me to say?' Salman bristled. 'That I'd be happy, that I'd be proud?'

'Many would be,' said Pasha. 'Many Muslims would have emotions that could be described as "mixed".'

'No one's gonna feel good about ordinary people losing their lives. You're talking rubbish,' said Aadam.

'Really? 9/11 sparked off all kinds of impromptu street parties across the world, didn't you know that? I've seen pictures of Arabs letting off rounds of ammo in celebration!'

People were rushing in and out of the various stores and countless grocers, getting stuff for the evening and beyond.

'Hang on,' announced Salman. 'I need to get some things. Anyone want to come?' And with that Aadam joined him in a halal butcher's whilst Pasha and Imtiaz hung back. Pasha rested up against the railings separating pavement from road, looking down the Parade. The headlights of passing vehicles were now mostly on. He struck a leisurely pose with arms outstretched, and next to him Imtiaz stood to attention. Two sassy young women came into view: all crinkly hair and prominent make-up, big round earrings and fags, handled with style. They stopped a few feet away, reading something in a newsagent's window. One girl wore tight pink jeans, with the letters C H E E K Y emblazoned across her behind.

'Does that mean you're a cheeky girl, or that you like cheeky boys?' He threw the girls a big smile and Imtiaz looked aghast. Pasha ignored him and stayed smiling, cheekily, whilst the girls whispered.

'You what?' said Cheeky's mate with a sneer.

'You heard,' snorted Pasha, undeterred, warming up nicely.

'Give over – you're old enough to be her dad!'

And with that the two exchanged derisory looks and moved on. Cheeky said nothing throughout. Pasha was stunned and shot a look at his brother. His mute irrelevance provided some consolation.

Salman and Aadam reappeared holding bulging plastic bags. They passed the *Lahori Kebab House* and Pasha insisted they go in even though no one wanted to eat. As a compromise they ordered *lassis* and made themselves welcome at a table for four, much to the chagrin of the head waiter.

'Can I get you anything else?' he asked pointedly on four occasions, receiving the same blunt response each time. Of course, what he was really saying was *order something substantial or kindly fuck off*, and eventually they took the hint and left.

Night had ascended her celestial throne. Still people hustled and bustled, streaming in and out of shops, those lighted fronts like beacons.

'Actually, I'd like to get a few things too,' said a circumspect Pasha, belatedly wanting to spend some money.

'What sort of things?' asked Salman, business-like.

'Stuff I can't get up in Cheshire. Could I get a *kadhai* here? I'm after a proper iron one, no aluminium rubbish. And a *tawa*?'

'Sure, you've come to the right place. You want to impress your missus, eh?' Salman wore a weak smile and checked his watch. 'Look, it's getting late. I'll come with you – I know where to get what around here. You two coming?'

'Yeah, why not,' Aadam said grudgingly.

'Actually, I'm a bit tired,' blurted out Imtiaz. 'I might go into that café.' He turned around and pointed. 'Can you come get me on your way back?'

'Sure,' remarked Pasha, surprised at his brother taking a firm stance.

'Look, on second thoughts I'll hang back too,' said Aadam. 'Don't be long – come and get us by six, OK?'

Imtiaz clasped a mug of tea as if he could die without the immediate transfer of heat. His gaze was steadfastly downwards, deep into his mug. The café furniture reminded Aadam of school: the chairs were plastic and red; kids-toy red. He shuffled backwards and was mildly surprised that it wasn't bolted to the floor. Two men – Tamils, thought Aadam – took up seats at the next table. Dishes of dhal and meat curry were placed down without ceremony, and soon they were tearing at *rotis* and dipping pieces into steaming bowls. Aadam felt a pang of hunger. He looked back at Imtiaz, who was still avoiding eye contact.

Oh boy. He sugared his tea in consolation, pouring rather than tipping from a spouted jar.

'I'm glad you spoke up back there. I didn't feel like walking about any more either.'

'Yeah,' sighed Imtiaz, looking up cautiously. 'I think we'd exhausted the pleasures of Northolt by then.' He wore a reluctant smile. Aadam responded in kind and looked around for some cream; his tea was going to have to pack an extra punch.

'You know one thing I regret?' remarked Pasha, inspecting two wok-like utensils. 'My Urdu is useless now.'

'No it's not,' said Salman quizzically. 'You've spoken well today. It sounded fine to me.'

'Yeah, all right, of course I can still converse but I'm talking about proper Urdu. You know, language can really expand the mind. I've lost that "high" Urdu.' Salman looked at his cousin. Despite himself, he was starting to feel a real connection. This Pasha, this 2004 Pasha, was so familiar and yet so strange. 'Your father was really into classical Urdu, and poetry.'

Salman put an arm around his cousin's shoulder.

'I know, *Bhai*, I know. I'm surprised you remember.'

'Why wouldn't I?' remarked Pasha. 'You should teach some of that to Taimur. We need to keep our culture alive.'

'Why did you leave when we were all chatting earlier? You should have come back down.' Aadam's voice was soft, suggesting concern rather than anger, yet Imtiaz shifted with discomfort. 'OK, look, forget it. I was just asking. I can't remember when we were last together, that's all.'

'How long have you been married?' Imtiaz made speculative eye contact.

'Two years now.'

'That's ... great. Oh, and I did come back down but you guys looked engrossed in some big talk. Anyway, I went into the living room instead.' His gaze dropped again and yes, *scared.* There was just no other word; the guy looked permanently fucking petrified.

'To be honest, I'm more interested in his religious education. Urdu poetry can wait. I'll enrol Taimur in an Islamic secondary school when the time comes.'

Pasha bit his tongue as he paid for his *kadhai*. They left the shop and Salman began marching with unnecessary haste.

'But why? Taimur and Aaliyah are growing up in London – it's a fantastic opportunity.'

'Really? You sound like a politician.'

'Things are different now. They can be proud Muslims and proud Britishers too.'

'Oh come on, whose glossy brochure have you been reading? You live up there in Cheshire. You have no idea what it's like for us here.'

'Maybe, but one thing's for sure – if you build some closed-off world for your kids, they'll fail in this country.' Pasha stopped for emphasis but Salman shrugged and continued. He ploughed on silently and Pasha had to canter to catch up. 'And anyway, what exactly is your issue? Do you want to protect them from others' prejudice, or do you just not want them mixing with these *kafirs*?'

'You know, I see Salman and Kahina all the time. Pasha I haven't seen since my wedding. But I honestly can't remember when the two of us last met. I still don't get why you didn't make more of an effort today.'

Imtiaz sighed and swallowed hard, his prominent Adam's Apple bobbing up and down. 'Kahina's really nice. Salman and her have two beautiful kids.'

'For fuck's sake, man, join me in conversation!' Imtiaz jumped. The Tamils turned around but Aadam ignored them. 'You're not a fucking cripple, OK? Stop acting like one.'

'Not in a traditional sense, maybe.'

Aadam waited for him to continue but he didn't. 'What's wrong, for God's sake? Why can't you answer a simple frigging question?'

'You know, you're lucky.'

'How's that then?'

'I ... I like Nazneen. You have a lovely wife.'

'I know. So why don't you get yourself a piece of the action?'

Imtiaz contemplated. 'What do you do, Aadam? I mean, for a living.'

'I'm a programmer. Banking software. You?'

'I work for the local council. I help run this Communities project.'

'So?'

'I live in a one-bedroom flat. I've never lived with anyone else since leaving home. I've never had a girlfriend.' His delivery was matter-of-fact and Aadam giggled nervously, waiting for a punchline.

'When you say *never*...'

'I used to cook: dinners for one. Have you ever done that? I used to make a real effort, just for myself. But I'm a ready-meals convert now.'

Aadam swallowed hard. 'Look, dude, just find yourself a wife. There's someone out there for everyone.'

'But I'm going to be thirty-five soon. I don't know how ... to satisfy a woman.' Aadam glanced at the wall clock, cursing its slow progress. 'So what should I do? I used to lead a good life – a simple life, at least. Everything was in order. But it just got harder.'

'You can't beat yourself up for losing interest in dinners for one! Why didn't you look for a wife before? I found Nazneen myself. Well, kind of stumbled across her, really, but Salman's marriage was arranged, of sorts. Didn't you have the urge earlier? Even just for sex?'

'No...' He gagged on the word. 'No. I knew that everyone around me was pairing off. But I never felt the need. Not back then, anyway. I'd left home, I had a place of my own, a job – it was all fine. And for sex.' Again he stalled.

'What? You polished the woodwork?' Aadam tittered before berating himself for the misplaced humour.

'Have you ever ... You've watched porn before, right?'

'Yeah, of course. There's not a man who hasn't.'

'And?'

'And what? Please, Imtiaz – no more being cryptic, huh?'

'Did you like it? No, wait. Do you still watch it?'

Aadam stared hard. He wondered what on earth had possessed him to hang back with this lunatic and not stay with the others. 'Er, no,' he stamped. 'I'm happily married, thank you. But yeah, it was kind of fun. Guilty pleasure.'

'Do you miss it?'

'No! Look, what is this? Why are you talking about porn now?'

'It's ... it's all I think about.'

Silence.

'What do you mean, exactly?'

Imtiaz drained the last of his tea, like he wished the action would last a thousand years.

'The others will be back soon – this is your chance. Say what you want. I'll not judge you.'

'What to say, Aadam? Please. There's nothing else. Work, eating, sleeping – I just go through the motions. But porn ... it takes me to another place. I hate it. I hate myself, but there's just nothing else.'

Aadam was lost. There was just no point of reference. But this was nothing less than a confession; he couldn't reject him now.

'Porn isn't damaging, Imtiaz. Not necessarily, anyway. The thing is you have no checks and balances. Look at you, man. You've got to turn this around.'

'But that's the thing. By the time I realised there was more than what I could see...' He just couldn't complete the sentence.

'It's never too late, Imtiaz. Never. No one expects you to go to a pub and start chatting up birds. We can help. The community can help.'

'Aadam, I'm terrified. I know nothing about women, real women. I know nothing about real sex.'

'You have to take a leap of faith. You don't have the luxury of time now.'

'You say others can help, but if the marriage is "arranged" it's kind of a business transaction, right? I have to bring something to the table. I don't know what I can offer.'

'Oh Imtiaz, *Bhai, tu kyaho gaya?*' Aadam rubbed his face, sadness spilling over confusion. 'Do you know how amazing being with someone can be? Even afterwards, couples talk. Nothing fancy – just checking-in with each other, really. Often I'll drift off to sleep like that. So tell me, how do you feel after a session on the Internet?'

For a moment Imtiaz looked livid, ready to launch a tirade. But then he started crying. He tried to regain composure but failed and quickly buried his head in his arms. Strangely, he wasn't even making any noise. Aadam looked on, nothing but a spectator. He looked around – those Tamils were gone and there was no one on the other side. Not that it mattered. Should he say something, hold him, offer him some water? He'd never seen a man cry like this before. The seconds passed. Imtiaz stayed slumped, cradled in his own arms.

'There they are,' pointed out Salman, on entering the cafe. Imtiaz was smiling and gestured them over.

'Did you get what you want?'

'Yeah, sure did. This dude really knows his stuff!' Pasha flashed a congratulatory smile and Salman acknowledged the compliment mutely.

'Come, let's go.'

They began walking when Pasha saw a bus: an old-style red double-decker. It was slowing down, pulling up at a stop about thirty yards in front.

'I thought they only have those in Central London now. For the tourists, and that.'

'True,' replied Aadam. 'Maybe their main fleet is getting a wash or something,' he added unconvincingly. Pasha knocked his shoulder and the pair tittered.

'110. I think this one passes Arwa Masi's.'

'Yeah, yeah – you're right.'

And with that the four of them pelted towards the bus and scrambled on-board just in time. Imtiaz was last on and looked put-out and out of breath.

'Come on, Imtiaz, this is fun! When did you last ride an old-style Routemaster?' chided his brother lightly. The four of them were bunched up by the entrance, waiting for those in front to take up seats.

'Oh leave it out, Pasha, you don't have to sell me a ride on a bus. It's a very small thing.' He was still catching his breath and was bent double, hands resting on knees.

'Look, bro, if you can't enjoy the little things then it really is all over.'

'Where to?' asked the West Indian conductor, his voice deep and gravelly.

'Erm, same as him,' said Pasha with a smile, pointing at Aadam in front. He was still holding the pole by the entrance and the conductor was using a manual machine to dispense tickets. The man wore a uniform, he had a hat on and there was a bag of change strapped to his waist. Tripping on the nostalgia, Pasha took his ticket and followed the others up the stairwell. It wasn't that packed on the top deck – just one group of lads right at the back and a sprinkling of individuals here and there. Pasha gazed out of the window and watched the Parade ease out of sight. He turned around. Salman was inspecting a packet of diced lamb.

'You know one thing I like about *halal* butchers?'

Salman braced himself, not knowing how many more cute comments he'd silently absorb.

'You see real meat, real carcasses. There's no squeamishness.'

Salman relaxed and laughed. Pasha had riled him constantly today, but he'd also been funny and warm. He didn't have to come out to him after he'd slapped Taimur – he'd not forget that. He remembered the two of them making their way home from school on buses just like this. It seemed like yesterday. It seemed like another life.

'Aye. Lamb comes from lambs, not some plastics factory in New Zealand,' said Aadam.

'*Wah*! Very cute,' applauded Pasha, and the two high-fived.

'So will you be rustling up some exotic dishes?' asked Imtiaz of his brother, gesturing at his new utensils.

'Oh, I might well take these babies out for a test drive,' he remarked lightly, clearly in high spirits. He removed the *tawa* from its bag and held it up, rotating it by the handle. 'Isn't it beautiful? Cast iron. I miss eating *rotis*. Naan bread is fine, but there's nothing like *rotis*. And I can now make my own!'

'So invite us all up once you've perfected them. We should be the first to sample your handiwork.'

Pasha was taken aback by Salman's suggestion. *Is he saying what I think he's saying?* Salman's gentle smile assured him that he hadn't misunderstood.

'You boys can expect a call from me within a month, then!' And with that Pasha turned to his brother.

'You'll come too, right?'

'Sure, *Bhai*, count me in.'

27

I'm bored. Aadam's not back yet. The boys have been gone for ages. The others are watching telly, the kids are getting ratty and Kahina's praying. Again. I tried joining them, all of them. But I was no good at reminiscing, playing *It* or talking about cooking and kids. I'm a damn spare part here. I mean, why bring me along, huh? Did I want to come? Was this my idea? It's always about him. He pretends to be all modern, that everything's shared, that we work as a team – but it's rubbish, really. In the end it's his call and I have to go along with it.

I go into the kitchen to see if there's anything to do, just to pass the time. I was playing racing cars with Taimur five minutes ago. Did Aadam not think to take me along? He didn't even ask. I'm like some porcelain doll – he takes me out to impress the guests and then stuffs me back in the cupboard. *I'm bored.* I'm not used to this, being treated like some show piece. I want to be adored. *I want to be adored.* Oh, Martin.

The sun is no longer visible up in the Colorado sky, now but a sheer veil on the day, set off by a soft peach glow. But as she gazes up into infinity, it looks as if a wounded sun has been staggering all over the heavens, leaving a blood trail. Several gaping wounds puncture the dim glow, clear evidence of the crime committed. She pays homage to the martyred, anointing herself under a blood-red sky. And the alien landscape lies stretched out below, an unleavened red crust opened up repeatedly by those mighty sandstone eruptions. The sheer expanse. Nothing else. Nothing. *She looks up again and the sky seems lower,*

*darker. She snatches her breath, scared. And those stone Centurions,
guarding since the dawn of time; and this descending red pall,
smothering her, above and below.*

'You OK?'

*Nazneen jumps on hearing Martin, a voice outside of the
Apocalypse she was witnessing. His hand is on her shoulder and she
snaps towards him, confused and frightened. He lays a hand on her
cheek, softly.* 'This place is just awesome, no?'

'Yeah – and a little freaky too!' *she adds with a nervous giggle. A
few loose strands of hair dance across her face, surfing on a small
breeze. He patiently collects them, smoothing them back into place.*

'Are you OK?' *he repeats a little louder, staring with concern. She
relaxes and smiles, taking hold of his outstretched arm.*

*A group nearby relax around a small fire, sipping liquor, listening
to soft music and chatting quietly. Some crackling raises hearty cheer
and a few raise a friendly hand as Martin and Nazneen pass by. The
glow from the fire soon passes and they find themselves staring into a
black void – the light in the sky has been snuffed out. Nazneen
instinctively stops, waiting for her eyes to adjust, and she turns back
to the wicked red flames, now dancing with naked abandon. Sensing
her unease, Martin pulls her closer, and with his arm around her they
slowly walk away. She looks up at him, open delight on her smiley
face. She's just so happy. She snuggles up, sheltering under him as
they meander down a smooth incline, just in from World's End.
Meanwhile, folk rhythms continue, giving the night comfort. Martin
starts singing, serenading her, letting the music still nearby dominate,
but as they walk away he becomes more animated, clicking fingers to
maintain the beat. He stops, abruptly, once the music is out of range.
He grabs her face, lit up now only by moonlight. They stand alone
and in complete silence, but for Martin's heavy breathing.*

I'd give this whole world,
just to dream with you, under these stars.
'Cause they'll be here tomorrow,
But we will never come back.

*Silence. Just the dull silence of blackness, filling empty space.
Nazneen's head is locked in his hands and his tight grip pulls her up,
forcing her onto tiptoes. He holds her eyes, his expression somewhere*

between pained and disturbed. Suddenly he kisses her, but he devours her face with such haste it's closer to being licked by a dog. He grabs her by the shoulders and starts driving her backwards, ramming her into a jutting rock face. She screams and he abruptly lets go, panting heavily. She moves back against the support, instinctively lying down across its broad surface.

'What did you scream for?' he snaps, looking back up the path nervously. He sees no one.

'What...what are you doing, Martin?'

Her face is barely visible but he can make out a terror etched there.

'I love you,' he whispers. 'I want you.' He takes one step forward and then stops, allowing her to get comfortable with his proximity again. Standing over her now he reaches out, deliberately leaving his arm hovering for her to breach the gap. She sees his quivering hand, opened, waiting for her touch. 'I need you...' She takes his hand and places it on her chest, the centre of his palm over her solar plexus. He steps in, his fractured, heavy breathing still the only sound, but despite himself, somehow, he keeps his hand still, pressing down on just the one spot. She props herself up a little, finding easy purchase on the gently sloping rock face; Martin inches forwards to stay connected. She leans in and kisses him and a current shoots through on the circuit completing. He bolts onto the surface and forces her right back, and on all fours considers his prey menacingly. Nazneen touches his face, trying to take some of the heat out of his fever but it's no good. He descends onto her to make the kill. Ripping her t-shirt upwards he buries his face in her stomach, smothering his mouth, nose, forehead and cheeks over her smooth, soft belly. Securing her centre, he works outwards both ways, biting flesh, pacifying limbs, tearing away clothing. She opens her eyes and looks skywards, a naked innocent splayed out on a sacrificial altar. He touches her, igniting delicate nerve endings, making calm waters stir. She shivers and covers her eyes, not wanting to watch the heavens watching her. Trickles flow and coalesce, each drop longing for the ocean. And the body of water builds, shaping slowly into a vortex. And he throws himself in, wanting only to die in this holy water. And she grips, pulling him; dragging him down, sinking him. He tries to resist but the current takes him instantly. He knows he's helpless. She gazes up again. The sky has become a black velvet drape, speckled with a billion stars. Again,

shame bites her. Those stars, observing everything, and she turns to avoid their censorious stare. But each movement of his – a torrent trapped in a storm, thrashing around in ever decreasing circles. The stars above join in the dance, at first swirling uniformly but then splintering into rival factions, competing for her attention. Nazneen faces the heavens squarely, surety replacing shame: this performance, this kaleidoscope sky – it's all for her. The beat becomes faster, faster still and the stars swoosh in a desperate frenzy, individual movements now blurring. She shuts her eyes and the vortex shatters, smashed apart under pressure. Her waters spill, overflow, and wash into his animal release. He collapses onto her, a dead weight. The kaleidoscope stops spinning and she soon feels a breeze, trespassing on her naked limbs. She folds arms around his lifeless body and in silence offers thanks. Today the gods have borne witness, on this, her High Noon.

Aaliyah was crying. She'd woken up suddenly after drifting off to sleep and Kahina thought the unfamiliar surroundings had frightened her. Nazneen was sitting alone in the kitchen before Kahina had burst in with babe in arms. And the kid's bawling wasn't stopping and Kahina kept talking in a rush, despite Nazneen not responding with even a word. And the worried mother touched her daughter's forehead before announcing that she thought she was getting a temperature. Expressionless, emotionless, wordless, Nazneen watched on. And Kahina came swiftly round and dumped the little girl in Nazneen's arms before returning with haste to the sink. She blathered on. Warm drinks, warm wraps, swaddles, blankets, hot water bottles. Nazneen gazed at the small child and held her out, as if to inspect. She observed the little girl's bawling intensify as she writhed in her arms, straining to get away from the stranger and call out to her mum.

28

'Pasha, Imtiaz, guess what? It's an *Eid Special* on Zee TV tonight – they're showing *Pakeezah*!' The four boys were in the kitchen, sipping tea and warming up. It was just past seven o'clock when Zakir burst in, heralding the good news. *Pakeezah* – Pure of Heart. The word lingered in the air, like dried dandelion on a summer breeze. The film was a masterpiece, a story about a tragedienne, a courtesan in Muslim Lucknow at the turn of the last century. Instantly they recalled: the swirling romanticism, the intoxicating songs and dance. Happier, simpler days.

'Wow,' whimpered Pasha. 'I loved that film.'

'Yeah, me too,' said Imtiaz, finally sounding like he was home. 'The music though, *Bhai*, the music – some of those songs will live forever.'

'*Yaar,*' continued Zakir to his boys. 'Your mother has a CD of the songs. It's right here, I think.' And he slid open a drawer underneath the worktop, picking up a batch of discs. And there it was: *Pakeezah* – Songs from the Movie. He handed it to Imtiaz who took it reverentially.

'Do you remember that song, *Chalte Chalte*?' asked Aadam, joining in.

'Yeah,' said Pasha. 'Look at the cover. Look ... She's about to sing that very song.' And there she was, Meena Kumari, dressed in pink. A sheer veil was covering her face and she was dancing. And the song? An ode to her mysterious lover: *Chalte Chalte*.

'I can't watch that film,' declared Salman.

'What? Why not? It was one of our favourites!' said Pasha.

'Come on, bro,' encouraged Aadam. 'I reckon Mum and Dad still have a tape of it somewhere. We all loved that one.'

'Look, I'm not interested, OK? You all go ahead.' He walked away, taking a seat by the breakfast table.

'What's the matter?' asked Nazneen. 'It's just some old film.'

'Yeah, a dumb, glossy story about a prostitute. *Pretty Woman* for Indians. It's hardly inspiring, is it? And besides, I'm not stopping you all from watching. Go ahead!' He sat alone and in relative darkness, frozen like prey in the predator's range.

Imtiaz broke the rising tension.

'Please, Salman. Why don't we all just go and watch it, eh? Tastes change. Maybe it'll be showing its age now. But it was part of our youth, right? What do you say?'

Salman looked up, convinced that the hub around Imtiaz had clustered a little tighter. Five pairs of eyes were on him. *Don't spoil this, please,* implored one. *What's wrong with you, you cunt?* swore another. A third just wore a look of mild contempt. He found that the most offensive.

'You know, you all surprise me. You talk big about Islam and politics, and yet you carry on in the same ways.'

'What the hell are you on about?' said Pasha. A giggle, however, crept into his blast, taking the edge off his indignation. Aadam, too, began to smirk.

Sensing the temperature getting too hot, Zakir did what he always did and got out. Imtiaz, though, went for one last throw of the dice.

'Look, we've had a lovely day. *I've* had a lovely day. Let's not spoil it now, eh? It doesn't matter about *Pakeezah* – it's only a film.'

'Oh no,' snorted Salman. 'It's much more than that.'

'Actually, he's right.' Pasha's heavy voice was pregnant with intent and the two exchanged looks of unguarded malevolence. Imtiaz walked out.

'You know, Pasha, you're a hypocrite.'

'And how's that?'

'Well, you talk about possible bombings on the Underground and you question Islam because of Bin Laden, but why not the other way round?'

'*Bhai*, we were talking about watching a Bollywood flick, that was all,' said Aadam, his face heavy with disappointment. Standing behind Nazneen he held her tightly across the shoulders.

'Bollywood Flick! How can you enjoy Indian culture? Don't you watch the news? Haven't you seen what those Hindus have done to our brothers and sisters in Gujarat?'

Looks of bewilderment were exchanged as Salman's question hung in the air.

'You're talking about Muslim pogroms in India, right?' asked Aadam.

Salman nodded weakly, his face turned away. Pasha began laughing – a mocking, bellicose, sinister laugh.

'So that's what this is about? You don't like Hindus because of Hindu-Muslim violence and so you don't want to watch a Hindi film? *Jesus Christ.*' He spat the Lord's name in vain, not knowing what else to say. Nazneen stepped in.

'But Salman, don't you get it? Hindi cinema, it's part of this amazing synthesis. It flourished once – still does over there, in part. Some of India's biggest stars are Muslim. At least they're clinging onto being secular; we gave it up after five minutes.'

'You're right, honey,' said Aadam, 'but he's got a point – that Gujarat violence wasn't the work of fringe lunatics. Those Hindu mobs were led by the rich and educated: doctors roamed the streets with government-supplied printouts of Muslim addresses. No wonder it's left such a bad taste in his mouth.' Nazneen prised herself out of Aadam's arms and walked over to the sink. An emboldened Salman continued.

'Our people are being humiliated over there. During the pogroms when they captured a Muslim, they'd taunt him by chanting *Babur ki aulad* or *Aurangzeb ki aulad,* before shoving tyres over him, dowsing him in petrol and setting him alight. And you want me to ignore all that and happily sit through a Bollywood flick?'

'Aurangzeb was a cunt,' said Aadam bluntly. 'He humiliated Hindus. And anyway, whose shoes would you rather be in? An Indian Muslim's or a Pakistani Hindu's?'

Pasha and Nazneen looked askance, clearly wondering just whose side of the debate Aadam was on.

'You kids all right?'

Everyone turned sharply. Bilqis and Arwa were standing by the door, Bilqis looking concerned and Arwa smiling mutely.

'Zakir told us you kids were squabbling.' She looked around firmly, demanding an answer. Awkward gazes fell to the floor.

'It's OK, Mum. We're just talking,' assured Aadam.

'Well can't it wait? The film's started. Come over when you get bored of all this rubbish.'

'OK Mum, we'll be over soon,' promised Nazneen. Bilqis didn't look convinced but said no more, and the two of them returned.

The kitchen door closed and Aadam began to giggle. 'What were you saying?'

No reply came until the silence caught Pasha's attention. 'Sorry, what's that?'

Nazneen, too, was now smirking. 'You were about to make a point – sounded big...'

'Oh, fuck it,' interrupted Aadam. 'Mum's right. None of this crap matters. It's Eid, remember? Let's go watch the film and stuff ourselves with chocolates. Salman?' He stared with wide eyes, just daring his brother to let him down again.

'Forget about it.'

'You're pathetic,' said Pasha.

'No, *you're* pathetic,' retorted Salman moronically, the insult clearly rattling him.

Aadam closed his eyes, disappointment assaulting his soul. 'Nothing is ever straightforward. But if we can't even enjoy a Bollywood flick, then it really is all over.'

'But why should I be understanding? All this talk about bombs going off in London. The day that happens we'll all be ... everyone'll hate us.'

'That's rubbish,' said Pasha. 'All the chiefs will go out of their way to differentiate between normal Muslims and the lunatics.'

'Oh come on, please,' cursed Aadam. 'Forget the official line, huh? This ain't *Candid Camera*. We can speak honestly. The day some mad, maverick Muslim walks onto a Tube with a bomb, we're all fucked.'

Nazneen scoffed derisively, blindsiding him.

'Really? A lot of our friends are non-Muslim. None of them rejected you after 9/11. Aren't you just being paranoid?' A stung Aadam searched his wife's face for clues but she just gazed back coldly.

'It's...it's not that simple. Sure, no-one just blanked me, but all of a sudden they had questions – questions which weren't there before.'

'Well you can't blame them for that. The men who took control of those planes and killed all those people, did so in the name of Islam. According to themselves at least. And all those trapped in the Twin

Towers? They were just ordinary people – like you and me. They didn't deserve to get caught up in all this stuff and lose their lives. It's bloody disgusting.'

'Of course it is. No one's saying anything different. But why should I be made to feel guilty?'

'Because you're Muslim, that's why. If a part of our house isn't in order, it's up to us to sort it out!' She again held his gaze, her expressionless face jarring with her words. Alarm seeped into Aadam's confusion. *Why is she acting like this? She was fine just before we left home.*

'Look, whoever the bombers turn out to be, one thing's for sure – they'll have gone underground to plan their attacks. But despite that the finger will be pointed at all of us.'

'And? I've already explained that one.'

'Well you talk about ordinary people, so what about those pilots bombing Baghdad from the skies? They'll have known they'd be killing a lot of ordinary people too, right? But they still dropped their bombs.'

'Make a fucking point, son. I'm getting tired of this.' Pasha stared hard at Aadam, straining to keep his anger in check.

'Look, if the Muslim nutter with the packed rucksack is brainwashed – which he is – then those pilots have been brainwashed too.'

'Oh fuck off, Aadam. I'm out of here, really. These guys have stressed the accuracy of their weaponry and how they only attack military targets.' Pasha took a mobile phone out of his pocket and began fiddling.

'You believe that? Cluster bombs? Cluster munitions? Daisycutters? Firebombs? These are weapons of pinpoint accuracy? Would you walk onto a Tube with a bomb?'

'Piss off.'

'Would you drop a bomb over the Baghdad skies?' Pasha stayed silent. 'Well?'

'You're really starting to get on my nerves, Aadam.'

'In both cases the outcome's the same – you'd be killing random strangers who've done you no harm.'

'So RAF pilots are brainwashed, are they? Exactly how does that happen?'

'We're all influenced by the currents swimming around us. The pilot is, the jihadi is. Just because one has a big plane and a shiny uniform and the other has rags and a fuzzy beard, it really don't mean shit.'

'All right everyone, that's it. Until next Eid, then.' Pasha doffed an imaginary cap and, putting the mobile back in his pocket, he turned to go.

'God. Who the hell are you, huh? I don't recognise you at all.' Aadam looked more wrought than confrontational and Pasha hesitated.

'Look, someday you guys will realise. All this is a dead end.'

'"You guys"? Well who the fuck are *you*, then?'

'I'm just me. I've never sought to embrace or reject anything, by design. These people – the British – I like them and they like me. That's it, really.'

'Yeah, me too,' conceded Aadam, his eyes downcast.

'So why get so worked up?'

'Can't you see, Pasha? Things are changing. And if I'm being told that a Muslim terrorist speaks for me – whether I like it or not – then I have every right to ask what the deaths of so many Iraqis says about this lot. What's the difference between an Anglo-American soldier and an Islamic terrorist?'

'There's more of the first lot and they kill more innocent people,' declared Salman, looking relieved to get a word in.

'And don't forget, this ain't no Bantustan. This is Great Britain – a fucking democracy. None of this could have happened without the British Street being basically on-side. I have far more right to tar all this lot with the same brush, than they have with us. And yet I've never approached a British person with a sour taste in my mouth. I've never fallen out of love with them, or started to hate them because of Iraq. But when those bombs go off on the Underground, we'll all be torched. I'm really starting to hate this country now.' Aadam panted, his gaunt face scarred with exhaustion.

'But you've just said you don't hate the British. Do you or don't you? You've never said this before. Why are you talking like this?' A bitter disappointment carried Nazneen's words.

'I love the British, and if truth be told I'm closer to them than I am to my supposed own mob. Anyone who tries to hurt them is an enemy of mine.'

'So what are you talking about? Exactly who do you hate?'

'Listen carefully,' croaked Aadam. 'I said I love the British people, but I hate their fucking country – there's no contradiction in that.'

'*Their* country? But you're British too,' she challenged. He was finding it hard to spit bile when answering his wife; he stared into space, hoping the void would absorb his anger.

'Yeah, *their* country. I love the British but I'm not British myself. It's not for me to claim that territory – it's for others to share it.'

'This country is a haven for Muslims,' said Pasha. 'There's complete freedom of worship here – even Muslim criminals get halal food in prison. Just how much more do you want them to give?' Aadam didn't answer and eventually Pasha asked another question. 'If you hate this country so much, why don't you leave?'

'I've been thinking about that a lot recently.'

Nazneen looked furious. 'What? Why am I hearing this for the first time?' Aadam turned away. 'Where are you thinking of going? Pakistan? Dubai?'

'Look, I believe in plurality. I want my children to grow up with different races, different religions.'

'Well this is the best place to stay, then, surely,' said Pasha.

'Not if they can't grow up confident in themselves first. We're second-class citizens now – they'll forever be apologising for things that they're not responsible for.'

'So just where are you planning for us to go?' Mockery had replaced the anger carrying Nazneen's previous words, and her eyes – for the first time ever – held him dispassionately. Aadam froze. 'Well speak up then...'

'Canada appeals to me. It's a nation of immigrants, a great leveller. I won't have to spend all my time worrying about the fucking natives.'

'Our future isn't here,' began Salman, like he was sealing the argument, 'whilst this country wages war against our own people, and in our own lands.' He leaned back in his chair, folding his arms theatrically.

Nazneen's face crumpled. 'You ostentatious f...'

'What?' Salman looked around confused, having missed the retort. Pasha pressed home the advantage.

'Understand one thing – if you live here, your first loyalty is to this country. The worldwide Muslim community doesn't override that.'

Aadam spat his contempt.

'The British shouldn't be suspicious of our *Ummah*. They, too, have their *Ummah*: New Yorkers, young Aussies partying in Bali, white farmers in Zimbabwe. And why not? I don't begrudge them that.'

'OK,' conceded Pasha. 'But at least you can differentiate. Salman hates Hindus so much he can't even watch a Bollywood flick. And you know what gets me? He's going to pass his poison onto his kids. I can understand some hick in Montana hating Muslims and I can see why some boy from a Peshawari Madrassa would hate infidels. But we're here – we should be leading the way. But no, he wants to hibernate. He just wants to hate.'

Rendered mute, Salman jumped from face to face, like he was searching for some clue.

'So what? What gives you the right to come down so hard on Salman? Don't demand from us what you wouldn't demand from the British.'

'Oh, but I can.'

'And how's that?'

'Because he's living in their country, that's why.' Pasha began coughing spasmodically, his hands cupped over his face. Walking slowly to the sink, he poured a glass of water, his face sombre. 'I just don't want to be associated with any of this. Put yourself in the shoes of the average bloke, sitting at home and watching the news, and seeing pictures from our own 9/11 stream in. What are they going to think? Can you blame them for hating you?'

'Fuck you,' spat Aadam. 'These bastards have demonised us. That makes you happy, does it?'

Pasha clapped in mockery. '*Wah!* And so the answer to Muslim grievance is terrorism?'

'Terrorism? Just what does that word mean? If you or I were in Baghdad at the start of the war, with the city being pounded from the air, wouldn't we have been terrified? What a fucking stupid word. If some madmen ever do let off bombs on the Underground, Britain will have no right to be outraged.'

Nazneen looked mortified. 'How can you say that?'

'Because they've killed so many more innocent people themselves, that's why.'

'So what are you doing to broaden their vision?' butted in Pasha.

'What?'

'How are you going to change things?'

Looking spent, Aadam shuffled over to the sink himself. Nazneen picked up the chase.

'That's a stupid question. None of us individually can make any difference. All we can do is live our lives, work hard and try and contribute.'

'Good answer,' complimented Pasha, before turning squarely towards Salman.

'And you?'

Salman looked towards Aadam, a plea for help written all over his face. Pasha wrenched him back.

'Answer me – how are you going to make things better? By mixing with the hardcore set down at the *masjid*? By sticking your kids in an Islamic school? By teaching them that Hindus are our enemies and that they shouldn't watch Hindi films?'

'Oh go to hell, Pasha, I don't have to justify myself to you.'

'No, but you have to justify yourself to the British.'

'No, I don't.'

'Yes, you do. Regardless of how they eat, drink, fuck and wage war, you still live in their country. You're a guest; we're all guests. We can't slouch on their nice sofa, take control of the TV remote and sit there farting and belching till the early hours. That's the road to hell – we'll end up overstaying our welcome.'

'No. Forget it. I'm not interested in these racist people.'

'Racist? Racist!' Pasha laughed in mock exaggeration. 'There are street names in the East End, written in Bengali. There's a larger-than-life bust of Nelson Mandela at the Royal Festival Hall. What more do you want from them?'

Salman thumped the table, startling everyone.

'I've had enough of this and I've had enough of you. You come back after all these years and all you can do is lecture? No longer just a dirty paki, like us.'

'Dirty paki or British. Choices, choices.' Pasha rocked his head, a measured, self-satisfied grin covering his face.

'You know, before you think to lecture us, you should put your own house in order.'

'And what do you mean by that?'

'How often do you see your mother?' Pasha's eyes widened. 'Do you know that whenever your mum comes round to ours, she ends up in tears?'

'Don't be ridiculous. Why would she do that?'

'Because she sees her sister with her loving family, and she has none of that.'

Pasha stepped back and gripped the edge of the worktop.

'I phone at least once a week, I see her three or four times a year. I do all I can.'

Salman laughed. 'Are you trying to convince me or yourself?' Pasha lowered his head. 'I mean, are you twenty years old? A student at uni?

You phone at least once a week!' He revelled in his mimicry before banging the table again. 'You think your mum's happy?' Silence. 'Your father's a complete bloody vegetable.' Pasha's shoulders slump. 'Why do you think your mum's so unhappy?'

'No, it's not like that.'

'Answer the question, Ibrahim Pasha Walayat. What do you think your mother wants more than anything?' Pasha's body jerked as he fought-back tears. 'Your brother's lost – God knows what his problems are. But you ... Just 'cause you've come down here today and helped her serve some dinner, doesn't change a thing. You've sacrificed her – your own mother.'

Pasha moved and the others instinctively braced themselves. But he simply walked out briskly, looking at no one as he left.

29

The kitchen door opened and Bilqis and Arwa were there.

'What's happened? Where's Pasha?'

'I don't know. I think he might have left.'

Arwa looked gripped with fear.

'*Nai*. No. Ibrahim? Ibrahim, *Beta!*' She turned and began running for the front door, and as she did so, Aadam caught the look on her face: it was beyond grief.

'You stupid kids! Could you not show love towards each other for even one day?' She stormed out to help her now grieving sister.

'Well done, Salman. That was a first-class show,' said Nazneen. She slow-clapped him and his eyes dropped, his victory instantly soured.

'Well what would *you* have done?' challenged Aadam. 'Just because we hadn't seen him in years, didn't give him the right to talk down to us.'

'He had some good points. He had every right to discuss them.'

'Sure he did, but his attitude ... The whole day he'd been sizing us up. Just who did he think he was?'

'And what about you? When were you going to mention you're planning your escape?'

'*Our* escape.'

Nazneen shrugged.

'Look,' Aadam began conciliatorily. 'It's difficult to explain. You won't understand.'

'What? *I* won't understand? It's you who don't understand. I've had enough.'

'Go on, then – tell me what I'm missing.'

'All this! Screw the War on Terror. I wish you gave *me* as much attention.'

'What?'

She blinked and held his hand in hers, like a prayer. 'Let's go away. Anywhere. Take a break.'

'Nazneen, where is this coming from?' He jerked in protest, shaking her off. 'You know this isn't the right time. There are things I need to do.'

She held him again. 'Aadam, please. Forget all this. Forget work, forget everything. Just remember us.'

'Well, where were you thinking of?'

'How about Colorado? Let's do something totally different. I'd love to learn how to ski. You ever been skiing? And they've got all these National Parks there. Have you heard of Red Rocks?'

He shook her off and laughed.

'Colorado?' He didn't stop laughing and she shrank back. 'America? You must be joking. Go all the way over there and spend all that money, only to be treated like a fucking terrorist? I can get that here for free. You know skiing is big in Iran – we can go there, if you like.'

He turned towards her, expecting an outburst, but she was once again expressionless – marble eyes offering no clue.

'Look, Nazneen, I'm sorry. I just want to get out. There's a shit-storm brewing, just getting ready to blow. Let's go. It'll be better for our kids.'

'Kids? Emigrating? I'm not going anywhere.' She stared impassively at the wall. He leaned in, touched her, but her marble eyes didn't turn.

'Nazneen? Listen.' He looked for some response but then noticed his stiff brother. He let go. 'If you're not willing to listen, why did you marry me?'

'Dunno. Maybe I felt sorry for you.' She turned, finally facing him; but there was no hurt, anger or even satisfaction there. She quietly stood up and walked out. He heard the jangle of keys and a few seconds later the front door again opened. Aadam expected a dramatic bang but it clicked shut – politely, gently. Still open-mouthed, he looked at his brother but found no answers.

Part Three

You are free; you are free to go to your temples, you are free to go to your mosques or to any other place of worship in this State of Pakistan. You may belong to any religion or caste or creed. That has nothing to do with the business of the State. We are starting in the days where there is no discrimination, no distinction between one community and another, no discrimination between one caste or creed and another. We are starting with this fundamental principle that we are all citizens and equal citizens of one State. Now I think we should keep that in front of us as our ideal and you will find that, in the course of time, Hindus would cease to be Hindus and Muslims would cease to be Muslims; not in the religious sense, because that is the personal faith of each individual, but in the political sense, as citizens of the State.

MOHAMMED ALI JINNAH
Presidential address to the Constituent Assembly of Pakistan
11th August 1947

30

He tore out of the place. He thought of his mother and heard her heart break, loud and clear inside his head. *Ibrahim, Beta? Where are you going? Don't go!* He considered running back and wiping the tears from her eyes; he considered running back and stabbing Salman through the heart. Neither was possible and he was consumed with self-loathing. He got to his car with keys in hand but he was fumbling – her pain kept raking through him, shredding all thought, paralysing his functions. *What have I done to her?* She would have heard the end of the argument, when the raised voices reached their crescendo. They all would have heard. *Why did no one come back?* No matter. He knew she'd suspend her confusion and bolt for the door. She'd soon be hobbling down the driveway and, if he saw her now, or even heard her call out his name, it was over – he'd never leave. He mustered some sense of presence and threw himself into the car.

As he pulled away he recalled that he was born in that house. He remembered the story, having been regaled with it a thousand times. He'd come early, unexpectedly. His mother was home alone, wailing with her contractions into empty walls. And she'd pushed and pushed but he kept on resisting, unwilling to leave his cocoon, until finally he arrived – limp, blue and silent; the life-giving cord entwined around his neck. And in the stress of being expelled he'd pooped himself, his tiny nostrils blocked by his own waste. Believing her child to be stillborn, Arwa cleaned his face regardless and pressed him tight to her breast, whereupon he suddenly began crying along with his mother. His focus snapped back to the road and he constrained himself to not look into the rear-view mirror. He kept on driving.

Finally, he hit the road that fed the motorway. It was a narrow, meandering lane, not unlike the country roads near his home. Home ... He pulled up and looked around, the sole light provided by his front beams. He'd not picked the best place to stop: just past a bend which sat atop an incline. But there weren't any vehicles in sight and he took his chance, unable to dwell further on such practicalities, sheer fatigue having ground him to a halt.

Silence and darkness; the night's guardians fanned out in a pincer movement, chilling the air into submission. Turning his lights onto full beam he saw the road dip as it bent, illuminating the motorway in the distance. It ran perpendicular and he followed the trace of distant headlights: heading north, heading south, heading north. It was a great view and one he'd lose if he went any further forward. He'd move on soon.

He looked down at his overcoat on the passenger seat and prised out a CD: *Pakeezah*. He felt childish about having just taken it, but he'd call in a few days, mention it to his mum. He'd give it back. His thumb caressed the cover, that dancing girl, her pain hidden under a veil. He wanted to hear her cry, absorb her tears. *Chalte Chalte*. He fed the CD unit, his senses heightened. And suddenly there was sound; a rippling, an undulation of Indian strings. His back arched, his spine reacting to being tickled; caressed with soft brush strokes. In reflex his eyes closed, the Hindustani devotional demanding reverence. Music that he'd not heard in years flooded his heart with sadness and joy. There was no singing yet; strings and flute set up the paean. Like partners they took turns, the flute playful and feminine and the strings yearning, longing. *Can such a thing be real?* they asked. Pasha was lost. Lost in a world that he never, ever saw: Indian splendour, Asian splendour, Muslim splendour. And he was now so close. The girl started singing, pining, and Pasha was sitting with the *Nawab*, watching her dance. *Why did you leave me, my Lucknavi Princess? Where did you go?* Raw folk drums dominated the sparse, barren sound but their heavy echo thundered into a hypnotic pattern, establishing a trance-like, spiritual feel. Pasha was really there, seated on a Persian rug, smoking sheesha: Mughal splendour. *Entrance me, My Princess, take me away. Make it all go away.*

A car approached. An oncoming beam, building in intensity. He didn't move, he didn't have to – it was on the other side. But then beams from behind ripped through – sudden, intense, blinding light. Instantly he knew – another vehicle had just climbed the peak behind him. *But why so violently bright?* wondered Pasha absurdly, like he had all the time in the world. A horn blew: heavy, deep and long but the oncoming car was nearly alongside and the juggernaut behind now couldn't go round. It was too late ... It was too late but there was a moment; a mere sliver of a moment when Pasha could have acted. If James Bond-like he had thrown himself out of the car and rolled, rolled, rolled like the boyhood hero, he could have saved himself. But Pasha wasn't James Bond. He wouldn't be sipping cocktails in half an hour with only a small cut above the eye and his tie hanging loose at a raffish angle, as evidence of his dance with death. He wouldn't be entertaining his chums or making good girls go moist with tales of his derring-do. He would drink from that cup no more.

'Please, God,' screamed Pasha silently, but he didn't move. He was so terrified his handsome features were now frozen in some grotesque contortion. A word formed in his mind: *mercy*. But there would be no mercy. The incline smoothed out and the juggernaut's headlights traced through horizontal – Pasha's body entered its final, spasmodic dance. And the behemoth kept surging forward.

Mum.

FLASH. The horn blasts. FULL BEAM.

That look, the love in her eyes.

The noise, the lights, the lights, the noise.

Forgive me ...

Bitter tears ran freely as the dancing girl withered and folded, like a rose in the gutter. Everyone's fate was sealed – no escape for her, no escape for him. The air was pregnant with energy. Just the slightest spark and ... the torrential release tore into the night. The kinetic snap spewed out heat, thunder and lightening, with the thunder rolling relentlessly on, gorging itself on the silence and dark.

Finally the night returned to claim her right.

We were once so beautiful, was Ibrahim Pasha Walayat's final thought.

31

Bindweed – also known as Love Vine, Witches' Shoelaces, Hairweed and Devil's Guts. It's a weak-looking outdoor climber; indeed, a parasitic weed, possessing the strange attribute of only having roots at the very start of its life. The plant grows from seed and sprouts from the ground, but on reaching its stem it looks for a host to latch onto. And if it doesn't find one it will die. Once it discovers a host it quickly entwines itself around it and subsequently loses all connection to the soil: its roots die and it now totally depends upon the host. It survives through little bumps on its stem – "haustoria". The Love Vine wraps itself tightly around its host and the haustoria press right up and push their way in. Through the haustoria the Love Vine pulls the nutrients that it needs to survive. Love Vines rarely kill their host, although they often stunt their growth.

It was cold outside. Aadam gripped the scarf tightly around his neck but the night-time chill still had bite. He was moving fast, heading for the Tube station. There were lots of Pakistani youths out tonight, all dressed to impress. Many were waving flags, big and small, and horns blew from the passing cars – Eid continued to be celebrated. A group of youths stood outside the *Punjabi Textiles House* singing *Who Let the Dogs Out*, but substituting "Dogs" for "Sikhs". With head down, Aadam continued briskly but one of them saw him and offered up his *Eid Mubarak* with a smile. Aadam looked at him, the smiling, well-dressed young man, his hand outstretched to shake that of a brother. Aadam almost spat in his face but stopped himself – the guy was well built and there were seven, eight, nine of them – he had enough battles to fight. He saw the Tube station up ahead and started groping around for his wallet. A police van screamed past, sirens blazing, and as he entered an officer approached.

'Excuse me, sir, we're stopping passengers for security.' Aadam took a long, hard look, considering the exact degree of contempt in which to hold him. 'Do you mind if I ask you some questions, sir?' the copper continued breezily, taking out a pad and pen and smiling, business-like but friendly.

He's quite young, Aadam re-thought. He couldn't muster the energy to hate him.

'Please, go ahead.' And he handed the copper his plastic bag. A car drove past outside, horn blaring.

'Don't tell him nuffink, bro!' came the cry from some youth hanging out of the window, waving a Pakistan flag like his life depended on it. Aadam turned back and the policeman was looking uncomfortable.

'Is everything in this bag yours, sir?'

'The natives are restless, eh?' quipped Aadam, feeling the need to apologise.

'No one but you has put anything in this bag?'

'No. No, it's all mine.'

'Is there anything sharp in here?'

'No,' he sighed.

The copper started removing the contents with forensic care.

'One pair of jeans. One wallet. One bunch of keys.' He paused and looked at Aadam with every item, like he was giving him an opportunity to object. 'One bottle of ... perfume?' He held the bottle up.

'Yes, it's perfume.'

'May I?' he asked with offensive politeness.

'Go ahead.'

The policeman unscrewed the top and sniffed the liquid suspiciously. Satisfied, he screwed the lid back on. Another officer approached.

'Excuse me, sir,' he said briefly, before turning to his colleague. 'Are you gonna take your break in the café upstairs or are you going elsewhere?'

He's a little plump for a policeman, thought Aadam, a faint smirk appearing on his face.

'Upstairs. And where are you travelling to today, sir?' The young copper turned back sharply, eager to get back to business.

'South London. Lewisham.'

'Hot or cold?' interrupted Tubby.

'What?' snapped the young copper, giving a serious stare.

'Do you want a hot or a cold meal during your break?' pressed Tubby, merrily. Aadam perked up with the sideshow, something which he didn't bother hiding.

'Hot,' the policeman stamped, after a long pause. He turned firmly back towards Aadam. 'Right, where were we? Ah yes, Lewisham. And this is the start of your journey today, sir?'

'Chicken or beef?'

'Oi, Frank! Make sure you don't get an erection this time!' The four lads started laughing, breaking the silence within the carriage. Some of the other commuters saw the funny side but most didn't – the sobriety of the Tube had been disturbed. Aadam checked his watch: it was nearly 9 pm and yet the Tube was still full of people. No Eid delights for them today. As the automatic doors were closing, four workmen had scrambled on board, noisily announcing their presence. Those closest dispersed somewhat, giving them room to down tools and preserve some personal space. Thus when one reminded another to keep his excitement in check, it wasn't strictly necessary. But still ...

Aadam turned to look at the newspaper being read next to him. A photo dominated the page: a picture of an Iraqi boy and an American soldier, both smiling. The soldier stood behind the boy, who in turn was holding up a small, wooden placard on which was written: *Lcpl Boudreaux killed my dad then knocked up my sister!* Skimming the article, the debate was over whether the photo was genuine – and therefore in poor taste – or a malicious piece of editing. Aadam looked away. It really didn't matter anymore.

Nazneen had taken the car. They had driven up together and now she was driving home alone. He had left soon after, regret and confusion tearing at him. He shouldn't have laughed at her "skiing in Colorado" idea – it wasn't that bad. But why had she been so vicious? She'd been fine earlier. He thought they'd settled that business with Kishore before even leaving home. He remembered their first date. They had arranged to meet in Leicester Square, outside the Burger King, and on arriving she'd announced that she had a top to return and promptly began marching towards Piccadilly. And from that moment on he'd been trailing behind her, all excited, trying desperately to catch up.

Getting off the Tube at Charing Cross, he walked along the tunnel connecting underground to overground. Would he get home before her? Would she get home before him? There might be traffic. There won't be any traffic. She'll definitely hit traffic. *Please, God – I can't lose her.* Each side of the tunnel was plastered with a seamless stream of posters advertising films, bands, events – London Life. So much information – too much information – but he couldn't resist sucking it in. One stood out – for a film, a French film. The poster was dominated by a woman, a stunning young woman. She was lying on a sun lounge, catching some rays. Delicious ... He recalled reading a review and remembered how awful it sounded – some boring characters mincing around and regarding each other with withering contempt. But he'd probably go see it anyway, because his will to live would be maintained by injections of lovingly-shot soft porn.

Nazneen. Please, I didn't mean it. What did I do wrong? A couple approached, hand-in-hand. *God, that boy's done well for himself.* He used to watch people watching them, the odd couple: her the serene and stellar beauty, and him looking like a refugee, clutching a winning lottery ticket. Another poster – the Band of the Moment, promoting their new album. There were two men – manish-boys, boyish-men: thin frames, jet-black hair, white, white skin. One of them was pouting with ruby-red lips whilst the other looked downwards, sallow-cheeked and wan. His bare, thin arm was outstretched, suggesting vulnerability if not substance abuse. *Heroin chic. Just who are they meant to appeal to? Men? Women? Boys? Girls?* He continued on, down this never-ending tunnel. A Muslim couple passed by. The woman was fully covered – her nose was covered, her mouth was covered. She was looking out onto the world through thin slits. Did she know fresh air, the scent of flowers on a pregnant summer's day, the sharpness of an autumn morning? *We've had a bad day. She's very happy with me. What if she's not happy? Is there someone else?*

Walking away from the top of the escalator he reached the barrier. He passed the tiny newsagent's which was still open (it's always open), and moved towards the escalators leading to the overland concourse. The homeless were bedding down for the night and there was a faint smell of urine and *Special Brew* in the air. *The Bag Assue, Bag Assue!* heralded one hardy soul. *Bless him*, thought Aadam, without buying a copy. *He's been repeating that all day.* Further along, two men were huddled side-by-side in sleeping bags.

'Spare any change, please, mate?' asked one with a grin. Aadam shook his head before rounding them and stepping away. 'Thanks, boss!' he heard the man say, now out of sight. 'Fucking paki!' his friend added, thus completing the exchange. Crossing the platform, another policeman approached.

'Excuse me, sir, we're stopping passengers for security.'

Aadam stared into space as a police vehicle could be heard tearing past on Charing Cross Road outside. 'Tea's up...'

'What?' exclaimed the copper, his bored look replaced instantly with aggression.

'I said, the kettle's boiling.' He enunciated slowly and clearly. The policeman continued staring, the silence between them speaking volumes.

'I have some questions to ask you, sir.' Aadam handed him his bag.

* * *

He checked the departure boards. There was a Dartford-via-Lewisham train due to leave in six minutes. As he made his way, a couple of Asian lads crossed his path. They were drunk, not paralytic but proper merry, and with arms around shoulders they were singing the chorus to *Kabhie Kabhie Mere Dil Mein*, like it meant something. They were probably Indian: no one's simply Asian anymore. It's a nice song.

Aadam got on at the first door and walked down the carriage. The train was less than half full though people were embarking at a brisk-ish rate. He saw the back of a man sitting by the window, all alone in a bay of seats. People continued streaming in, in ones, twos and threes, but this chap remained by himself. Strange. Finally, Aadam pulled up alongside and the mystery was solved. Of course, he was black. Feeling a sense of solidarity, Aadam took up a nearby seat. He closed his eyes and saw Nazneen. Loving her had come so easy: his life, his priorities, his needs – they all got flipped in that one instant. He just couldn't imagine her not being there. The same wasn't true the other way round, of course – he wasn't stupid, he'd always known that. But he thought that with marriage, in the fullness of time, she'd grow to love him. He opened his eyes. There was a suited guy sitting opposite, checking some papers. It looked like work. *Fucking hell,* this man was still working. Within a few hours the guy would be back at his desk, probably staring at the very same papers. Aadam, too, would be at his desk. *What do we all do it for?* Still, right now he could relax. At least he wasn't driving. *Let the train take the strain,* as the ad used to say. Too fucking right. The most overrated pleasure in life? Driving a car.

The rapid beeps sounded and within seconds the automatic doors closed. And as so often, in fact almost without fail, he saw a couple dive for the door only seconds too late. It was a lovely little piece of theatre – that final dash up the concourse, the leap for the open door and then the *clunk-clunk* finality of them shutting in your face. They were out of puff. They'd been dashing, maybe pushing people out of their way for the last ninety seconds, and all for nothing. Aadam felt their pain.

Pulling out of Charing Cross under cover of darkness, he looked out lazily into the blackness. He knew the London Eye was there and, flipping across, he saw the River Thames, or rather its lit-up banks. The river was quite wide at this point and the swooping lights all along the Embankment looked majestic. He loved this city – he felt pride at being a part of it.

Arriving at Waterloo East there was a lot of activity: swarms embarking and disembarking. A cacophony of youthful banter arrived in the shape of two young men – Australian – and two young women – English. They looked in their early twenties and, from their conversation, they'd not known each other long. The girls were laughing regularly, on-demand, little shrill shrieks accompanying every Aussie utterance. *Slam dunk.* The two lads were tanned, tall, athletic – real fair-dinkum Aussies; the English girls were punching well above their weight. No wonder they were trying so hard. And they were competing with each other: *Don't want her, want me,* pouted each girl eagerly. Something snapped. He bent forwards and held his head, his palms over his eyes. He wanted to stop – stop seeing, stop hearing, stop thinking. He was trying to find some stillness inside but he didn't know how. He just couldn't shake this really bad feeling. The train of thought was relentless. Well fuck it, fuck it all: fuck French cinema and its existential nausea, and fuck the "Lucky Country", which wasn't so lucky for the Abo's. And fuck the Muslims, with their desert hearts and desert nations. And fuck Britain, with her oh-so-glorious past and her maggot-infested future. All he wanted was her. *Please Allah, please.* He opened his eyes as Southwark Cathedral approached. By day it was impressive but by night it was transcendent; a balm for the soul. Huge lamps at its base threw light up the cathedral's walls and the effect was utterly beautiful. It looked haunted – less a House of God, more a memory of a House of God, in a Godless land. The train moved on but Aadam felt a little calmer as they pulled into London Bridge.

He was home and sitting in his living room all alone. The light from the ceiling was insufficient, produced as it was by a 25W bulb. There should have been a 60W bulb there – at least a 40W – but when the old one went they only had one left in the cupboard. He was meant to get some more but he'd forgotten.

On reaching, he'd immediately noticed that their car wasn't there and that no light was on indoors. But did that mean Nazneen hadn't yet got back, or that she'd come and gone? He went straight to their bedroom and the first thing he looked for was her suitcase above the tall cupboard. It was still there. He then went to the chest of drawers and pulled open the top one, and held a handful of her knickers to his chest.

Suddenly a key entered the latch. At first he thought he'd imagined it but then he heard the front door swing open followed by the sound of someone climbing the stairs. The steps had a softness, a lightness, a familiarity to them. Aadam was mortified. *Be a man*, he told himself – whatever was about to unfold. She entered the living room but stayed standing by the entrance. Aadam bolted to attention. *Be a man.*

He studied her face as she moved towards him. Would he be reprieved or was he about to be condemned? *Be a man.* He was trying, he was really trying. They were staring at each other but her expression remained blank. He started trembling and he leant to offset it, trying to affect a casual pose. It didn't work, though; he looked more awkward. She now stood right in front. He was still trying to hold his ground but it was getting too much. His head dropped; too many conflicting messages. He was desperate not to cry but he'd failed to hold it back, his dread spilling over. His face crinkled, a quite pathetic attempt to conceal a quivering lip. She decided to end it. She put her arms inside his and wrapped herself around him, resting her head on his chest. Instantly he pulled her close, burying his face in her neck, her hair veiling him.

'It's OK,' she said softly. She knew he didn't make her eyes catch fire, the way they should, but at times she did feel love for him. Sort of. They rocked together to and fro, arms interlocked and bodies meshed, if not quite souls fused. He started whispering her name – not mantra-like, more wish-upon-a-star.

'I'm not letting you go now,' he whimpered. She felt bad that his love hadn't melted her more.

'I love you, Aadam,' came the reply, and she still didn't know what those words meant.

32

Nazneen had been sitting in her car, two minutes' drive from home. Her and Aadam's home. But she couldn't go there yet. She needed time to figure out what to do, what to say, what she wanted to hear. The streets were empty, not a soul in sight. She could drive off right now, just keep on driving ... She thumbed her mobile, teasing the *call* button, a number already loaded. A new number, saved from earlier today.

'Hello?' His voice sounded unfamiliar, in a neutral tone.

'Hi, Martin.'

'Nazneen...' He almost whispered her name, stretching it out like he didn't want to let go.

'I ... I remember Red Rocks, too.' She giggled self-consciously, thinking she sounded ridiculous.

'Red Rocks?'

'Yeah. You mentioned it this morning, when you called.'

'It was a pretty special time, huh?'

'God, yeah. You know, I'd not forgotten. But life goes on, I guess.' Through the windscreen she peered up into the blackened sky, as if searching for clues. There were no stars adorning the London night and the naked heavens seemed reduced, stripped of all mystery; just a mechanical device, ticking pointlessly on.

'I know I shouldn't have called you today. I knew you'd have moved on, settled down, but...'

'Go on, Martin. Talk to me. I'm here.'

'You know what I remember most about Red Rocks? The stars. And standing tall on that soil and looking hard in every direction.

Nothing but earth, sky and stars. A billion specs of light, whispering a symphony.'

The Scooby Doo air freshener was lying prostrate on the dashboard and grinning right at her. *He won't stop fucking grinning.* She grabbed it firmly, constricting its rubber body, and tried to break its head off with her thumb but it was too elastic and it snapped back, its grin undimmed.

'Nazneen?'

'How did things get so fucked up? Can you tell me that?' She slammed the air freshener down by her feet. 'I mean, this isn't real. You're not real. All we're left with is damn memories.' With trembling hands she fumbled for a hanky, wiping the regret that was oozing out of her, staining her face.

'Shhh. It's OK, it's OK.' His voice, so formal on picking up, was now swaddling her.

'Sorry, it's just ... today. I wasn't expecting any of this today. Why resurrect this now? I wish you hadn't called.'

'What? Oh, I get it – just 'cause it's inconvenient for you. I should fuck off now, should I?'

'No! Sorry, I didn't mean that.'

'Oh, have I upset you? Disturbed your cosy little life? You know I've never even come close to recreating what we had. I've spent the past three years trying to forget you.'

'Martin, don't. I'm sorry...'

'Sorry? Is that the best you can do? You know, you never actually explained to me why you left.'

'Please, stop it...'

'No, hang on – one moment we lived together, studied together, planned today and tomorrow together. And then all of a sudden you ended it. Why?'

Silence. She remembered her gran, and Ramazan arriving one year and it suddenly meaning something.

'We'd had a great time at uni but it'd finished, right?'

'What had finished? The good times or just uni?'

'Martin, please. You must've had a reason for getting back in touch. And I've not returned the call by mistake.'

'But I need to know. I mean, all couples bicker but I don't remember us tearing chunks out of each other, or us drifting apart and getting bored.'

'And you think I've forgotten? Why the hell do you think I've called you?'

She let go of her hanky and it fell by her feet, her sorrow now running freely.

'Look, it's OK. Forget it. I don't want it to be like this. I just wanted to hear your voice, one last time.'

'Wait! Don't go. Let's just talk for a while, huh? There's no harm.'

She adjusted the rear-view mirror and studied her reflection; her earlier glow from Eid, a day of pure celebration, completely washed away.

'I didn't mean to upset you, Nazneen.'

'I know. Hey, I reckon that's probably our first proper fight!' She giggled innocently, her relief for the change in mood blinding her to the irony.

'Great timing, huh? So what about you and your husband – do you fight?'

'If you were, you know – getting intimate with someone – and a friend unexpectedly popped round, what would you do?'

'You what?'

'Oh, it doesn't matter.'

'But he loves you, right?'

'Yes, yes he does. He's crazy about me. It's just he's so ... I think he's forgotten how to live. So have I.'

'And do you love him?'

'What the hell is love, huh? Will someone please explain that damn word to me?'

'Shhh, Nazneen.' Again, swaddling her. She giggled briefly and bent to pick up her hanky and found the Scooby Doo by her feet. Holding it up, she carefully lifted off some debris collected from the floor mat and planted a kiss on those ever-wide lips.

'It's OK,' Nazneen conceded. 'It doesn't matter anymore. So tell me, how are you finding life in the Big Smoke?'

'Oh, I'm still a small-town boy from Branscombe. For most of my life even Bournemouth was a dizzying metropolis; London's a crazy place.'

'So you like my city, then?' Her voice was playful, all tension gone.

'It's all right, my dear. Very cosmopolitan.'

'So what can't the small town boy get used to, eh?'

'It's been crazy round my area today. Really mad.'

'Oh yeah? How's that?'

'The Asians. There's lots round here. There's some festival every other week.'

'Eid,' she underlined. 'Today's festival was called Eid. That's why you caught me when you called this morning. I'd have been at work otherwise.'

'Right, right. But you were never into all of that, were you?' There was an edginess, a stiffness in his voice.

'No ... Yes ... Things change, you know? Haven't you changed?'

'Not really. I like the same things, I dislike the same things. Actually, there is one way in which I've changed.'

'Yeah? How's that then?'

'I was always an easy-going guy. You know, happy-go-lucky; I could get on with anyone.'

'Yeah, totally. Being with you was like a ticket to anywhere. That's still you, though, right?'

'Look, I take people as I find them. I mean their colour, their race, where they come from – it's all irrelevant bollocks to me. But religion? I ain't got no time for that one.'

She closed her eyes, a numbness surrounding her.

'Why are you telling me this?'

'I always took you as you were – you should know that. I never thought of you as Asian or ethnic or Muslim. You were just you.'

'And you were unique. My lover, my finest friend. And yes, I do love my husband, but what me and you had ... Don't get bitter, please. Think of what we shared. Colorado, Keystone. Do you remember that lake? It was so beautiful, right? We used to go swimming and biking up in the hills. And Red Rocks? Think back to our last night, Martin. World's End, under the stars.'

'Those memories are a fucking prison. You left me because I'm not Muslim, didn't you?'

She recalled speaking to Nikki in the morning, and her trying to wish her a happy Eid, and flicking idly through magazines in their Colorado hut and suddenly wanting to torch the world.

'Don't you love your culture? I love mine.'

'Our culture's the same; *was* the same. But I didn't ask you about culture. Are you into your religion?'

'So if I said "yes" you'd see me differently, would you? I wouldn't just be me any more.'

'Basically, yeah. Look, if people want to believe in fairies or Father Christmas, let 'em. I won't interfere. But when they start believing that they're gonna go to some heaven and get seventy virgins to fuck till eternity, and all for killing Infidels, Jews and Hindus, then I got some serious problem with that. How can you love that?'

There was simply no answer.

'How can you go back to that? Did we reject you? Did Britain reject you? This country gave you everything.'

Nazneen sat still, letting herself drift into the void.

'It's no good saying it's all the media's fault, focussing only on the nutters. I live around these people. I see it all with my own eyes.'

'What, you see Muslims on street corners, distributing leaflets on how to kill Jews and Hindus?'

'Don't be facetious – you know what I mean. The Hindus and Sikhs – they're all right; they just get on with their lives. They work hard; they want to fit in. It's just ... it's just the Muslims.'

FUCKING JEWS, FUCKING HINDUS, FUCKING MUSLIMS. *It's so hard to love, there's so much to hate.* Hate, hate, HATE, *HATEHATEHATEHATEHATE* ... She pressed hard on her scalp, wanting to rip it apart.

'Goodbye, Martin.' She brought the phone down and held it in her lap; paused, for one last moment, and then ended the call. It was time to go home.

33

'Pasha, Pasha!'

Salman cups hands to his mouth and shouts at the top of his voice. They'd been hunting for clues, scrapping and running for hours through woods and down bridle paths, across streams and farmland. Old Spam Head, their Scout master, had sought special permission – not everyone got to trample all over the English countryside like them. And here he was, young Salman, the first to reach the hilltop checkpoint.

He breathes deep, greedy for fresh air and looks down at the chasing pack, which includes Pasha. Surveying green fields with cows out to pasture, he stretches up towards the English summer sky – a light, fresh blue with lots of fluffy, white clouds.

'Come on, Pasha!' His cousin needs all the encouragement he can get – at eight he's a year younger than the others and a right skinny little runt. Still, it's lovely out here, in the country. He'd like to live somewhere like this one day.

The chasing pack closes in and Pasha crosses fourth. He was heading the others until the final ten metres or so. He collapses onto the earth, panting heavily, as Andy, Rob, Clem, Jon and all the others sprint for the finish, throwing themselves forwards for the last two yards.

'Well done, lads,' bellows Old Spammy, patting down each of his boys as they spread out over the slope, quenching their thirst and replaying every trivial incident of the day. Pasha looks upset but Salman goes to him and he soon cheers up. He really looks up to his older cousin.

'Right!' Old Spammy commands after their panting subsides. 'Last leg now, lads – back to base camp!' He puffs full of purpose and his boys dart up and mount their backpacks. 'Blue team, yellow team – you got your maps?'

'Yes, Spammy!' chipper back bright, unbroken voices.

'OK!'

And with that his young charges break free, leaving him to keep watchful guard from the rear.

Soon they are back in the forest, lost in another world – one in which dense trees lock horns, making daylight unwelcome. A riotous nature fans out: moss smothering bark, wet and dank, and fern leaves weaving an emerald carpet, shrouding a subterranean world. Unseen birds chipper and squawk and a mist freshens the air, cool and alive. But the lush, flat earth soon dips – imperceptibly at first, with the gradient starting to challenge as the terrain morphs – lustrous greens giving way to a powdery red, holding nothing but loose stone, atrophied vegetation and dead roots. The boys stumble, caution each other, continue with renewed resolve, for they are determined to solve this riddle, of how life and death can mock them; taunt them by appearing as comfortable neighbours, ignoring the human need for a mighty ocean to keep them apart.

The decline levels out and they stand again on even ground, panting in silence, quenching their thirst, and finally, cautiously looking out. Water, clear and trickling, moving softly over pebbles. A wide bank sits either side, uncut grass and reed bending uniformly with a gentle breeze, the benevolent sun making everything shine. Horses arrive. From where it is unclear, as they are in a valley, with each apex touching the horizon. The herd approach leisurely: four, five, six of them, heads bobbing with their gentle pace. They come right up, seeking contact, and a couple of the boys back away, turning towards Spammy for reassurance. Standing deliberately back he simply nods, giving them the confidence to touch the beasts, stroke their flanks, and immerse themselves in this strange encounter. The horses nicker and snort, letting them all take their turn before moving off, back toward the stream. Their pace again is so gentle the boys consider it an invitation, and thus follow the herd into the middle of the valley, to the stream, hopping over the larger stones, the water rippling on regardless. They look around, survey the space, the *sheer expanse making them at first dizzy but then heady, intoxicated with their achievement in making it down here.*

Clem picks up a stone and hurls it up into the air, and they watch its flight, high, high into space, before hurtling back down. Immediately the boys all dart down to grab their own, with Salman and Andy making for the same one.

   'Oye!'

   'Leave it – it's mine!'

They tumble and roll, neither of them willing to let go. The others enjoy the scrap, cheering on both of them. It's in Andy's hand but Salman manages to prise it out of his grasp.

   'Leave it, you paki!'

Suddenly a big hand grabs each boy roughly by the collar, yanking them apart.

   'Right, you pair of monkeys!' Old Spam Head looks angrily at each of them, and despite both feeling aggrieved and wanting to protest, neither dares say another word.

He clasps each boy firmly, one to each side. Their heads are bowed, cheeks glowing with anger.

   'Look,' he booms, but both heads remain defiantly downcast. He tightens his hold of each boy, leaving them in no doubt that disobeying twice is not an option.

   'Look out there,' he commands, and both heads are reluctantly raised. They look out but don't really see ... The expanse of lush green, the horses playing, cantering, blind to the fragility of what they have; of the barren, infertile drop flanking them, bearing down on them, locking them in.

'You see that?' he begins, his eyes moving from the wasteland they descended to the oasis of the valley itself. 'All this.' He waits until silence rings around. 'These horses will be here till the end of time. No matter what surrounds them, God will provide. God or Allah – 'cause it's all the same, in't it?' No response comes forth and he re-applies pressure. 'In't it?' He looks down to his left and right.

   'Yes, Spammy,' muffles a chastened Andy.

   'Salman?'

   'Yes, Spammy.'

'Good ... Good. Right, shake hands.'
And Andy extends a speculative hand which Salman takes.

Salman was back home and alone in the kitchen. It'd been a silent return drive and everyone had gone to bed within minutes of reaching. Salman, though, needed to think. Sipping water, he sat by the kitchen table, flicking through the day's paper. One article grabbed him: an interview with one of Iraq's few remaining Jews. He was an old man, one who could remember his thriving community from years gone by.

'Why don't you leave for Israel?' the interviewer had asked the Arab Jew.

'Because this is my home. I was born here and I'll die here.'

Salman stood outside his son's bedroom. He couldn't hear anything and, presuming Taimur to be asleep, he was about to walk away, not wanting to disturb him after such a long day. But then he heard some sounds. Salman pressed up against the door to hear his son in animated conversation with himself.

'*Sergeant, we're under attack! Rat-at-tat-tat.*'

He opened the door a little and peeked in. Taimur had his back to his father and was playing war. His motley collection of toys were all out, forming two random armies. Not in any advert would you see a homemade Humpty Dumpty, a twenty-five-year-old train set and some camp-looking toy soldiers collaborating in war games. Taimur was holding the gun given to him by Aadam, like his life depended on it – he was clearly excited by this latest addition to his arsenal. Salman wondered where his own present was. He knew that Taimur would never pick it up without his mother or father pestering him to do so. But he was only eight – the Holy Book could wait.

Salman shifted his weight and the floorboards creaked. Young Taimur turned abruptly, a little startled. It was only his daddy, though, and he gave a big smile. Salman entered, remembering that he smacked him today. He knew that his son would always remember that: the Eid day when his father hit him. He sat down on the carpeted floor and Taimur hopped up onto his dad's lap.

'Do you like Aadam Uncle's present?' he asked.

'Yeah, Dad! It's the best ever!' he said, his small voice scaling octaves. 'When I grow up, Daddy, I want to be a soldier!' His eyes glistened and his cheeks shone with health.

'And why is that?'

'Because they have big muscles and big guns!'

Salman laughed, his heart instantly filled with joy. But then a question.

'And who will you fight for?'

Taimur considered it, his little brow furrowed. 'I don't understand, Daddy.'

Salman said nothing – he just held his son. He kissed and tickled him and Taimur squealed with delight.

'Daddy?' asked Taimur after a while, now back on the floor and making adjustments to his battlefield.

'Yes, *Beta*?'

'Michael from school is having a birthday party on Saturday, round his house. Can I go?' There was silence as Taimur continued tweaking, now bringing his Action Man into the equation. 'Daddy?' persisted Taimur.

'Sure, son. Why not.'

34

Imtiaz sat with his mum. They were in the kitchen by the breakfast table and he was trying to comfort her. Arwa was wiping her nose with a scrunched-up tissue, her tears all spent. The evening had unravelled so fast – Pasha, Nazneen and Aadam all leaving abruptly, without any goodbyes. They'd heard raised voices when watching the film and Arwa was ready to go back in but Bilqis had suggested that they stay away.

'They'll get tired soon,' she'd assured her sister. 'Let's enjoy the film, yes?'

She had run outside to catch Pasha; to beg her son not to leave like this, but it was too late. By the time she had reached the pavement his car was hurtling down the road. Bilqis and the others had only just begun consoling her when they saw Nazneen leave – without Aadam. Husnain went into the kitchen to find Aadam half-crying and half-fighting with his brother, and before he could establish what had happened, Aadam, too, had left. Arwa's special day didn't so much finish as get aborted – it was simply flushed away.

And here she was, alone with Imtiaz.

'I'll give Pasha a call tomorrow. It'll be all right. He'll be back down before you know it.' Arwa didn't answer but continued wiping away the last of her tears and mucus. 'He wouldn't have meant to upset you. He'll be feeling really bad right now.' His expression jarred with his words, being more diplomatic than emotional.

'You boys have failed us, failed us as parents.'

'Actually, it's more the other way round. But never mind.'

Arwa looked at her son, surprised but not hurt. She sniffed back some more.

'You know, your father never supported me. I could see that things were going wrong but I couldn't do anything by myself.'

'Never mind,' said Imtiaz, sounding a little bored.

'I've always loved my boys. I have a lot of love, a lot of *pyar* to give you both.' She leant towards him, clearly seeking reciprocity.

'I don't want your *pyar*,' he said, and with that he put his specs on and walked out.

Before getting on the train, Imtiaz went into a petrol station; one combined with a small supermarket. He was cold and uncomfortable but once inside he relaxed, unbuttoning his coat and unfurling from his hunch. He didn't particularly want anything but nevertheless he took his time, browsing the various shelves. There was so much in here – nappies, watermelons, fresh spinach and jam. Not that long ago it was novel to pick up a coffee and a paper with your fuel and now you could choose between Galia and Honeydew melons. It truly was fucking amazing. Imtiaz strode leisurely towards the freezer section, where he picked up some luxury ice cream. He was pretty sure he had some at home but it'd been a bloody long day and he deserved a treat. With small tub in hand he began his journey to the tills, making one final stop by the magazine section. A lifetime's instinct made him look up towards the top shelf, but these days all the adult mags were sheathed in an opaque, plastic covering. His gaze fell to about halfway down, to the lads' mags. Cover after cover featured openly lustful women. It still seemed so bold, this unleashed, raw, female sexuality. *Where do they find them? Are these girls real?* They were all striking some sort of pose and dressed in gear that was guaranteed to flick that switch. Imtiaz swallowed hard. There was a blonde girl – a tall, leggy fantasy of a woman. She was half-squatting and wearing nothing except elbow-length black leather gloves, knee-length black leather boots and black tassels over her nipples. And nothing else. She was looking at Imtiaz kind of menacingly, as she held the fingertips of one glove between her teeth, ready to rip it off. Imtiaz shivered. He looked around nervously before picking the magazine up. He held it unopened, reverentially, and could feel his heart smacking into his ribs.

'*It's never too late,*' he remembered Kahina saying. '*We can help you find someone.*' But this cover girl was looking so mean, so damn dirty. *Someone has actually enjoyed this woman*, he contemplated. *Probably several men, maybe a dozen or more.* Imtiaz felt dizzy as the thought scrambled his mind. He opened the magazine. Flicking impatiently from page to page he gorged on the pictures; there was so much flesh but he wanted more. Breasts were good, nipples were great and smooth legs, stomachs and arses were devoured with relish, but his appetite was just increasing. He bought the magazine and walked with haste to the train station. Making sure no one was in sight he went through it a second, third and fourth time, stoking his hunger until there was nothing else – just a meat feast.

'It's never too late.' *It is too late. What does she know? Go ahead, son. You deserve it.*

Imtiaz got off at Oxford Street before jogging down to Wardour Street, towards Soho. Soho – the word, the promise. Right now he wanted this so much. Despite the cover of night he could see everything clearly, as he still had his specs on. The start of Wardour Street was quiet and dark but West End life soon made its presence known: bustling cafés and swanky bars. He passed a pub and glanced into its warm hearth, catching a sliver of the glow therein. Gentle laughter, glasses clinking, soft conversation – he'd missed out on so much. Still walking briskly, he passed a woman standing outside some office building, having a fag. She was stamping her feet, trying to keep warm. She was clearly not comfortable but she wanted that fag more; Imtiaz knew how she felt.

'*Porn isn't damaging, Imtiaz. Not necessarily, anyway. The trouble is you have no checks and balances.*'

Yeah, Yeah. You enjoy yourself. Everyone needs to cut loose every now and again. A couple walked past arm-in-arm, full of the goodness of life. There were lots of people swilling around now, heading in all directions. Everyone looked so young, even those clearly older than him.

He took a right into Peter Street and finally he was there. Neon lights, winking at him. *LOVELY SEXY GIRLS.* Blues, pinks, reds and greens spoke their message, leaving him in no doubt – this was truth. He continued on and approached a small entrance. *LOVELY YOUNG MODELS.* Discreet pieces of cardboard informed him that heaven awaited, on the second and third floors. He stopped, transfixed by those little cardboard signs, and the promise of something lovely and something young. He was seeing frilly things; soft, velvety things.

Itsy-bitsy things. He entered. The stairwell was putrid, the stench of urine strong. He continued upwards, past the first floor. And then he was there. The door to the second-floor flat was decorated: lots of glitter, lots of colourful little hearts, lots of promises. *SLIM SEXY MODEL HERE TODAY. NO RUSH – GOOD TIME.*

It's never too late. He hesitated for just a moment before pressing the doorbell. An ample-sized woman wearing bra and knickers opened the door – *the advert says "slim", but ...* With hands on hips she gave a little wiggle and smiled generously.

'Twenty for sex, twenty-five for French and sex,' she stated casually. *Bloody hell, that's cheap.* Imtiaz said nothing: he was just standing there, gawping.

'You coming in?' she prompted. More silence. Her smile quickly faded and she was now looking serious, making Imtiaz uncomfortable. 'Wanker!' she shouted, before slamming the door. He heard her continue to cuss, but now in a language that he didn't recognise. He turned around and walked back down the stairs. He took a left into Walkers Court and entered a sex shop. Rows and rows of DVDs pulled him close on an invisible string. *Forget them all, forget it all.* Everywhere he looked, just everywhere ... what a feast. His penis was hard and he put his hand down his trouser pocket to discreetly readjust. He picked a few of the empty covers up and flipped them over. A montage of clips revealed things that he'd seen a thousand times before, but he was just not getting bored. Actually, that wasn't quite true – it wasn't as pure as it once was but for sheer intensity, nothing else could compete. Once you are in that zone, pornography is peerless. Sport, work, art, politics – interests come and go and aptitudes vary, but porn is imperious. It's so simple, it's egalitarian – porn is for everyone, the poison of poisons. Oddly he found the front covers more alluring than the back – the anticipation of the wrapped up gift. He left the shop without buying anything, though that would come. This, though, was the best part. He'd had the foreplay of the train journey and now this was it – the heat of passion. He'd keep upping the pressure, moving from shop to shop until he could take it no more. And then he'd make his choice. Coming back into Walkers Court, Imtiaz strode purposefully. He was mentally mapping a route, thinking of the various establishments he'd go into. He fully intended on lasting the course tonight – it'd been such a trying day. And then an accident. Two men tore past, one knocking him straight down with his shoulder. He was thrown to the pavement and he banged his forehead hard on the ground. The suddenness of the impact stunned him and for several seconds he was disorientated: *I'm all right, I'm all right,* he tried to reassure himself. From lying prostrate, he moved to squat before crawling to the side of the walkway. Nobody came to his assistance but he understood – you were on your own here. He checked his possessions. His wallet was still in his back trouser pocket but his glasses had come off. Scanning where he fell, he saw them in the middle of the path and he scurried to fetch them. They were broken. The left lens had been shattered and the frame was bent – they were beyond repair. The shock of the injury was now subsiding, allowing the physical pain to take over. He had scuffed the fleshy part of his left palm badly: the skin there was torn and he was bleeding. There was some grit mixed in with the open wound and even though he tried rubbing it off gently, it burnt like hell. Two doormen standing outside a strip joint up ahead burst out laughing. Self-consciously he looked up but the joke was not on him. With some effort he stood and gingerly continued. Coming to the end, he hit an opening: Brewer Street cutting across with Rupert Street. There was a lot of activity and a real festive feeling hung in the air. Everywhere he looked he was seeing groups of people: twos, threes and fours, making their way here and there. Everyone looked normal. Even here, in what was meant to be a lonely man's paradise, he was the odd one out. He looked up into the night sky and inhaled. Returning his gaze to street level, he slowly moved on but he was now only interested in going home. His urgency, his earlier appetite had been drained. He walked past another new bar – Latin or Spanish sounds emanated. Soho was becoming gentrified, with the smut being moved out. Approaching the next building along some graffiti caught his eye: *Without my depression I'd be a failure – with it, I'm a success on hold.* He paused to consider the point ... *Die before you die,* whispered the wind without notice, picking up around his ears. He sensed death and shuddered. He looked around but, without his glasses, his vision was no longer clear. He checked his cut hand again, though he was now aware of a burning sensation in several other places: his forehead, his left knee, his hip. He continued onwards, though with increasing difficulty – his muscles and joints were tightening up. Towards the apex of his vision he made out another *GIRLS GIRLS GIRLS* and an *XXX*, restoring something of the natural order for the area. The two signs were overlapping, though; an illusion brought on not only by the distance, but also by the absence of his glasses. He squinted, trying to get a clearer picture, but tears were now starting in his eyes and it didn't really help. It was all just one big blur.

END

The world is a bridge. Pass over it, but build no houses on it. He who hopes for an hour may hope for eternity; the world endures but an hour. Spend it in prayer, for the rest is unseen.

JESUS CHRIST (AS)

Inscribed above the *Buland Darwaza*,
the Grand Entrance to Fatepur Sikhri, India